KOLWEZI

By Ritchie Perry

KOLWEZI

RITCHIE PERRY

PUBLISHED FOR THE CRIME CLUB BY
DOUBLEDAY & COMPANY, INC.
GARDEN CITY, NEW YORK
1985

All of the characters in this book
are fictitious, and any resemblance
to actual persons, living or dead,
is purely coincidental.

LIBRARY OF CONGRESS CATALOGING IN PUBLICATION DATA
Perry, Ritchie, 1942–
Kolwezi.
I. Title.
PR6066.E72K6   1985   823'914
ISBN 0-385-23004-4

Library of Congress Catalog Card Number 85-1567
Copyright © 1985 by Ritchie Perry
All Rights Reserved
Printed in the United States of America

First Edition

I would like to thank Alan Tipler and Peter Tyson for the valuable assistance they gave me in the preparation of this book.

KOLWEZI

LONDON, ENGLAND

There were no decorations on the whitewashed walls or any windows to allow in light from the outside. Shoheibi was sitting at a table in the centre of the room. As the unshaded electric lightbulb was directly overhead he had to hold his hands over his eyes to protect them from the harsh glare. Although it wasn't particularly cold, he'd begun to suffer from uncontrollable spasms of shivering, physical expression of his total exhaustion. In the seventy-two hours since his capture the teams of interrogators had been working non-stop, not allowing him a moment's rest, and there was no sign of an end to his ordeal.

"I've told you everything."

When he spoke, Shoheibi could hear the desperation in his voice.

"Come on now." Parker's voice remained as gentle as ever. "We both know better than that."

"What more do you want from me?" Bitter self-disgust had replaced the desperation. "You know everything I've done since I arrived in England. I've betrayed my friends and my people. What more do you expect?"

"The truth, Hassan. That's all we're after."

"So far we've simply been scratching the surface." Weissmann, the third man present, was an Israeli. He was there as a courtesy. "You've only told us what you had to. We knew most of it already."

Ordinarily Shoheibi would have told them nothing at all. He flattered himself that he could have withstood torture if necessary. What he hadn't bargained for was the sheer weight of evidence against him. His own flat had been clean, of course, but they'd obviously had him under surveillance for weeks. Leila's place, a supposedly safe house, had been a gold mine for the British. The weapons alone were sufficient to tie him in with the killings at St. John's Wood and Orly. Then there had been the passports, the other forged documents and, most damning of all, his account book. Shoheibi had always known it was a form of suicide but he'd had no real say in the matter. His paymasters had insisted on knowing where their money had gone. Nowadays, even terrorists had to keep up with the bookwork.

"You still don't seem to appreciate the situation, Hassan." It was Parker speaking again. "At the moment, you're completely outside the legal process. We can do anything, and I mean absolutely anything, we like with you."

"For instance, we could even send you back to Beirut."

Shoheibi was glad that his hands were back over his face again because

he wouldn't have liked them to see how the Israeli's barb had struck
home. Death itself didn't frighten him so much. It was what went before
it. There was nothing quite so terrible as the wrath of former friends,
especially if those friends happened to be Arabs.

"Now, Hassan." Suddenly Parker was all business as he sorted through
the photographs on the table in front of him. "Tell me about this woman."

As soon as Shoheibi took his hands away from his face, the pain in his
eyes started again. It was almost as though his eyeballs had been
sandpapered. Even so, he only had to glance at the photograph to recognise the subject.

"She's a friend of Leila's," he said. "She works at the Embassy with her."

"Name?"

Parker was sitting with his pen poised. Although the interrogation was
being taped, he was a compulsive note-maker.

"Monica Heller."

"Ending *er?*"

"I think so."

The name went down on the pad in front of Parker.

"OK. You met her at Heathrow last Wednesday. What were you doing at
the airport?"

"I've already explained why I was there."

"So refresh our memories."

The order came from Weissmann. If he ever had the opportunity,
Shoheibi intended to kill the Jewish bastard. However remote, the prospect gave him something to hang on to.

"Tripoli had sent word for me to hit one of the El Al flights. I was at
Heathrow doing the reconnaissance. I had to find a suitable site for the
rocket launcher."

"When was this attack scheduled?"

"It wasn't. The operation was still at the planning stage."

"We already know about the launcher." This was one of the weapons
which had been found at Leila's house. "How about the team? Who were
you going to use?"

"I hadn't decided. They'd be flown in once everything was ready."

Weissmann's grunt reflected his scepticism. Parker, however, was forg-
ing on.

"Where exactly did Miss Heller fit in?"

"Mrs. Heller." Shoheibi corrected him automatically. "And she didn't
fit in anywhere. She was at Heathrow to meet her daughter—I think she's
at a finishing school in Switzerland. We bumped into each other in the
concourse."

"The meeting was by chance?"

Now it was Parker's turn to be sceptical.

"It was a coincidence. I was surprised to see her there."

Parker looked across at Weissmann and the Israeli gave an almost imperceptible nod of his head to indicate that they should move on. The El Al operation was something they'd be returning to later.

"What about this man?"

Shoheibi was being offered another photograph and this was the moment he'd been dreading. Ever since he'd realised that the British had photographed everybody he'd been seen with over the past few weeks, he'd known it must come. He hoped his face had given nothing away.

"Jan-Carl Ramirez," he said. "Revolutionary manqué."

"What the hell is that supposed to mean?"

"Ramirez talks a great revolution. He'd change the world if he wasn't too busy drinking and whoring."

"By the sound of it, you don't like him very much."

Shoheibi shrugged with assumed indifference.

"Ramirez is all right. He gives good parties and he's generous with his women too, once he's finished with them."

"So what's your connection with him?"

Another shrug.

"Tenuous. I think he contributes to a couple of the South American groups. I know for a fact that he talks about Marighella as though he was God. That's as far as it goes, though. He's not what you'd call committed."

"How did you meet?"

"At a party. I was introduced by a friend of mine."

"Name?"

"Ernesto Larra. He's the Cuban cultural attaché in Paris."

"Does that mean Larra is DGI?"

Shoheibi deliberately hesitated. He'd far rather talk about the Cuban Dirección General de Inteligencia than about Ramirez.

"Possibly," he conceded.

"Yes or no?"

"Yes."

Parker made another note.

"What's his field of operations?"

The questions went on and on and on. Now, however, Shoheibi had one small source of satisfaction. He might have given an awful lot away but at least he'd managed to hang on to his most important secret. For the time being Jan-Carl was safe.

Paul Atkinson was a tall, gangling man in his late fifties with a slight resemblance in both appearance and manner to James Stewart. As head of the department he could have held himself aloof as his predecessors had done but this wasn't his style. He wanted people to be able to talk to him when they had something to say. This was why Parker had no hesitation in joining him at his table in the canteen.

"How's it going, John?"

Atkinson had noticed the purple smudges under the other man's eyes. He knew Parker had been driving himself hard.

"You've heard the tapes, sir. With Shoheibi's help we should be able to clear up every act of terrorism since Cain killed Abel."

"Maybe. I suppose you've heard the news from Paris."

Parker snorted disgustedly and stabbed viciously at a potato with his fork. A two-year stint in Paris had made him the department's resident Francophobe.

"It's no more than I'd have expected. So long as it isn't on their doorstep, the French don't mind where the shit lands."

"Some of them do. The head of the DST phoned me to make his personal apologies."

"How very considerate of him." Parker didn't bother to mask his sarcasm. "I suppose that makes everything all right. We drop a dozen terrorists in his lap, he promptly lets them go but he does apologise afterwards."

"It wasn't his decision, John." Atkinson kept his tone mild. "Pierre didn't want to deport them but the order came down from the Ministry of the Interior. Pierre has promised us complete dossiers on all of them."

"That's a fat lot of use when they're on the loose again." Parker refused to be mollified. "Those bastards change their identities as easily as most people change clothes."

Atkinson decided it was time to change the direction of the conversation. Unlike the younger man, he knew that banging his head against brick walls gave him a headache.

"How about the loose ends over here?" he asked. "Are they all being tied up satisfactorily?"

"We've dealt with most of them as they cropped up. About the only one we're holding fire on is that Ramirez character. I'm not entirely happy about him."

Atkinson nodded to show that he was in total agreement.

"Weren't Special Branch any help?"

"Not really. Their file on Ramirez more or less confirmed what Shoheibi told us. It's the same with the Israelis. Weissmann checked back with Tel Aviv and he's clean there as well."

"But you still have your doubts?"

Parker shrugged unhappily. It was always difficult to put hunches into words.

"I just don't know. On the face of it, Ramirez is strictly small fry. He's a playboy who gets his kicks from associating with big, bad terrorists. At the same time, I can't help feeling he's a little too good to be true. His stint at Lumumba University in Moscow worries me. Then there's the way Shoheibi reacted. I'm almost positive he was holding out on us. He was too keen to change the subject."

"I noticed that when I listened to the tape. Do you have any idea how you're going to handle it?"

"Some. Surveillance hasn't turned up anything one way or the other. I thought I might go along and take a look at Ramirez myself."

"When?"

"Tonight. If it's OK with you, I'll take Shoheibi with me. It might be interesting to see how they react."

"That's a good idea. Put the two of them together and you might strike a few sparks. I'll be interested to hear how it goes."

Atkinson was gathering his plates together as he spoke. Despite what they'd said, neither man was expecting a great deal from the confrontation. It was all simply routine.

Departmental regulations clearly stated that all officers should check in their weapons before they went off duty. On this, the last night the regulation was in force, Parker was feeling lazy. So was Roberts, the operative who was accompanying him. The visit to Ramirez was their last assignment of the day and, as neither man fancied the journey back across London, they checked in their automatics before they left headquarters. Weissmann, as a foreigner, was also unarmed.

Once they'd collected Shoheibi from the detention centre, the four of them drove in Parker's Volvo to the luxury apartment block off Park Lane. Ramirez's flat was on the ninth floor and when they exited from the lift, Parker took Roberts to one side. From where they were standing they could clearly hear the sound of music coming from the flat.

"I'll go in alone to soften him up," Parker said. "The rest of you can come in when I'm ready."

"What about friend Mustapha here?" Roberts jerked his head in the direction of Shoheibi. "If we keep him cuffed, the neighbours might start talking."

"Let them. Atkinson will do a hell of a sight more than talk if he isn't cuffed and he does a runner."

"Point taken. Make it as quick as you can, though, will you? I'm on a promise tonight."

Parker agreed to do his best. Then he headed towards the door of 9C while Roberts and Weissmann moved their prisoner out of sight.

Ramirez was obviously on far more than a promise and he was still zipping up the fly of his trousers as he opened the door. Stripped to the waist, he wasn't a particularly impressive figure. Although he'd only just passed thirty, years of soft living had already given him a belly which sagged down over the waistband of his trousers. Facially, he was exactly what the photographs had suggested, plump-cheeked, bespectacled and going a little thin on top. By way of a contrast, the blond who was modelling a bath-towel in the bedroom doorway was only plump in the right places. Parker spared a second to examine her appreciatively before he introduced himself.

"John Parker." As he spoke, he flashed his identification card. "I'm with the anti-terrorist squad."

"Guy Fawkes," Ramirez answered amiably. "I'm fully booked for November."

Ramirez was holding out a hand to be shaken and, taken by surprise, Parker accepted it. He found the grip to be as weak and flabby as the rest of Ramirez looked.

Once he was inside the flat, Parker decided to cut the interview even shorter than he'd originally intended. He no longer had much faith in the hunch which had brought him there. Although he'd been in the anti-terrorist section long enough to know that his quarry came in all shapes and sizes, he was a great believer in first impressions. Ramirez was clearly a buffoon with more money than sense and everything he'd seen so far tallied with what Shoheibi had told him. Parker only had to look around him at the extravagant furnishings, or at the blond, to see where the playboy image had come from. He'd never seen anybody who looked less committed.

"Drink?"

Ramirez had already poured a large whisky for himself.

"No thanks. I'm on duty."

"That sounds heavy. Which of my friends has been up to something naughty? Or is it those parking tickets I've been collecting? Has somebody finally seen through my masterplan to disrupt traffic in London?"

Although Ramirez spoke English with an accent, it was so slight as to be hardly noticeable.

"I've come in connection with Hassan Shoheibi."

"Ah, the dangerous Arab. What's he been up to then?"

"That's what we're trying to establish. As you're a friend of his, we thought you might be able to help us. We're hoping you can add something to what we've already learned about him."

Ramirez didn't even pause to think.

"Well, I do know he's a terrorist, of course."

"You do?"

Parker was caught off-balance by the man's apparent naivety.

"It would be hard to miss, wouldn't it? I mean, nobody could possibly look as furtive as Hassan does without being up to something anti-social. Are you sure you won't have that drink?"

It took Parker less than five minutes to admit to himself that the visit had been a complete waste of time. It would be worth keeping an eye on Ramirez, if only because of his admitted terrorist connections, but this was all. He'd stage his little confrontation to keep Roberts and Weissmann happy, then they could drop Shoheibi off at the detention centre and clear off home.

"There are some colleagues of mine waiting outside. Is it all right if I invite them inside?"

"Why not? The more the merrier. If you like, I'll rustle up some more women and we can all have a party."

Somehow Parker managed to dredge up a smile. He was beginning to understand Shoheibi's attitude towards Ramirez—the man was an unmitigated pain in the arse.

While Parker went across to the door, Ramirez headed for the bathroom to collect his shirt. He also retrieved the Czech 9mm M75 from his washbag. Ever since Hassan had dropped out of circulation, he'd realised that he might be in trouble. Only the certainty that Hassan wouldn't talk had kept Ramirez in London but since Parker's arrival he was no longer so sure. Although it had gone smoothly enough so far, he wasn't prepared to run any risks. To be taken in for further questioning would be a disaster.

By the time Parker returned, Ramirez was back in the living room, doing up the last button of his shirt. The sight of the manacled Shoheibi standing between the two newcomers hit him like a hammer blow and the Arab's obvious uncertainty told Ramirez all he needed to know. Hassan had talked in order to save his own skin.

"Hello, Jan-Carl."

Like his smile, Shoheibi's greeting was tentative. He was only too well aware of how dangerous Ramirez was.

"It's good to see you, Hassan. I'm led to understand you haven't been behaving yourself."

Even as he spoke, Ramirez was pulling the automatic out from beneath his shirt. Nothing which had gone before had prepared Parker for what was happening now. It was so unexpected, so totally unnecessary, that he could only stand and watch as Ramirez put the first two bullets into

Shoheibi's chest. The next two hit Roberts and Weissmann in the head and it was only now that Parker started to react, instinctively throwing himself at Ramirez. His thrill-seeking playboy had been transformed into an ice-cold killer before his very eyes and, as he saw the automatic swing towards him, Parker knew that Ramirez wouldn't miss. This was his last coherent thought before the fifth bullet tore into his throat.

"Jan-Carl," the blond shrieked from the bedroom doorway. "What are you doing?"

"I'm killing people, you stupid bitch. It's what I do for a living."

On his way to the door, Ramirez paused long enough to put the remaining bullets in his clip into Shoheibi's head. Only then did he start to run. As he raced for the stairs, the girl began screaming inside the flat which had been his temporary home. She was still hysterical when the first police arrived some five minutes later.

CHAPTER ONE

It was already warm inside the curtained room and it was warmer still after Ricky had switched on a couple of the big arc lights. However, the heat wasn't the reason the young West Indian in the corner had stripped to his underpants. Ricky had never gone in for elaborate costume dramas and when he made a skin flick, skin was what he showed. Under his direction, interior shots took on a whole new meaning.

"Come on, Erroll love," he lisped. "Let's have the knickers off as well. We're all boys together so there's no need to be shy."

It was a wonder that Ricky managed to keep a straight face when he spoke because he had almost as many female chromosomes as Maggie Thatcher. Come to that, he probably had more. I might have made some comment myself if Ramona hadn't been there to save me the bother.

"I think I ought to resent that, Ricky," she said from the sofa. "Either that or you need your eyes tested."

Ramona was already stripped for action, which was a very persuasive argument for not blinking more than necessary. Whatever his other faults might be, Ricky definitely believed in giving value for money and all the skin he put on display was top quality. Ramona was sleek and smooth and tanned with full breasts which were still capable of resisting gravity on their own. In fact, they were doing a hell of a sight better than my stomach since I'd been desk-bound in London. She caught me looking across at her and smiled. I smiled back before she returned her attention to the magazine she was reading.

"Would you look at that, Philis," Watson breathed in my ear, leaning uncomfortably close. "Sling it over his shoulder and he could disguise himself as a petrol pump."

I grunted noncommittally and wished Watson somewhere else. I found him only slightly more amusing than bubonic plague. In any case, Erroll wasn't the reason we were out visiting. We'd come because of Ramona and I went back to watching her, trying to understand why what she did for a living hadn't left some mark on her. Perhaps it was the prude in me but it seemed indecent somehow, far more so than the hardcore films she starred in. Ramona still looked as fresh and wholesome as she'd done four years previously, back when I'd first recruited her. This was probably why she was so successful in her chosen profession. And why she was so useful to us. I couldn't think of any better bait for a honey trap.

"Do they really do it?"

"Do what?"

I really didn't like Watson very much. This probably had something to do with his red hair and freckles. And the fact that he had a mental age which made the average gate post seem bright. How he'd ever found his way into SR(2) was a complete mystery to me.

"I mean, is the sex for real or is it faked?"

"Most of it's for real."

"Jesus Christ."

All Watson's attention was reserved for the two actors and he was oblivious to the hostile glare Ricky was beaming in his direction. Ricky was the producer, director, cameraman and financier for the epic which was about to be filmed and firmly believed he was in the vanguard of art and culture. This meant self-delusion had to be one of his strong points. On a cultural scale of nought to a hundred, Ricky wouldn't have registered.

"Now, dears," he said. "You're both quite clear about what you have to do, aren't you?"

"If they aren't, I'll be happy to draw a few diagrams."

Although Watson laughed appreciatively at his witticism, nobody else could muster a smile and the aside did nothing to boost his general popularity. It rather surprised me that Ricky had managed to keep his temper for so long. I suspected that this was only out of deference to me.

"Ramona," Ricky went on. "Try to remember that you're acting under duress. You're only doing it to save the child. Let's have you looking ashamed and frightened."

"That shouldn't be too difficult." Watson had insensitivity down to a fine art. "The way he's hung, I'd be bloody petrified if he came anywhere near me."

Ricky had finally had enough. He took his work seriously and Watson's asinine comments had finally broken his self-control. He was about to say something but I managed to beat him to it.

"OK, Watson," I said. "You'd better get outside now."

"Outside?"

Watson wasn't sure he'd heard me correctly.

"That's what I said. Somebody has to stand guard duty. We don't want the police bursting in here while Ricky's at work, do we? It might be embarrassing."

He didn't believe my explanation for a second, which all went to prove there was sense in him somewhere, and for a moment I thought he might actually object. Then he looked at me again and reconsidered. All the same, he made sure he slammed the door behind him when he left.

"I'm sorry about that," I said. "With any luck, he'll grow out of it eventually."

Ricky shrugged.

"It's not your fault, Mr. Philis. You can't choose who you have to work with."

He went on with his instructions to the two principals and I continued to watch Ramona. The complexities of our relationship worried me a little. Although I'd been thinking about the problem all morning, I still wasn't sure of the best way to handle her. Ricky was easy. A few threats and a bit of cash were all that was needed to keep him in line. Besides he liked being dominated and it wouldn't really matter whether it was me or Watson doing the dominating. Ramona was different, though. The threats had long since lost any edge they might have had and she didn't need the money. It disturbed me not to know why she agreed to work for me and only one thing was certain. Telling her that I was no longer her control wasn't going to be easy.

I was still brooding about this when the telephone started ringing in the corridor outside. Ricky muttered something obscene, then minced off to answer it. It was no more than a few seconds before he reappeared.

"It's for you, Mr. Philis."

"I was afraid it might be."

I pushed myself out of the armchair, automatically compensating for the stiffness in my left knee. This was the reason I'd been desk-bound for so long. A lot of people assumed it was an injury I'd collected in the line of duty and I hadn't bothered to put the record straight. Shooting myself in the leg on the SR(2) range hadn't been the cleverest thing I'd ever done.

"Don't start filming yet," I told Ricky. "It could be I'll have to mess up your schedule a bit more."

Although Ricky pulled a face, he didn't voice his annoyance. He was always very careful not to upset me. I closed the door behind me before I picked up the phone.

"Yes?"

"It's Farrell here. What's it like to be a voyeur?"

"Terrific. Is that all you wanted to know or is there something else?"

"The old man wants to see you."

Now it was my turn to pull a face.

"Urgently?"

"What do you think? I wouldn't be disturbing you otherwise."

"Tell him I haven't finished here yet. See if he can manage without me for another couple of hours."

"I'll try, Philis, but I can't promise anything. Pawson knew where you were when he told me to phone."

While Farrell was checking, I picked up the address book which was lying beside the phone and idly flicked through it. Nearly all the names inside were masculine. If Ricky had been a few years younger, we could have used him for a lot more than his camerawork.

"Philis?" Farrell sounded slightly out of breath. "Pawson says he'll allow you an hour. You're to go straight up when you get back to headquarters."

"Fine." This was longer than I'd expected. "Tell him I'll try not to be late."

I could hear Farrell laughing as I hung up. Nobody in the department was ever late for an appointment with Pawson, not unless they had a death wish. Do that and you were likely to be rewarded with a six-month assignment in Vladivostok.

"It's not your lucky day, Ricky," I announced once I'd rejoined the others. "I have to speak with Ramona now."

Erroll laughed, Ricky looked upset and Ramona rose from the sofa. She looked even better standing up than she had sitting down.

"Do you want me dressed?" she asked.

"It would do my blood pressure a favour. Besides, you're going to attract an awful lot of attention on the street if you don't."

Ramona smiled, then headed for the bedroom. She seemed completely unaware of her nudity, which was more than I could say for myself.

"How about me?" Ricky inquired. "Am I needed as well?"

"Not this time. You can stay here and give Erroll some more coaching."

"In that case I'd better get dressed myself." The West Indian had almost as good a smile as Ramona. "I'd hate Ricky to get any ideas."

"Perish the thought, dear. I'm as straight as they come."

Somebody might possibly have believed him if he hadn't leaned across to fondle Erroll's knee.

Although the sun was shining palely, there was a fresh breeze which made me wish I'd brought an overcoat with me. Ramona, dressed only in a thin sweater and jeans, seemed to be oblivious to the cold. She'd taken hold of my arm and, even through the material of my jacket, I was aware of the warmth of her. I could also feel the soft pressure of her breasts against my arm and it was one of those times when I regretted the nature of our relationship. What little authority I had as her control would have been undermined by any real intimacy.

It would have been nice if we hadn't had Watson tagging along with us.

The silly smirk he was wearing showed that he'd misinterpreted the significance of our linked arms. I'd tried to explain something about Ramona to him before we'd left headquarters and even then I'd suspected that I was wasting my time. I also suspected that Pawson had made a mistake when he'd instructed me to pass Ramona on. OK, I was a field agent and controlling the casual labour wasn't what I was paid for. There was no arguing with this but Pawson had overlooked one salient point. Ramona was tied to me, not SR(2), and I didn't think she'd take kindly to working for anybody else. This could simply be vanity but I didn't think it was.

Once we were inside The Feathers, I rewarded Watson for his smirk by leaving him up at the bar. I could sense his resentment as I escorted Ramona to a table by the window and this didn't bother me at all. The wind had put some colour into Ramona's cheeks and she was looking younger than ever. Her files said she was nearly thirty but there were times when she could pass for a teenager. This was another element in the equation that I had to allow for. I found her attractive and it was no use pretending otherwise.

"Well, Philis," Ramona said, pushing a strand of chestnut hair back from her forehead. "Who is it this time?"

The photograph was in an envelope, the name typed underneath. She only glanced at it for a few seconds before she handed it back to me.

"Is he an Arab?"

"What else could he be with a name like that?"

"True. When do we meet?"

"He's going to a party in Mayfair on Friday night. So are you."

"On my own?"

"No, you'll have Watson as an escort. He'll point you in the right direction. After that it's up to you."

This was the fifth occasion I'd employed Ramona on the department's behalf so she knew most of the right questions to ask. In return I gave her some of the answers and it took less than ten minutes to cover the important ground. Then Ramona came up with the question I'd known I wouldn't be able to avoid.

"How about reporting back?" she inquired. "Will we be keeping contact in the normal way?"

"Not quite." I was trying to use my beer glass as a shield. "There's a slight change in procedure."

"What is it?"

She had clear green eyes and her level stare was rather disconcerting. Her defences had gone up immediately. Men had been trying to feed her a line since puberty and Ramona could spot a lie before it was properly hatched, even when it came from an expert like me.

"You'll be reporting back to Watson."

"You mean you're handing me on?"

"Not at all." I was George Washington Philis, as honest as the sky was pink. "I'll still be your control."

"My remote control."

This was an accusation.

"It's nothing for you to be upset about. I'll still be available in an emergency."

"Bullshit." Elegant or not, this was a pretty fair summary. "I think I need another drink."

Watson collared me when I approached the bar, wanting to know whether we were ready for him to join us. I said that we weren't and left him muttering darkly to himself about social outcasts. It seemed he was getting the message at last.

"I'm not going to do it, Philis." Ramona had barely allowed me time to sit down. "I refuse to be passed from one member of your department to another."

"You're over-reacting."

"So what? That's a female prerogative."

I sipped my beer and thought how proud of me Pawson would have been. There had to be a worse way I could have handled her but I couldn't think of it offhand. I decided to change my tactics slightly.

"I'm not doing this from choice, you know."

"I am, Philis. That's the difference between us. I choose to work for you. I choose not to work for a little prick like him."

Her contemptuous jerk of the head was directed at the bar.

"You're doing him an injustice. After all, I've seen him in the showers."

"Very funny."

My attempt to lighten the mood was being treated with the contempt it deserved.

"Watson's not so bad when you get to know him." He was worse but I'd been taught to stand up for my colleagues. "Besides, like I said before, I'll still be your control."

"Like I said before, bullshit."

This should have been the moment for me to apply a bit of pressure, remind Ramona how vulnerable she was. There was only one minor drawback. When it came right down to it, Ramona was one of the least vulnerable people I'd ever met, a feature of her character that I'd always admired. Besides, I was fast running out of time. In a few minutes I was due back at headquarters for my meeting with Pawson.

"OK," I decided. "Let's leave it for now, Ramona. Forget I ever mentioned any change. We'll keep contact in the normal way."

"That isn't good enough, Philis."

Ramona's sudden smile suggested that everything was all right again. Now she'd had her own way, we were back on an even keel.

"Let me guess. You want me to grovel as well."

"Oh no." Ramona was shaking her head. "I expect a much higher price than that. You're going to be my escort to the party on Friday night."

She didn't have to twist my arm very hard because her cooperation was far too valuable to risk. In any case, I hadn't wanted to hand Ramona on to Watson in the first place. This would have been almost as much a waste as feeding pearls to swine.

Pawson was going through his Oxbridge phase. At least, that was the only reason I could think of for the way his office had been redecorated. Vinyl oak panelling had been tacked up on the walls, his bookshelves were suddenly filled with meaty Victorian tomes and he'd taken to sitting behind a huge, battle-scarred desk which properly belonged to the days of quill pens. For all I knew, he had a mortar-board and gown hidden away in one of the cupboards. I sipped my sherry and did my best to ignore the telephones and the computer terminal which were there to shatter the illusion. Like most things connected with Pawson, it was all a front anyway. Whatever his surroundings, he remained the same shark at heart.

Good as it was, I'd already classified the sherry as a danger sign because Pawson's hospitality was usually of the Last Supper variety. He only ever bothered to be nice to me when he had something lined up which would make crucifixion seem like a peaceful holiday. Quite apart from the sherry, his attitude was all wrong. He was being affable, friendly and relaxed, all characteristics which were totally alien to him. Greeks bearing gifts were trustworthy compared with Pawson.

I took another sip of my sherry and watched him suspiciously. Despite the new setting, he still looked far more like a fading Riviera gigolo than an academic. His dapper moustache, oiled grey hair and sun-lamp tan gave him the appearance of the kind of man mothers ought to warn their daughters against. Not that I'd ever make the mistake of considering Pawson a figure of fun. He had power and he had ability, not to mention almost as many scruples as a bull had udders.

"How did it go this morning?" he inquired.

"Badly," I told him. "I'm afraid I blew it."

Pawson laughed, yet another danger sign. Mistakes were occasionally tolerated but they never, ever amused him.

"I'd have put money on it. Your problem, Philis, is that you lack detachment. You always have to get yourself personally involved."

"Detachment be damned. Like I told you before, it's more a matter of trust. Ramona likes me. She feels safe working with me."

"That shows how little she knows you, Philis." Pawson was gently mocking me. "Next thing you'll be telling me she looks on you as a father figure."

"Brother figure, if you don't mind. I'm not that old."

"Whichever it is, I hope she approves of incest. Let's face it, Philis. If she wasn't so attractive, you'd have dropped her like a hot potato."

"If she wasn't so attractive, she wouldn't be any use to us. You can't bait a honey trap with somebody who looks like the back end of a bus."

"That's true, I suppose."

I drank the last of my sherry and looked up at the Landseer print which now graced one wall. It was hideous enough to fit in well with the decor of the revamped office.

"What's the flap about?" I asked. "Farrell implied that it was urgent."

"Jan-Carl Ramirez," Pawson answered succinctly. "He's surfaced at last."

Although this was most inconsiderate of him, Pawson hadn't really answered my question.

"Since when has he been our problem? I thought Atkinson's mob were the ones with the vendetta. They've been waiting years to lay their hands on him."

"Ramirez isn't in Britain. He had a bit more sense than to come back here."

This explained it because Atkinson's anti-terrorist brief was purely domestic. Considering the thugs he employed, this was probably just as well. The British image abroad was bad enough as it was.

"Why not feed Ramirez to the Israelis then?" I still failed to understand why he should be our problem. "They have the odd score or two to settle with him."

"It was the Israelis who fed him to us."

"They did?"

Now I was really surprised. Normally the Israelis were most meticulous about washing their own dirty linen themselves.

"He's popped up in Oslo," Pawson explained. "Norway is a very sensitive area for Mossad at the moment."

It had been ever since the debacle at Lillehammer. The Israeli intelligence agencies didn't make many mistakes but those there were tended to be spectacular. Killing the wrong man had been bad enough; getting caught had been unforgivable. It would be some time before Tel Aviv authorised any more clandestine operations on Norwegian soil.

"OK, that lets them out. It doesn't explain how we came to be elected."

"We weren't. I volunteered to handle the operation."

"That was very generous of you."

"I thought so too."

Pawson was smiling at me. I'd have been doing the same if I'd been in his shoes, because volunteering was no great chore for him when he was going to be sitting safe and sound in London. From the sound of it, I'd be the poor fool risking life and limb in Oslo. Carlos the Jackal might have received more publicity but Ramirez was up there in the same league.

"I'm not a hit man," I said.

"You do surprise me, Philis." This was a glimpse of the real Pawson. Sarcasm always had been his substitute for wit. "How exactly do you explain the trail of bodies you manage to leave behind wherever you go? In any case, this isn't a sanction. We want Ramirez taken alive."

"What's happened to our extradition treaty with Norway?" I was still refusing to accept the inevitable. "Surely the Oslo police could pick up Ramirez for us."

"They undoubtedly could but we don't want Ramirez's capture advertised. Do that and British Airways is likely to have half its fleet hijacked. You're forgetting that Colonel Gaddaffi has placed Ramirez under his personal protection."

I nodded gloomily. Libya was the international terrorist's equivalent of a holiday camp anyway but Ramirez was a special case. He was the man who'd snared Majid Zaltan.

Most of Gaddaffi's opponents had long since had the sense to get out of the country. Although this didn't necessarily mean they were safe, they did at least have a chance of survival provided they were careful. Majid Zaltan had been the nearest thing to a leader that these Libyan emigrés had had. A one-time professor at the university in al-Bayda, Zaltan was intelligent and articulate and his non-stop sniping from his new home in Paris had been a constant irritant to the government in Tripoli. This alone would have been sufficient to earn him a place at the top of Gaddaffi's death list but Zaltan hadn't relied on words alone. He'd actually had the temerity to organise two separate attempts on Gaddaffi's life.

The newspapers in Tripoli and Benghazi had responded with editorials which portrayed Zaltan as a cross between Jack the Ripper and Genghis Khan. On a more practical level, efforts to dispose of him permanently were stepped up, but none of them met with any success until Ramirez had intervened. On the morning of April 27, 1977, Zaltan had boarded a plane in Paris for the short flight to Geneva, where he was supposed to address a pan-Islamic conference. Six hours later his Air France Boeing had landed in Tripoli, hijacked by a team led by Ramirez.

Almost overnight, Ramirez became a Libyan national hero. He was publicly decorated by Gaddaffi and appointed as his personal bodyguard. According to the hysterical Libyan press, Ramirez was Superman's big brother and nothing had changed since then. Every new exploit had only added to Ramirez's prestige and reputation within Libya. If Gaddaffi was God, Ramirez stood at his right hand. There'd been so much propaganda that the Libyan leader would have to react to any news of Ramirez's capture and, at the very least, he'd let his National Youth fanatics off the leash. This was a prospect which did nothing to add to my enthusiasm.

"It's going to be very messy."

I always had tried to look on the bright side.

"Not necessarily. The whole idea is that Ramirez quietly disappears. We shan't be advertising where he's gone to."

"You won't need to. However careful we are, it won't be a secret for long."

"Maybe not." When it came to shifting his ground, Pawson was an expert. "There's still no cause for pessimism. If the worst comes to the worst, there are one or two levers Whitehall can pull to calm the Libyans down."

"It won't matter how many levers they have. Gaddaffi isn't exactly famous for seeing reason easily."

"But he does have a modicum of common sense, Philis. He knows he can't afford a major confrontation with us."

Pawson didn't believe this any more than I did. Gaddaffi was a certified maniac and the men working for him were even worse, which meant any operation involving the Libyans almost inevitably ended up a bloodbath. This seemed as good a reason as any for asking Pawson for another sherry.

I should really have asked Pawson for the bottle, because the further he went with the briefing, the less I liked it. Until now I'd never had reason to go into Jan-Carl Ramirez's background in any detail so nearly everything I knew about him had been gleaned from the popular press. As usual, this was only a small part of the story. Ramirez wasn't simply an international terrorist and a cult figure for the lunatic fringe. It seemed he had a KGB connection as well.

From 1968 to 1970 Ramirez had been a student at the Patrice Lumumba University in Moscow which, together with the Institute of International Relations, was renowned as one of the chief recruiting grounds for the Komitet Gosudarstvennoe Bezopasnosti. It was estimated that as many as 90 per cent of the faculty were moonlighting for the state security service, so it was hardly surprising that many of the more promising Third World students graduated to further training with Department V of the KGB. What made Ramirez special was that he hadn't travelled the direct route. If he had, he'd have been closely monitored from the moment he left Russia and would never have had the opportunity to take Atkinson's men by surprise.

The incident which had lulled everybody's suspicions had also helped to establish Ramirez's reputation as a playboy. In January 1970 he'd been expelled from Lumumba University and kicked out of the country, charged with "anti-Soviet provocation" and a generally dissipated lifestyle. In retrospect, of course, this could be seen as a classic example of KGB disinformation and, since Ramirez had emerged from the closet, it had been established beyond any reasonable doubt that he still retained close links with Moscow. As far as I was concerned, this was the icing on the cake.

"Let's get this straight," I said. "The actual mission is to snatch Ramirez and spirit him out of Norway."

"Right."

Pawson was nodding his head in agreement.

"OK. Now even if we're successful, there's no way that Gaddaffi is going to let it go. We can be pretty sure that the Libyans will take reprisals, either against SR(2) as a department or the individuals responsible for the abduction. Would you say that's a fair assessment?"

"Only if we presuppose that the Libyans discover that we're responsible. The whole idea is to arrange matters so that the blame can't be pinned on us."

"I'm looking on the dark side and one reason for that is that you've said the KGB will be lined up against us as well."

"I haven't said that at all, Philis. There's virtually no danger of any direct Russian involvement. They have their image to think about. They can't afford to acknowledge Ramirez as one of their own."

This was undeniably true because Moscow had always been very sensitive about its supposed links with international terrorism. Besides, the KGB was run by pragmatists and the loss of Ramirez would be very small beer indeed. The danger lay in quite another direction.

"Does Gaddaffi know about the Russian connection?" I asked.

"Almost certainly."

"In that case, as soon as Ramirez goes missing Gaddaffi will turn to Moscow for help and the KGB aren't likely to turn him down. They'll cooperate, even if it's only to feed their computers with an analysis of how the operation was handled. However careful we are, they'll piece it all together sooner or later and my money is on sooner. What we're talking about here is a potential disaster. Ramirez simply isn't worth all the hassle."

For a moment or two Pawson didn't say anything. He seemed to be absorbed in an examination of his immaculately manicured fingernails. When he did raise his head, his sincere, I'm-telling-you-the-truth expression had settled into place and he was looking me straight in the eye. This was when he was at his most dangerous.

"Normally I'd be inclined to agree with you, Philis. It probably is going to be messy. There may well be unpleasant repercussions. Unfortunately, there's no real alternative because Ramirez the terrorist is simply a minor side issue. At the moment he's involved in something far more important. Perhaps vital would be a better word. Whatever the cost, Ramirez has to be picked up and it has to be done quickly."

"I suppose it's no good my asking why."

"I'm afraid not. If it's any help, I can tell you I'm working on the express orders of the JIC and the Foreign Office."

It certainly helped to frighten me because if operational control went that high, I really did have something to worry about. Pawson I could trust within certain limits. He wouldn't ever get me killed without a damn good reason, if only because of the expense involved in training a replacement. With the big boys in Whitehall it was very different. They measured casualties in thousands and losing Philis wouldn't bother them at all. Me it would bother a hell of a lot.

"I'll need protection after we have Ramirez," I said. "I don't fancy being a target for the Libyans. How will I be covered?"

"That's already being arranged. As of today, you're officially transferred to Cairo. The paperwork is already being processed. Naturally you're due the fortnight's transfer leave."

The old ploys were usually the best, otherwise they didn't become old. While I was in Oslo, a stand-in would be enjoying a touring holiday in the Highlands of Scotland. He'd be using my name, credit cards and car. The KGB might be able to pin responsibility on the department but, unless I was very unlucky, I should be in the clear. Now this was settled, I could afford to consider some of the other practicalities.

"Do we know what Ramirez is doing in Oslo?" I inquired.

"I do and that's all that matters." Pawson allowed himself a thin smile. "It's totally immaterial as far as you're concerned."

I translated automatically. What Pawson was saying was that the less I knew, the less I could give away if things went wrong.

"You mentioned that speed was important. Exactly how long do I have?"

"Until yesterday. Ramirez is using a rented villa in Oslo. He's paid in advance until the end of next month but we'd like to have him well before then."

It was sounding more like a cowboy operation by the minute.

"Do I get to pick my own team?"

"Depending on availability, you'll have a completely free hand."

"In that case I want Bayliss."

"Bayliss?" My request had taken Pawson by surprise. "It's not really his line of work."

Bayliss was paid to kill people. It could even be what he enjoyed doing.

"I disagree. You're not going to tell me that Ramirez is in Oslo on his own. He'll have bodyguards."

"Yes," Pawson admitted. "There are three of them."

"Well I shan't be running a package tour. I'll need Bayliss to keep them out of my hair."

"All right."

Pawson had conceded the point.

"When can I talk to him?"

"He's in Lisbon at the moment. I'll have him on a flight to Heathrow tomorrow."

"Fine. I'll sort out the rest of the team this afternoon."

"Do that."

For the time being there wasn't much more to say. All the same, I felt I owed Pawson at least one last gripe.

"I don't like Cairo," I said.

"Who does?"

"It's bloody close to Libya as well."

"Exactly. That makes it the last place any sane person would want to run to. You bother about Ramirez. Your cover will be fine."

I sincerely hoped Pawson was right. Perhaps it was my imagination but the hounds in the Landseer seemed to be sneering at me as I went out.

LISBON, PORTUGAL

Although the unseasonable heatwave showed no signs of abating, it was pleasantly cool inside the Estoril Sol once the glass doors had slid closed behind him. Slipping his sunglasses into his jacket pocket, Peter Bayliss walked through the foyer and into the downstairs bar. It was deserted apart from the barman and Bayliss selected a stool at the back of the horseshoe which commanded a view of both the bar and the foyer.

Gradually, over the next half an hour, the bar began to fill up. First in were a couple of middle-aged matrons. Once they were seated and had their drinks in front of them, they made no secret of their interest in the solitary figure at the bar but Bayliss ignored them. He was well aware of the effect he had on women of a certain age and the knowledge neither disturbed nor flattered him. Next to come in was a group of soberly suited businessmen. They were soon engaged in an animated conversation on the far side of the bar, only interrupting it when something female passed through their range of vision. Bayliss ignored them as well.

He was well into his second Campari soda, and the bar was almost full, when the woman he'd been waiting for finally put in an appearance, sitting out in the lounge with her two friends to drink her coffee. All three of them were in their thirties and, to Bayliss's mind, typical of the upper strata of Estoril society—chic, attractive, expensively coiffured and strangely sexless. Portugal was a country where they still locked up their daughters and sexual awareness often came too late to be enjoyed.

From past observation Bayliss knew it would be almost an hour before the women left. Nevertheless, he finished his drink and settled the bill immediately. Outside the hotel, he checked where the Stag was parked, noted that the hood was down as usual and then went across to his own car. While he was waiting he smoked a cheroot and thought about the message from London. It must mean Pawson had another job for him, an urgent job because he could normally count on at least a fortnight's leave between assignments. The prospect neither excited nor worried him. Bayliss was aware of his limited emotional range and regarded it as a strength.

It was almost five o'clock when the woman emerged, the bright sunlight shimmering on the material of her trouser suit. For a minute or two she remained at the top of the steps, saying her farewells. Then she went across to the Stag and Bayliss switched on the ignition in his hired Fiat. As expected, she was heading towards Lisbon and Bayliss kept close behind her, making no attempt at concealment. It didn't matter anyway but he doubted whether she used the driving mirror for anything other than checking her hair and make-up.

His opportunity came sooner than he'd expected. They caught the lights outside the Casino and Bayliss was able to pull right up beside her. As the Stag was a right-hand drive, only a foot or two separated them and the woman couldn't fail to be aware of the way Bayliss was looking at her. She chose to pretend he wasn't there.

"Senhora Simao," Bayliss said softly.

When she started to turn, Bayliss picked up the pistol from the seat beside him and, very precisely, shot her once in the head. As he released the brake and stamped on the accelerator, Bayliss could see that her face was already a mess of red.

Simao's outer office had been decorated with delicacy and taste and the receptionist had been carefully chosen as well. She was a mulatto, either Angolan or Brazilian, and the blood mix must have been just right when she'd been conceived.

"Yes?" Her voice had a lovely deep timbre to it which perfectly matched her looks. "Can I help you?"

"My name is Peter Bayliss. I have an appointment with Senhor Simao."

"Of course. Will you take a seat?"

The walk, like the smile, was especially for Bayliss because she could have used the intercom on her desk. Standing up, she was taller than Bayliss had expected and she moved with the feline grace of one of the big cats.

It was only a matter of seconds before she returned to announce that Simao was ready to see him. She deliberately held the door so Bayliss had to brush against her as he went past, catching her body scent in his nostrils. He thought it was a shame she had to be so obvious.

"Do sit down, Mr. Bayliss."

Simao's English was flawless and grooming and breeding were stamped all over him, from his silver-grey hair down to his hand-stitched shoes. He looked more like an aristocrat than a gun-runner for the IRA.

"What can I do for you?" Simao asked. "When we spoke on the telephone, I wasn't quite sure what it was you wanted."

"Let's just say I've come to make you an offer you can't refuse."

"That sounds intriguing."

Either Simao had never seen *The Godfather* or he was deliberately being obtuse. Bayliss decided to be more direct.

"I understand that your wife was the victim of a practical joke yesterday afternoon."

"How did you hear about that?"

Now Simao's entire attention was focussed on Bayliss.

"I was there outside the Casino when it happened. In fact, I was in the car next to hers."

With detached interest, Bayliss watched the outraged expression slip into place on the other man's face. Simao was so furious he could hardly speak.

"It was you, wasn't it? You were the man in the Fiat."

Bayliss nodded, vaguely amused by Simao's anger. As Simao reached for the telephone, Bayliss stretched out to take hold of Simao's wrist. He

squeezed until he could feel the bones grating against one another and
Simao yelped with pain.

"I want you to think about something, José." Bayliss had eased the
pressure slightly. "I could easily have used a real gun, not a toy. Then it
would have been blood on your wife's face, instead of red dye. Do you
understand what I'm saying?"

Despite the pain, Simao managed to nod.

"And there are your daughters to consider as well. Some very nasty
things can happen to attractive young girls nowadays."

"What do you want?"

Simao's voice was hoarse and he was having to fight to keep the tears
from his eyes. Bayliss released his wrist and started to explain, feeling
reasonably optimistic. If Simao saw sense, there would be time to drive
out to the little restaurant in Monte Estoril before he had to catch his
flight to London. Manuela's king prawns in brandy sauce were a treat he
wouldn't like to miss.

CHAPTER TWO

President Marcos obviously didn't believe that imitation was the sincerest form of flattery because he was demonstrating his democratic zeal by arresting the opposition Laban leaders for sedition, coercion and intimidation. The Israelis were telling anybody who cared to listen that the use of cluster bombs in southern Lebanon was a necessary act of self-defence. On the far side of the Atlantic in Washington, President Carter was still fighting with his conscience over the neutron bomb.

I was watching the Nine O'Clock News on BBC, checking that everything was all right with the world. I was also trying to eat the rock salmon and chips that I'd picked up on my way home from the Chinese chippy down the road. If there'd been any market researchers around, I'd have told them that the Chinese ought to stick to their laundries, restaurants and aphrodisiacs. The rock salmon had been battered insensible and the chips were limp and soggy. It was the first meal I'd had for a long time which made my own cooking seem tolerable.

The weather forecast was almost as depressing as the news so I switched off the television before I went through into the kitchen to dispose of the last of the congealed chips. I was still trying to remember where I'd put the coffee jar when the doorbell rang. There was a woman outside, an attractive young woman in designer jeans, trainers and a sweatshirt which claimed to have originated in St. Thomas in the Virgin Islands. In her right hand she was carrying a suitcase. Although this was better than a baby wrapped in a shawl, I was temporarily at a loss. The face was vaguely familiar but that was about all.

"Yes," I said hospitably.

"You are Mr. Philis, aren't you?"

"That's right."

"I'm Andrea Montgomery. You're supposed to have been expecting me."

"I was but not until tomorrow." The penny had finally dropped. "You'd better come in."

She followed me inside and dropped her suitcase on the floor. If she was impressed by the flat, it certainly didn't register on her face. Mind you, if she had been impressed, I'd have known there must be something seriously wrong with her. My flat wouldn't have made Ideal Home even in the days when most people lived in caves.

"I caught an early plane," Andrea explained. "I thought it was easier to come here than to book into a hotel. Is that OK?"

"It's fine if you don't mind sleeping in the spare room. Would you like a coffee? I was just about to make one."

She would and I located the coffee behind the bread bin. It only took me a minute or so to boil the kettle and rinse out a couple of cups. Then I took the drinks through. Andrea had installed herself in the most comfortable armchair. She seemed to be remarkably self-possessed.

"What's happened to your hair?" I asked. "In the photograph I saw it was much darker."

"I invested in a bottle of Revlon. Does it bother you?"

"Not at all. It suits you. I'm more interested in how much you were told before you were dragged down south."

Andrea pulled a face.

"Nothing. I was given your address and told to treat you as my lord and master until you said otherwise."

"That seems to allow me plenty of scope." When I smiled, she responded. Her file said she was 28 but without make-up she looked much younger. "The basic idea is that we play Happy Families for the next few days. Our passports will say we're Mr. and Mrs. Hemmings. Apart from being my ever-loving wife, you'll be the communications link with London."

"Where exactly are we going?"

"Oslo. I'll give you a full briefing tomorrow. Is it all right if I look through your suitcase?"

"That rather depends. Is this some personal perversion or is it connected with the job?"

She was smiling at me again.

"It's strictly business," I assured her. "I gave up stealing knickers from washing lines years ago."

Going through her things didn't take me very long. Although the clothes she'd brought with her were fine for a young spinster, they were a trifle flamboyant for what I had in mind.

"You'll have to do some shopping in the morning," I told her. "Get yourself a new wardrobe, smart but on the drab side. We don't want any heads turning when you go by."

"I should be so lucky." Andrea was doing herself an injustice. "Who picks up the tab?"

"The department so don't stint yourself. And you'll have to pop into headquarters. Do you know Farrell?"

"Only by reputation."

"Well he's not really that bad. He's going to be your link in London. The two of you will have to establish procedures."

"OK. What special equipment will I need?"

"Farrell will handle that." When I glanced at my watch, I saw that it was nearly half-past ten. "Look, I'll have to leave you to settle yourself in. Your bedroom is through that door there. The sheets are in the airing cupboard in the kitchen. If there's anything else you need, just help yourself. I'm afraid I have to go out."

My meet with Bayliss was at midnight which seemed appropriately cloak and dagger. The SR(2) training school might have taught him all the right moves but his style was pure Ian Fleming. According to what I'd heard, Bayliss hadn't been born like us ordinary mortals. He'd emerged ready-made from an Action Man packet.

I knew all about the Theory of Probability and roulette which was why I was using a modified Labouchere system on all the even bets. Provided you had long arms, a mind like a computer and unlimited capital it was virtually impossible to lose. Unfortunately, all I could manage was the long arms. When a long sequence of even red numbers sent my losses plunging towards the amount I could reasonably expect Pawson to authorise on my expenses, I called it a night.

Needless to say, Bayliss was winning. The bar overlooked the casino and I had a clear view of the table where he was playing. He already had a sizable pile of chips on the baize in front of him. As I watched, the croupier pushed some more in his direction. Bayliss appeared totally indifferent to his success. If anything, he looked bored. Knowing him, he'd have looked exactly the same if he was losing heavily. Bayliss had an emotional range which would have made a block of wood seem temperamental.

If I was honest with myself, I didn't like the man. On the other hand, I didn't dislike him either. I'd never bothered to check but I suspected that this was how most people felt about him. Bayliss certainly didn't have any close personal friends within the department and I didn't know of any enemies. He was too self-absorbed for that, too preoccupied with his own image. Sometimes I wondered whether Bayliss had ever done anything badly. There had to be flaws somewhere but they were bloody well hidden.

The only weakness I was aware of was also one of Bayliss's main strengths. It was his emotional sterility which made him so good at what he did. And he was good, there could be no doubt about that. Inevitably, there were any number of rumours about him floating around headquarters, a fair number of them concerning his sexual predilections because Bayliss was certainly no monk. The consensus seemed to be that he was absolutely superb between the sheets, his technique and control faultless, which was no more than I'd have expected. The sole criticism appeared to be that he had all the commitment of a clockwork dildo. I'd no way of knowing how true this was but it fitted in well enough with what I knew of the man. Bayliss himself would probably have been pleased by the assessment.

It was another ten minutes before Bayliss pocketed his winnings and came to join me. Several heads turned to watch him as he walked across the casino, most of them female. Tall, athletic and blond, Bayliss had it all. The Greeks had used to make statues of men like him and his immaculate DJ made me wish I'd had my own suit pressed more frequently. I bought him a drink and he offered me one of his specially imported cheroots in return. It only took a couple of puffs to make me feel light-headed. I'd been trying to stop smoking and my body was starved of nicotine.

"I'm glad I'll be working with you, Philis," Bayliss said.

"The same goes for me, Peter."

This exchange of platitudes helped to define our relationship. Bayliss would have said the same whoever his partner had happened to be.

"Any thoughts on how we play it?"

"One or two."

In actual fact, the way Pawson wanted it handled didn't leave us with a great deal of scope. The emphasis was on speed, not elaboration. Apart from Bayliss and Andrea, I'd decided on a team of six and the first three of them were already in Oslo. The rest would be leaving in the morning, although I wouldn't be flying in with Andrea until the day after. Then it would be a matter of monitoring Ramirez's routine and establishing some means of access. I was only allowing a few days for this phase but, of necessity, I had to be flexible. In this line of work there were no hard and fast rules.

The one point I was definite about concerned Bayliss himself. He wouldn't be needed during the initial phase. He'd earn his money when we actually grabbed Ramirez and this meant I had to strike a balance. Although I needed Bayliss close to hand in case we could move faster than I'd anticipated, it was pointless to have him in Norway any longer than was strictly necessary. Pawson's main priority might be to lay his hands on Ramirez. Mine was to ensure there were no obvious targets available when the Libyans began thinking about reprisals.

We spent the best part of an hour hammering out the details. Bayliss would drive one of the department's vehicles up through Holland, Germany and Denmark. He'd cross into Sweden on the Helsingor-Helsingborg ferry, then travel up the west coast to Uddevalla. The way he drove, Bayliss should easily manage this in a couple of days. Uddevalla was close enough to the Norwegian border for our purposes and there should be sufficient tourists around for him not to be an oddity. For the actual job, I'd arrange for a car with Oslo plates and all the appropriate documentation to be ready for him in Uddevalla. The weapons would be in Oslo and I'd handle their disposal afterwards.

"How long will it take me to drive to Oslo from Uddevalla?" Bayliss asked.

"I don't know the road myself but it shouldn't take more than three hours. I'll have somebody make a couple of dummy runs to find out."

Bayliss nodded, apparently satisfied.

"How about my cue? I won't want any messages from Oslo."

"I shan't be sending any. Your starting orders will be local."

I'd be moving most of my team out of Oslo before Bayliss and I went after Ramirez. One of them could stop off in Uddevalla.

"Do I exit by the same route?"

"Hopefully. Our part is finished once we have Ramirez. Pawson will have another team to take him out of Norway. There shouldn't be any problem but I'll have alternative routes set up just in case."

Once again Bayliss seemed satisfied. He knew there were no guarantees I could give him. Although I'd try to arrange it so he was back in Sweden before everything hit the fan, this might not be possible.

"Will you have an inside contact?" Bayliss inquired. "Somebody close to Ramirez."

"Possibly."

"It would make things a lot easier."

"I know."

I also knew it would be bloody dangerous. This was something I was still thinking about when Bayliss returned to the gaming tables.

I didn't like parties very much. I never had and I didn't suppose I ever would but it did help to have Ramona standing beside me. Tonight she'd elected to play the young innocent. Her hair hung loose over her shoulders, she was wearing very little make-up and her white dress was modesty itself. I doubted whether there was a red-blooded male present who wouldn't have liked to deprave and corrupt her. At least, this was the way I felt and I happened to know she'd learned all about depravity and corruption before she was properly into her teens.

"Don't you want to dance, Philis?"

"You must be joking. At my age I'm lucky I can still walk."

"Your poor old thing." Ramona was laughing. "You'll need a better excuse than that."

"How about my knee? In case you hadn't noticed, I'm still limping."

"I know. It gives you that irresistible Byronic look." Ramona was determined to dance so I didn't have any real say in the matter. "Come on, Philis. It's a nice slow one. I promise to return you in one piece."

All the other couples were gyrating a couple of paces apart but this wasn't Ramona's style. She preferred to be in close, pelvis to pelvis, where she could be sure I'd know exactly what I was missing. Considering what she'd forgotten to wear under her dress, I soon had a pretty fair idea. During the couple of minutes we spent on the dance floor, my blood pressure must have doubled.

"There, that wasn't too bad, was it? You'd be quite a good dancer if you weren't so stiff."

There was nothing innocent or virginal about the smile which accompanied her remark but I ignored it and accompanied Ramona back to the bar. The group had disappeared for its mid-concert fix and the disco had taken over again, the music so loud that conversation was virtually impossible. It was far less effort to sip our drinks and watch the gyrations of the other guests. I was slowly developing a headache. Being blinded and deafened wasn't my idea of fun.

"Shukri is here. He's on the far side of the dance floor."

Ramona had to mouth the information in my direction, relying on my skill as a lipreader. I nodded to let her know I'd spotted him as well. So far I hadn't had an opportunity to tell her I had something far more important lined up for her and Shukri was no longer her concern. We were forced closer together when a group of young men bellied up to the bar, all of them modelling leather, chest hair and gold ornaments. The stench of aftershave and body cologne was almost overpowering.

"I suppose it's time I went to work." Ramona was shouting in my ear. "Unless, of course, you're going to insist on another dance."

"In my day it was the men who did the asking."

"That's one of the things I like most about you, Philis. You're so stuffy and old-fashioned."

Ramona accompanied this with an affectionate peck on my cheek. The alcohol was percolating through my system by now and I wouldn't have objected to something a bit more full-blooded. Another three or four drinks and my cool, professional image would have sunk without trace.

"Let's get out of here," I suggested.

"We're leaving? What about Shukri?"

"You can forget him. Come on. I'll explain somewhere quieter."

I started breaking a way through the sea of bodies blocking our route to the exit with Ramona following close behind. She was probably thinking I'd finally weakened. To be honest, I wasn't so sure I hadn't.

The music had been so loud, it was a couple of minutes before my ears started functioning normally again. Fortunately, Ramona was in no hurry to talk. She preferred to sit back in her seat and watch me drive. As always, her lack of curiosity was rather disconcerting.

"How do you fancy a holiday abroad?" I asked.

"So that's it. You'd be surprised how many men your age make the same suggestion."

"This will be a working holiday."

"What they had in mind would have been hard work too."

I laughed. Most of the conversations we had together seemed to be heavily laced with sexual allusions. Ramona was irritated by my refusal to acknowledge the GO signals she kept flashing in my direction. Me it simply frustrated.

"Can you make coffee?"

"If I really put my mind to it."

"Let's go to your place, then. We can talk there."

I hadn't visited Ramona's flat before. While she was busy in the kitchen, I prowled around the living room, poking and prying without really learning a great deal. Apart from a few books and her record collection, it was almost totally impersonal which didn't really surprise me. Ramona's acting, if it could be called that, was no more than an extension of her normal life. Her lack of a permanent identity had always intrigued me.

After Ramona had come through with the coffee, I gave her the bare bones of the Oslo operation. They were very bare indeed because I didn't tell her anything of the real purpose of the mission. I didn't even give her Ramirez's name. All Ramona needed to know was that she might or might not be expected to find her way into somebody's bed. Inevitably, the very lack of detail told her a great deal.

"This is different, isn't it, Philis?"

"Yes and no." I was trying to be reasonably honest with her. "If I do decide to use you, your basic role will be the same. There will be one or two new complications, though."

"Will it be dangerous?"

Her tone was matter of fact. As far as I knew, there weren't many things which frightened Ramona. Apart from her looks, it was this inner strength which was her greatest asset.

"Possibly," I conceded, "but it's nothing for you to worry about now. If I do need you, you won't be sent in blind. I'll give you all the background when I name the target."

"You're going to be in Oslo too?"

"Naturally. I've taken what you said about remote controls to heart."

We smiled at each other and my professionalism was slipping again. When a man and a woman started developing their own private jokes, it was a sure sign that one foot was on the slippery slope. I was honest enough to admit that the foot belonged to me. If it hadn't been for the special nature of our relationship, I'd have been quite happy to let myself slide.

"When do you want me in Norway?"

"Tomorrow night. I'll handle the travel arrangements and accommodation for you."

Ramona pulled a face.

"That's very short notice."

"I know but it can't be helped. We don't have a lot of time to play with. Do you want to know the financial arrangements?"

"Not really. I think I can trust you not to do me down. There is one thing, though. If I'm leaving tomorrow, Ricky will be upset. It'll mess up his shooting schedule."

"That's tough on Ricky." I finished my coffee and stood up. "I'll be in touch first thing tomorrow."

Ramona had stood up too.

"Do you have to go, Philis? It's still early."

"I'm afraid so. I have a lot of things to do."

It hadn't occurred to me before that Ramona might be lonely and this was something I thought about on the way down in the lift. Some of the conclusions I reached were rather disturbing. When it came right down to the bottom line, I was lonely too. I didn't need Pawson to tell me that there was no fool like a lonely fool.

OSLO, NORWAY

As he stroked her short, blond hair, Ramirez felt quite fond of the girl. She might be a whore but she certainly believed in giving value for money. He felt much more relaxed now, the tension temporarily drained away.

"I'll settle up with you outside," he said, swinging his legs out of bed.

"You've finished with me now?"

Her English was as good as his.

"I'm not sure. Wait here a minute and I'll find out."

Abboud and Hosni were sprawled in the main room of the rented villa, watching television. Zomor, the third of his bodyguards, was presumably outside with the dogs. He seemed to prefer canine company to human.

"How was she?" Abboud inquired.

"Good," Ramirez told him. "Very good, in fact."

"Can we try her?"

Ramirez shrugged indifferently.

"Why not? She's booked for the night."

Once the two bodyguards had gone through to the bedroom, Ramirez walked across to the window and peered out into the darkness. The girl had been a welcome diversion but he'd been cooped up in the villa too long and he was already bored with the waiting. Besides, he was sure he was on a wild goose chase. The rumours about Mobutu taking a private holiday in Norway were simply the product of somebody's over-developed imagination. Ramirez would be glad when the signal came for him to leave Oslo for Luanda. That was where the real work was.

The London flight had only been half-full and Parun wasn't really interested in the disembarking passengers. His work at the airport had been finished when he'd seen Zarkov safely off on the plane to Stockholm. Even so, he found his eyes drawn to a couple standing near the head of the queue. The woman was attractive enough for Parun to be positive he'd never seen her before. However, the tall man with her seemed vaguely familiar. He definitely didn't figure on any of the current Scandinavian lists. Parun ran a last check through his mental filing cabinet but he was already sure of this. When it came to names and faces, his memory was exceptional. All the same, the man was definitely familiar, a face from the past. Although it was none of his business, Parun was nothing if not conscientious.

"Over there, Carl," he said to his driver in Russian. "The man eighth in line."

Carl's lips moved as he counted.

"The tall, dark-haired man in the suit?"

"That's the one. Find out where he goes."

"Do you want a photograph?"

"You have a camera with you?"

It was very rare for Carl to surprise Parun.

"It's in the car."

"Excellent. In that case you'd better photograph the woman with him as well."

Parun had other, more important work to do and it was late evening

before he returned to the Embassy. He found the two photographs waiting for him on his desk, together with Carl's report. It took him less than
ten minutes to match up the man's photograph. He clipped it to Philis's
file with a brief note before he tossed it into the tray. It would be passed
upstairs in the morning. The woman was more difficult. There was nothing about her in Parun's records so he arranged for her photograph to be
transmitted to KGB headquarters in Moscow. Then Parun dismissed the
matter from his mind. It was simple routine, nothing more, and he didn't
really expect to hear anything more about it. He would have been most
surprised to learn of the far-reaching consequences his diligence was
destined to have.

CHAPTER THREE

It was raining, a steady, continuous downpour which had begun before I'd arrived in Oslo and looked like continuing for ever. Conditions couldn't have been much worse when Noah had decided to build the Ark. Even with the windscreen wipers of the Volvo going full blast, visibility was terrible.

"The villa is coming up on the right," Gilbert informed me. "It's the one with broken glass on the wall and the double gate."

"I've got it."

Gilbert was holding the speed steady at about twenty. Even so, I only caught a fleeting glimpse of the house through the wrought iron of the outer gates before we were past. It was simply an indeterminate, rain-shrouded mass in the middle distance. A mile further on, the road curved round to the lakeside, ending in a small parking space. There were four boats moored at the jetty. Ours, a cabin cruiser, was the smallest and tattiest. Once again it was Gilbert who did the driving. A small, sandy-haired man in his forties, he was in charge of the surveillance team.

"Keep well out in the lake," I instructed.

"I was planning to but there's one minor snag. With all this rain we're not likely to see much, even with the binoculars."

"We might strike lucky." I'd read somewhere that it was a leader's responsibility to keep up morale. "The weather forecast said something about sunny intervals."

"It always does. The Norwegians are all bloody optimists."

The wet weather was even keeping the fish at home. Although we spent a couple of hours with the rods out, pretending to be fishermen, we didn't get a single bite. Nor did I get a decent view of the villa. By the time we agreed to call it a day, we were both soaked to the skin. We were also chilled to the marrow and thoroughly fed up. My sole consolation was that I didn't have Gilbert's cold to contend with. His coughs and wheezes proved just how beneficial the climate was.

On the way back in the Volvo, I caught another brief glimpse of Ramirez's hideaway, then I directed Gilbert back into Oslo proper. The

Danish aquavit I bought him put a bit of colour back into his cheeks. By the second one, I was beginning to thaw out as well.

"Summarise what we have so far," I suggested.

"Bugger all."

Gilbert had had his answer ready.

"Perhaps you'd like to type that out in triplicate. I'll send a copy back to Pawson."

"What else am I supposed to say, Philis?" He was grinning at me across the table. "There's no routine for us to latch on to. Ramirez stays stuck inside the villa and that's it."

"I don't know." Now it was my own morale I was trying to boost. "Lunching out seems to be a habit."

"Sure, and so far he's used a different restaurant every day. We don't know where he's going until he actually arrives."

"At least it gives us something to work on."

Gilbert still looked unconvinced and I tended to agree with his assessment. This was why I waved the waiter across for a refill. The alcohol might not stimulate any new ideas but it might make the old ones seem better.

Whatever Pawson might think, it would probably have helped to know exactly what Ramirez was doing in Oslo. Gilbert evidently thought so, because he'd requested permission to break into the villa while Ramirez and his bodyguards were out and to plant a few bugs. Although I'd been sorely tempted, I'd vetoed the suggestion. Pawson had made it very clear that we were in Norway to snatch Ramirez, not collect information. Besides, there was no guarantee we'd have time to tidy up afterwards. Loose surveillance might have its drawbacks and frustrations but it was much, much safer. There was less chance of alerting Ramirez and we wouldn't be leaving anything for interested parties to latch on to afterwards. If there was an afterwards, that is. To date we didn't appear to be making a great deal of progress.

"How would you do it, Ray?" I asked.

"I wouldn't. I'm too bloody ill."

Gilbert sneezed violently to prove his point. I sipped my aquavit and waited for him to recover. Gilbert wiped his nose on a large, red handkerchief, then sneezed again. By the looks of him he was running a temperature. If there'd been more time, I'd have had a replacement flown in.

"Look, Philis," he said. "The way things seem now, it would have to be very public. We could grab Ramirez from his car or at a restaurant. Either way we'd have to take out the bodyguards. That means it would be very messy."

It also meant witnesses, with the additional possibility that innocent bystanders might be hurt. None of this had been part of my brief from Pawson.

"You're ruling out the villa?"

"Aren't you?" Gilbert sneezed again. "You and Bayliss couldn't handle it on your own. You'd have the same three bodyguards to deal with, plus a couple of damn great Rottweilers. The only safe way to hit the villa is in force."

Gilbert wasn't simply allowing his natural pessimism through to the surface. He was giving me his considered opinion.

"OK. Let's leave that for the moment. How's the woman situation?"

"I get my share. At least, I did until I went down with pneumonia."

"Not you, you fool. Ramirez."

The aquavit made smiling easier.

"One of the bodyguards drove in a brass the other night. Apart from that, nothing."

"It's not like him, is it?"

"Not if his reputation is anything to go by. Mind you, he did have a longish spell in Libya. All that sand could have caused problems."

"Let's hope not. Anyway, we'll give it another thirty-six hours. If nothing develops by then, we may have to think again."

Gilbert and his team didn't know about Ramona yet. I was still hoping we wouldn't have to use her.

"You're the boss. Incidentally, how does married life suit you?"

He accompanied the question with a leer.

"You have a dirty, evil mind, Ray. Andrea and I have a purely professional relationship."

"Of course you do. How much does she charge? Or is it the other way round?"

He'd already left before I could think of a suitable rejoinder.

Thirty-six hours went by and Ramirez still wasn't doing anything to help us. Apart from his lunchtime excursion, he remained closeted in the villa while Gilbert's team hovered discreetly outside, waiting for a break. It didn't come so I decided to force the pace a little. Andrea had already passed on a couple of messages from Pawson reminding me that I was supposed to be working against the clock.

It was a considerable help to discover that Ramona hadn't been idle. The very nature of her role meant she needed more cover than anybody which was why, at my suggestion, she'd made the trip to Norway a working holiday. Scandinavia was still a centre for the porno film industry and I'd been able to provide her with several addresses. There was no language problem as the dialogue wasn't exactly a vital part of the films she made so it was no real surprise to learn she'd been offered far more work than she could possibly handle. I suggested that she ought to accept at least one of the roles. Although Ramona didn't know it yet, at some time in the near future the Norwegian police, and others, would be taking a keen interest in her. Her credibility would be very important.

Unfortunately, there was very little I could do to help her with the main problem. There was no way I could provide Ramona with proper access to Ramirez. Worse still, she'd only have the one shot at him.

"Why is that?"

"Lunchtime is the only occasion he ever leaves the villa. And he doesn't stick to any one restaurant. So far he's eaten in a different one each day. It might look a tiny bit suspicious if you followed him on a culinary tour of Oslo."

"I can see what you mean." For once Ramona was completely serious. "How long will I have to work my feminine wiles?"

"It's impossible to say but I doubt whether you'll have much more than an hour. The moment we know the restaurant he's using, the word will be passed on to you. Then it's up to you to get there as fast as possible."

"You have somebody following Ramirez?"

"Yes."

"In that case, why don't I go with them? It would speed things up."

I was shaking my head before she'd finished speaking.

"It would also ruin your image as little Miss Clean. It's important that you can satisfactorily account for every minute of your time here in Oslo. I'd rather lose a few minutes than risk compromising you."

"And I didn't know you cared."

Ramona seemed relaxed and confident.

"If I can, I'll try to arrange it so you have a table close to Ramirez but that's the best I can do. Otherwise, you'll be completely on your own. Do you think you can handle it?"

Ramona shrugged.

"You say Ramirez is heterosexual?"

"Very. Promiscuity is almost a way of life."

"Is he involved in any heavy relationships at the moment?"

"Not that I know of. He certainly hasn't got anything on the boil here in Oslo."

"In that case, it should be all right."

Perhaps Ramona was over-confident. This was why I sounded a note of warning.

"It will be lunchtime, don't forget. His libido isn't likely to be at its most active."

"Maybe not but it can always be stimulated. I'll give you a demonstration if you like."

Generous as it was, I turned the offer down. Ramona didn't need the practice and I was supposed to be a married man.

Good though I knew she was, I didn't share Ramona's optimism. Ramirez wasn't in Oslo on a social visit and the amount of time he spent in the villa showed he was intent on maintaining a low profile. I wasn't at all sure he'd allow himself to be picked up. As a dedicated womaniser, he was bound to notice Ramona at the restaurant. Unless there was something seriously wrong with him, he'd undoubtedly find her attractive. Whether or not this would be sufficient to prise him out of his shell was something else again. It would all depend on how bored Ramirez was. And on how secure he felt.

We did get one break in our favour. Ramirez's restaurant of the day was off the Karl Johansgate in the centre of Oslo, only five minutes from Ramona's hotel. This meant she was already there by the time I arrived outside the restaurant. There wasn't really anything for me to do but the whole operation could hinge on how successful Ramona was and I wanted to see how she did. I also wanted to take a good look at the bodyguards. A lot was going to depend on how good they were.

The hour I'd allowed for stretched to ninety minutes. Either the service was slow or something was distracting Ramirez from his normal schedule. Although I'd no way of knowing what was happening inside the restaurant, I had a clear view of the entrance from a café opposite. I spent the time sipping over-priced coffee and watching the rain come down. I was also wondering what to do next if Ramona failed to pull it off.

I was doing her an injustice because she obviously had everything well under control. When Ramirez eventually appeared in the doorway, Ramona was beside him and they were both laughing. Better still, Ramirez was in no great hurry to tear himself away and I couldn't say I blamed him. Ramona's dress suggested modesty but the carefully applied make-up hinted at the wanton below the surface. Ramirez wasn't to know this was one of her stock roles. He stayed with her under the canopy for almost five minutes, engaged in animated conversation while his two bodyguards suspiciously scanned the passing pedestrians. As usual, the third bodyguard had stayed at the villa to man the fort. When they did say their goodbyes, they parted like old friends.

It was a good moment for me and even a touch of jealousy couldn't spoil it. Ramirez appeared to be hooked. Now it was simply a question of reeling him in.

The first thing I did when I was back at my hotel was to put a call through to Ramona. I might have been a witness to what had happened but I was interested in the details. Besides, Ramona would probably want to boast a little.

"How did it go?" I inquired.

"Not too bad." She sounded smug. "I think he's interested."

"You only think?"

Ramona laughed.

"That was me being modest. Ramirez definitely has designs on my fair English body."

"So you'll be seeing him again?"

"Unless he changes his mind. He wanted me to go over to his villa for dinner tonight but I told him I already had another engagement. I didn't want to seem too much of a pushover."

"That's fine as long as you don't play too hard to get. What alternative arrangements have you made?"

"Nothing definite. I didn't want to commit myself until I'd had a chance to talk to you."

"But you are in contact?"

My sudden concern must have shown through because Ramona was on to it in a flash.

"Don't worry, Philis. I'm an expert at this, if you remember. I'm supposed to phone him at the villa later this afternoon. He wants to know whether I can manage tomorrow night."

"Try to persuade him to take you out somewhere. Don't make a big thing out of it but it would be a help. We want to winkle him out of the villa if it's at all possible."

"Your wish is my command, O master. I'll do my best."

On past form, this should be more than good enough.

"Fine. I'll phone back later to find out what arrangements you've made."

"Why not come on over? I'm free this evening."

No conversation with Ramona was complete unless she managed to introduce an element of sexual needle into it. Even over the phone it had been a passable imitation of Mae West.

"That's not a very good idea," I told her. "We shouldn't be seen together."

"We don't have to go out. You could always sneak up to my room again."

"I still think it's safer to telephone."

"Coward."

At least, this was what I thought Ramona said before she hung up. True or not, the accusation did nothing to spoil my good humour. The waiting was nearly over. At long last, everything seemed to be slotting into place.

My good humour lasted for all of two hours and it was Gilbert who ruined it for me. I could tell his cold was worse the moment I walked into the bar where we'd arranged to meet.

His face had a waxy, unhealthy sheen which was almost greenish under the strip lighting. They put healthier-looking people than him into coffins.

"You look terrible," I told him.

"That's what I like about you, Philis. You always go out of your way to cheer people up."

Gilbert took time out to demonstrate his hacking cough. When the spasms had died down, he examined his handkerchief suspiciously. He was probably counting the pieces of lung tissue.

"Mind you," he went on. "You're going to feel bloody terrible as well once I've passed on the glad tidings."

We were interrupted by the arrival of the waiter. Gilbert was still sticking to his aquavit but I settled for a beer.

"Your little scrubber did well," Gilbert commented once we were alone again. "Ramirez didn't know what had hit him."

"I know. I was there."

"So Toomey told me. You should have seen her in action, though. You could almost hear the fly-buttons bouncing off the ceiling. Even Ramirez's ears were standing to attention."

"You had some bad news for me."

I was being very patient.

"You won't want to hear it."

"Try me."

"OK. Your sex bomb was wasting her time. Ramirez is leaving."

"Leaving?"

I wasn't practising to be a parrot. I simply couldn't believe what Gilbert had just told me. Rather, I didn't want to believe it.

"One of his bodyguards popped out to a travel agent's this afternoon," Gilbert explained. "He picked up four tickets for Luanda. That's in Angola in case you didn't know."

And Angola was in Africa.

"When are the tickets for?"

"Thursday."

"This Thursday?"

Gilbert nodded with gloomy satisfaction. It meant we had less than forty-eight hours to play with.

"Shit." I was irrationally pleased with the amount of feeling I managed to put into the single expletive. "Why the hell would Ramirez suddenly want to go to Luanda?"

"I wouldn't know, Philis." Ill as he was, Gilbert didn't intend to miss the

opportunity to remind me that he'd told me so. "If you remember, I did
suggest bugging the villa. It was you who vetoed the idea."

"OK, OK." If I sounded graceless, this was the way I felt. "How long will
Ramirez be staying in Luanda?"

"Your guess is as good as mine. They were single tickets."

The situation was becoming worse by the minute.

"How about the villa?"

"It's paid for in advance until the end of the month."

This was no help either. All I could do was present the situation to
Pawson because he was the one who'd have to decide whether to abort or
not. Whatever his decision, one fact was painfully clear. My carefully
orchestrated operation was already falling apart at the seams.

GUERRILLA BUILD-UP NEAR BORDER

Kinshasa—A government source in Kinshasa today revealed that
there had been increased guerrilla activity in Shaba province during
the past few days. There have been three separate attacks on police
and FAZ barracks. The same source said there was also evidence of a
continued build-up of FNLC rebel forces in their base camps in
Angola.—Reuter.

NETO DENIES CHARGES BY MOBUTU

Luanda—President Agostinho Neto denied accusations from Zaire
that he was plotting against President Mobutu's regime or giving aid
to its enemies. In a speech to the Chamber of Commerce here today
he said such accusations were simply a smokescreen to hide President
Mobutu's own ambitions in Angola. Neto once again charged Zaire
with launching last month's raid against Caianda in the salient between Zambia and Zaire.

In a speech before Parliament, Premier Lopo do Nascimento said
he had conclusive proof that the government in Kinshasa was sending aid to the UNITA rebel forces in the south of Angola.—Reuter.

CHAPTER FOUR

I didn't really need one but I took a shower anyway. I was that sort of person. Besides, it helped to pass the time while I was waiting for Andrea to return with Pawson's decision and standing under the jet of water was good conditioning for the Norwegian climate. Outside the hotel, the rain was still bucketing down and there was no sign it ever intended to stop. All the local weather forecasters were agreed that it was the wettest Spring since records had been begun. As this was the only Spring I'd been in their country, this nugget of information did nothing to persuade me that my luck was in.

When Andrea came back, I was just rinsing off the soap. If she knocked at the bathroom door before she entered, I certainly didn't hear her. There wasn't even a chance for me to grab a towel before she pulled back the shower curtain. Modesty wasn't one of the words in her vocabulary.

"There are certain things a man likes to do alone," I told her.

"That way you'll end up blind. You're not embarrassed, are you? After all, I've seen naked men before."

"Not all of them have my heroic build." By now I had the towel and I was wrapping it round my waist. "I'd hate you to be overcome with passion."

"I must say it all looked pretty ordinary from where I'm standing."

"That's simply the effect of the cold water. What did Pawson have to say?"

"We're to proceed as planned."

"But we don't have a plan. That's the whole point."

"It's no good blaming me. I'm only the errand girl. Pawson says you're to try for Ramirez before he leaves Oslo. It's vital you don't allow him to leave for Luanda. The stress was on the 'vital.'"

"Damn." I was moderating my language for Andrea's benefit. I was also using a second towel to dry my hair. As I'd have to go out, this was almost certainly a waste of time. "You'd better arrange another meeting with Ray Gilbert. He's expecting me to call."

"Gilbert will have to wait his turn. Pawson wants you to see a Major Forbes first."

"Who the hell is he?"

"One of the military attachés at the Embassy."

Under normal circumstances, this would have suggested Forbes was with military intelligence. Either that or he'd been seconded to the Foreign Office unit.

"Did Pawson explain why?"

"Not really. I think he wants you properly motivated. From what I can gather, Forbes is supposed to give you more of the background."

It was a bit late in the day for this. The last thing I needed at the moment was a bullshit and patriotism session but I didn't have any choice. And, looking on the bright side, there was always the offchance Forbes might accidentally tell me something useful.

"How do I contact this Forbes character?"

"It's already fixed. You're meeting him in three quarters of an hour at a house on the Lillestrom road. I have all the directions for you."

"OK. While I'm getting dressed, you'd better contact Gilbert anyway. Tell him to stand by. I'll be in touch as soon as Forbes has finished with me. And phone Ramona as well. I'll have to find time to see her tonight."

"I thought you might squeeze her in." I wasn't entirely sure whether Andrea was being bitchy or not. "Am I coming with you to see Forbes?"

"I don't see why not?"

After all, married couples were supposed to spend time together. If Forbes should object to her presence, Andrea could always sit out in the car.

Forbes didn't immediately strike me as a military man and this wasn't simply because of his civilian clothes. Although he had the confidence and self-assurance which so often marked the officer class, he displayed none of the other outward signs of army life. His fair hair was on the longish side, his clothes were sloppy and unregimented and his north country accent wasn't something I normally associated with Sandhurst.

On the whole, my first impressions were favourable. Forbes evidently felt the same about Andrea but this didn't stop him sending her to another part of the house while he talked. What he had to say was for my ears only. The house we were using apparently belonged to a Norwegian friend of Forbes who was out of the country on business. He must have been a close friend because Forbes had no reservations about making inroads into our absent host's stock of whisky.

"I've been told everything is about to hit the fan."

Now he'd seen to our drinks, Forbes was ready to begin.

"You could say that. Ramirez is scheduled to leave the country on Thursday."

"That doesn't give us a great deal of time to play with. Exactly how far have your plans progressed?"

"They haven't." There was no harm in giving it to him straight. "Ramirez hasn't done anything to make it easy for us."

"It's access, isn't it? I understand that Ramirez doesn't leave his villa much."

"That's it in a nutshell."

"So how will you handle it?"

"Unless my orders have been changed, we'll have to go into the villa after him. Trying for him anywhere else would mean going public."

"You must avoid publicity at all costs." Now the military was showing through because this was a direct order. "There are any number of reasons, quite apart from your own protection. I realise this makes it more difficult for you but it's absolutely imperative for you to seize Ramirez before he leaves Oslo. We'll be standing by to take him off your hands the moment you have him."

"If we have him."

"No 'ifs' are allowed." Although Forbes was smiling, he meant exactly what he'd said. "You have to capture Ramirez and you have to capture him alive."

"So everybody keeps telling me. Until now, though, nobody has been prepared to explain why."

"That's my job. I'm supposed to impress you with the urgency of your mission."

"Go ahead and impress me then. And make it quick, will you? There's a lot to do in the next twenty-four hours."

"I'll do my best. Tell me, precisely how much do you know about the current situation in Zaire?"

Not a lot, was the honest answer. I did know that President Mobutu doubled as a supporter of democracy and, according to rumour, as one of the most corrupt rulers in Africa. While Zaire itself tottered on the verge of national bankruptcy, Mobutu was supposed to have several billion dollars salted away in Switzerland. I also knew that the previous year Mobutu's opponents had sponsored an abortive invasion of Shaba province. This, however, was the sum total of my knowledge and Forbes was only too happy to fill in the gaps.

To begin with, Forbes concentrated on the attempted invasion. Apparently, a large proportion of the 2,000 members of the rebel army had been gendarmes back in the balmy days of Katangese independence. They'd fled to Angola after Tshombe's overthrow in 1963 and spent the intervening years plotting their revenge. Fortunately, or unfortunately, depending on your point of view, they hadn't plotted well enough. Although Mutshatsha, in the west of Shaba, had fallen without a fight and large areas of the province had been occupied, the rebels had won no major engagements. Worse still, the main rebel drive had petered out twenty miles short of its primary target, Kolwezi. At the same time, the defeat of the rebels had hardly been a triumph for President Mobutu. If the rebels hadn't won any famous victories, nor had the Zairian armed forces. It had taken 1,500 crack troops provided by King Hussan of Morocco and flown south by the French air force to drive the rebels back over the Angolan and Zambian borders.

Nobody, not even Mobutu himself, had believed that this was the end of the matter. Failure though it might have been, the invasion had served to demonstrate just how vulnerable Mobutu's regime was. In particular, the performance of the Zairian army had been shameful. Faced with a ragtag band of poorly equipped rebels, the FAZ had caved in completely. Many of the soldiers had refused to fight at all, despite their superior firepower. They'd preferred to run away or, in some cases, actually desert to the enemy. It had been made painfully apparent that the FAZ alone was incapable of defending Shaba. If the Western bloc wanted to keep its most important supporter in Africa in power, it would have to be prepared to supply Mobutu with muscle in any new emergency.

The widespread support of the civilian population in the areas they'd occupied had been equally encouraging for the rebels. Kinshasa and the national government were half a continent away from Shaba and in Zaire the old tribal divisions were never very far below the surface. As for President Mobutu, his personal prestige had never been at a lower ebb. He and his supporters were seen as being far more interested in feathering their own nests than in the welfare of the people they ruled. Another better organised and better equipped invasion might cause the whole structure of government in Zaire to collapse. The entire country might dissolve into the tribal rivalries which had caused so much bloodshed in the years immediately after independence.

It was also apparent that any second invasion would have some powerful backing. Despite Mobutu's accusations of Cuban assistance, the FNLC rebels had been left pretty much to their own devices on their first attempt. Now they looked like potential winners, the situation was very different. The simple fact that Mobutu was one of the western democracies' most fervent supporters in Africa would have been sufficient to guarantee the involvement of the Soviet Union at some level. The opportunities for disruption were simply too great to resist.

Even if Mobutu himself remained in power, the seizure of Shaba province alone would be a dagger thrust at the country's heart. The very name

Shaba was derived from the Swahili word for copper. The mines in the province produced most of Zaire's copper, cobalt, uranium, zinc, cadmium, silver, germanium, coal, gold, iron, manganese and tin. Over 75 per cent of the country's wealth was concentrated in a single province. Cutting off Shaba from the rest of Zaire would leave the country rather like a chicken without a head.

If this wasn't enough, the Americans seemed intent on handing Zaire to the eastern bloc on a platter. As Forbes put it, President Carter would have done the world a service if he'd stuck to peanut farming. Whatever the moral basis, nonintervention was a disaster when it was put into practice. Despite repeated pleas from Mobutu during the first invasion, Carter had refused to lift a finger to help. The Russians could safely rely on his doing the same if there was a second attempt. No matter how much assistance they offered to the FNLC rebels, there would be no risk of a major confrontation. The most they had to fear was a bombardment of moral platitudes from Washington.

Codenamed Operation Dove, plans for a second invasion had gone on to the drawing board almost immediately. There were conferences in Havana, Algiers and Tripoli. Training camps were established in Angola, Algeria and Libya. The Soviet Union provided vast quantities of modern weapons, either directly or through the Cubans, and agents for the FNLC rebels went on shopping expeditions in Europe. The warning signs were there for everybody to see—a second invasion of Shaba province was only a matter of time.

"Two questions," I said. I hadn't interrupted Forbes because he was boring me. It was simply that I was acutely aware of how little time I had left. "Firstly, how does all this affect us?"

"Quite simply, we can't afford to have the invasion succeed. God knows, there's little enough stability in black Africa as it is. If the invasion is successful, the whole powder keg could blow. When the FNLC do make their move, there has to be an immediate response. As the Americans won't do it, it's up to us."

"You mean British troops will be sent to Zaire?"

For a moment I thought Forbes had ventured into cloud cuckoo land. It was a relief when he laughed.

"Certainly not. We're leaving that to the French and the Belgians. The Congo basin is their traditional sphere of influence and we don't mind them grabbing the glory. But don't make any mistake about it, Philis, it will be a joint operation at the highest level. Our role is to supply logistic support when and if it's necessary. That includes intelligence and Ramirez should be able to provide us with the most important information of all. He knows the FNLC battle plan and, even more important, he knows the date the invasion is scheduled to take place."

This led neatly to my second question.

"Ramirez is a terrorist," I pointed out. "He's a paid assassin. Why should he be privy to such high-level information?"

"Gaddaffi." Forbes's answer was succinct. "You know what he's like. He sees himself as the African messiah and wherever there's any trouble he has to stick his oar in. The situation in Zaire was tailor-made for him. That's why he volunteered Ramirez's services. Ramirez was at the first planning conference in Havana and we can definitely place him as one of the Mongyua group in charge of strategy."

"But what exactly does he have to contribute?"

"Infiltration. This is only guesswork but it's pretty accurate guesswork if you know what I mean. The one thing we can be certain of is that Kolwezi will be the main target. It's right in the heart of the mining complex and it's a fairly soft target. We're pretty sure there are several hundred FNLC men in the town already. If we've read it right, they'll have taken jobs in and around the mines. They've probably established arms caches around Kolwezi and they'll be trying to recruit local Luanda tribesmen. We're pretty sure Ramirez was in charge of training the infiltrators. That's one area where he is an expert."

I nodded and took another look at my watch. With so much to do, I couldn't afford to wait very much longer. Besides, I doubted whether Forbes had much more to tell me. He wouldn't go into specifics even if I wanted him to.

"Two more questions," I said. "Do you know why Ramirez is in Oslo?"

"No."

Forbes's answer was unequivocal.

"Not even any guesses?"

"Not really. There was a rumour a few weeks back that Mobutu might be making a private visit to Norway. There could be a connection but that's pure conjecture. To be on the safe side, we made sure Mobutu forgot all about the trip when we discovered Ramirez was here. Mobutu might not be much but he's all we've got. What else do you want to know?"

"Why doesn't Mobutu beef up his defences in Shaba if he knows there's going to be another invasion?"

My question made Forbes laugh.

"You obviously don't know anything about the FAZ. There's been some attempt to beef it up over the past year but it's still a bloody shambles. Ninety-five per cent of the army is barely fit for garrison duties, let alone serious fighting. Those units which are combat-prepared never move very

far from the President. Another invasion doesn't worry Mobutu nearly as
much as an internal coup would. When it comes right down to it, he
knows we can't afford to allow the invasion to succeed but a coup might be
a different matter. Is that everything?"

"It's everything I have time for."

I drained the rest of my drink and pushed myself out of my chair.
However, Forbes hadn't quite finished.

"I hope you understand just how important your mission is now, Philis.
Your Mr. Pawson thought you might make the safety of your team your
primary consideration. That's why he asked me to brief you more fully.
There are probably only a dozen men who know all the details of Operation Dove. Ramirez is the only one we can reasonably hope to lay our
hands on so he has to be captured, regardless of the cost. I trust I've made
myself clear."

"Crystal clear," I assured him.

And I'd still do it my way. If there were any sacrifices to be made, they
certainly wouldn't be on my conscience.

As soon as I was back at the hotel, I was on the phone to Ramona,
checking that she'd firmed up arrangements for the following night. She
had and this was all I needed to hear for the time being. I repeated my
instructions for her to stay in her room until I came over, then I went off to
meet with Gilbert. It was a different café this time but the schnapps tasted
exactly the same.

The orders I had for him were very specific. Half of his team were to
leave Oslo straight away, one of them departing via Uddevalla. He could
advise Bayliss of the situation and start him moving Oslowards. I left it to
Gilbert to arrange accommodation for Bayliss when he arrived. Provided
there were no more unexpected developments, I wanted the rest of the
surveillance team out of Oslo by the following afternoon. Only Gilbert
himself was to stay behind and he could book himself on a night flight to
London.

Gilbert obviously wasn't happy about the arrangements but, as I explained, I wasn't happy either. Rush jobs were almost invariably messy.

"All I can say is rather you than me, Philis." Gilbert was at his comforting best. "Have you decided yet where you're going to take Ramirez?"

"There isn't much alternative. We'll have to go for him at the villa."

"Jesus Christ." Gilbert was really putting himself out to cheer me up. "I
thought the villa was strictly a last resort."

"That's where we're at in case you hadn't noticed. Can you name
anywhere else we can guarantee Ramirez will be?"

"He's going to see your little dolly bird, isn't he? Can't you arrange anything there?"

"Not without compromising her, I can't. And it would have to be very public."

"I suppose so." Gilbert raised his glass in salute. "Good luck to you then. I'd better be off and hustling."

Now I only had Ramona left to see and I'd deliberately been saving her for last. She was the one bright spot in a grim day.

"He sounds like quite a guy," Ramona commented.

"He is, believe you me. I've only told you the half of it."

If only for her own protection, I'd had to give Ramona a clearer picture of what she was getting into. Although I'd been a trifle concerned about her reaction, I needn't have worried. She'd taken it all in her stride.

The role I'd assigned her was straightforward enough. She met Ramirez as arranged and she packed him off on his own at about midnight. No matter how insistent he might be, Ramirez wasn't to be an overnight guest at the hotel and Ramona wasn't to accompany him back to the villa. How she entertained him until he was packed off was Ramona's concern but this was to be the full extent of her involvement. Later on the police and other interested parties would probably be checking her out. Ramona's cover had to be as solid as possible.

"Is he dangerous?" she asked.

"Not to you. He doesn't have a record of playing rough with his women."

Ramona stood up and went across the room to the window, pulling back the curtains so she could look down on the lights of Oslo. They hardly rivalled those in Piccadilly Circus. Oslo was sometimes called the biggest village in the world which was as nice a way as I could think of for saying it was bloody boring.

All the same, I wasn't objecting to the view from where I was sitting. Ramona had the long legs and taut buttocks which looked so good in jeans and there was nothing much wrong with the rest of her either. She was standing in semi-profile so that I could see the shape of her breasts beneath the flimsy white top, her nipples making miniature mounds of their own against the soft material. When Ramona turned suddenly and caught me staring at her, she smiled. She didn't have to be a mind-reader to guess what I was thinking about. She could see the LU in one eye and the ST in the other.

"You like?"

Her response was immediate, her voice low and throaty.

"It's not too bad, I suppose. If you happen to like that sort of thing."

"Be honest, Philis. It's prime quality and you do like. Is this the night you don't run away?"

"It takes time for the yellow streak to rub off." Although I'd risen from my chair, I'd done so without a great deal of conviction. "Besides, I still have things to do."

"The same old excuse."

Ramona had allowed the curtains to fall back into place. Perhaps I should have kept going to the door, tossing some meaningless pleasantry back over my shoulder on the way, but I didn't. Every time I saw her my hands-off policy seemed more like an act of masochism and an insistent voice inside my head was saying what the hell. It was Ramona who was doing the moving while I remained where I was. When she rested her hand on my bicep, it felt as though her fingers were burning into my arm.

"Well?"

"OK, OK. I do like you a little."

"You don't find me totally repulsive?"

"Not totally, no."

By now Ramona had pressed her body in against mine. I had to put my arms round her to stop us overbalancing.

"I'm glad about that, Philis, because I like you too." Her voice had become a purr. "Don't you think it's about time we did something about it?"

"Well, if you happen to have any suggestions."

"I do so admire a dominant male."

As she spoke, Ramona began steering me towards the bed. Or perhaps I was the one doing the steering.

"What exactly are you doing, Philis?" Bayliss enquired.

"Protecting myself."

Once I had the padding adjusted to my satisfaction, I rezipped my fly. Even Nureyev would have been jealous of the effect.

"I thought you might be trying to impress somebody." Bayliss was almost smiling. This was his equivalent of somebody else's belly-laugh. "I assume it's not simply to save you from predatory females."

Now he was attempting a joke. I'd never known him to be so jovial before.

"The Rottweilers are attack dogs," I explained. "It's only the police and armed forces which train dogs to go for the forearm. Other handlers have different ideas."

Bayliss appeared to lose interest in the subject. When I'd outlined the situation to him, he'd agreed that the villa was the only practicable place to try for Ramirez. I'd given him a plan of the building and grounds and he went back to studying it, impressing the details on his memory. Although Bayliss hadn't said so, I knew he didn't relish going in blind. However detailed I was, this wasn't the same as seeing it for himself. I sympathised with him because in my own mind it had become a cowboy operation. We couldn't even finalise our plans until Gilbert phoned in.

When he'd finished with the diagrams, Bayliss went through into the bathroom. I could smell the smoke as he burned the paper, followed by the sound of the cistern flushing. He stayed to flush it a second time before he rejoined me.

"How good is the tranquillizer?"

Bayliss was standing behind me as I finished the final weapons check.

"The Skelopane is pretty effective if it lives up to its specifications. With a dog the size of a Rottweiler, it's guaranteed for a minimum of half an hour. Maximum duration is about twice that long."

"How long before it hits the dog's system?"

"The Skelopane can put an elephant to sleep in ninety seconds. It won't take more than a second or two with a Rottweiler."

The information made Bayliss pull a face.

"A lot can happen in a couple of seconds," he pointed out.

"I know. That's why I'm using the padding."

This was a subject which no longer amused Bayliss.

"It might be an idea to find an obliging stray we could test it on."

"It would be if we had the time."

Just to prove my point, this was the moment the phone started to ring. Bayliss and I exchanged a brief glance before I went to answer it. If he hadn't been with me, I'd have had my fingers crossed.

"Ramirez has just left the villa," Gilbert told me.

"With his bodyguards?"

"There are just the two of them. Zomor stayed behind with the dogs."

This was what we'd anticipated. I'd have preferred it if all three bodyguards had gone but previous patterns suggested one of them would stay. Zomor was the dog-handler so he was the obvious choice.

"OK," I said. "Thanks for your help, Ray. You'd better start moving."

"I'm already on my way. Be lucky."

When I put the receiver down, Bayliss had finished stacking the weapons in the holdall. It was time for us to be moving as well.

The boat drifted in with hardly a bump. Bayliss climbed ashore, then held the boat steady while I joined him on the jetty. It was very dark, with a light breeze stirring the trees. Although we both had tranquillizer guns in our hands, there was no sign of the dogs.

"Perhaps they're in their pen," I whispered.

"Perhaps they've been properly trained."

Bayliss had a valid point. There was no cover at all on the jetty. Between it and the villa was a small forest of trees and shrubs. Once we were amongst them, we'd have very little warning of any attack.

After the boat was secured, I took the lead. I had a better idea of the terrain and I had primary responsibility for the dogs. Bayliss was going to deal with their handler and at least we knew where Zomor was. For once it wasn't raining and, even from the lake, the night-glasses had enabled us to pinpoint him in one of the downstairs rooms. The flickering reflections on the glass of the window suggested that he was enjoying an evening's television.

When we reached the end of the jetty, I could understand why the Rottweilers hadn't come to greet us. The last section was a metal grille, similar to those used to keep cattle from wandering. The Rottweilers would have been risking a broken leg if they'd ventured out on to it. I paused for a moment, scanning the trees ahead. There were any number of patches of deep shadow which could have concealed a slavering beast. The only thing I could be sure of was that the dogs must already be aware of our presence.

"Remember," Bayliss breathed in my ear. "If they both come at us together, the lead dog is yours."

He could have saved his breath because this wasn't the kind of detail I was likely to forget. Wherever possible, I kept to the grass beneath the trees, moving quietly so I'd hear the Rottweilers when they came. They were heavier, more powerful dogs than Dobermans and equally fierce. They made me nervous. Humans could often be persuaded to back off but this didn't apply to well-trained guard dogs. Once they attacked, their commitment was total. Fifty metres from the water's edge wishful thinking began to set in again. Perhaps my original suggestion had been correct. Maybe the dogs were in their pen after all.

Ahead of us was a wide, open stretch of lawn but I wasn't afraid of being seen. Our side of the villa was in darkness and there was a screen of trees which would have concealed us even if it had been daylight. The grass was spongy underfoot and the rain had made it slippery but I was moving faster now. The first of the Rottweilers waited until we were in the middle of the lawn before it began its attack. He came out of the bushes silently and hard, driving over the grass like a giant, black shadow.

"To your right, Philis," Bayliss hissed urgently.

His warning was superfluous. I'd already swung round to face the danger and the tranquillizing dart from the specially adapted shotgun must have hit the beast somewhere in the chest. The Rottweiler didn't even break stride. He was bearing down on me as fast as ever and, ten feet

away, he sprang, eight stone of ferocious teeth and muscle. I automatically dropped and rolled, hearing the jaws snap together at the point where my throat had been an instant before. I even caught a whiff of his fetid breath in my nostrils.

He hadn't finished with me yet, already twisting in the air. The beast only needed one stride to build up momentum, then it leaped again and this time there was nothing I could do to avoid it. I was still down on one knee and the best I could do was throw up one arm to protect my throat before he crashed into me. We went down in an untidy heap with the Rottweiler on top. He'd found a firm grip on my forearm, teeth working, before the Skelopane finally hit its system. Even then I needed Bayliss's help to prise the jaws apart.

"I didn't know two seconds could last so long."

My voice was shaking as much as the rest of me. There had been a nasty moment when I'd been sure the dart must have missed.

"And we only had one of them to deal with. How's your arm?"

"Bloody sore. If that dog could swim, he'd give Jaws a good run for his money." I'd been examining my arm while Bayliss had been talking. The heavy padding of my jacket had protected me from any serious damage. "Get the dart, will you?"

While Bayliss was retrieving it, I kept a wary eye open for the second of the Rottweilers. It still hadn't put in an appearance by the time we reached the wooden verandah running round the outside of the villa. By now we were reasonably certain that it must be inside with Zomor.

"That's a nuisance," Bayliss whispered.

With him, understatement was a way of life.

"Any bright ideas?"

"You're the boss, Philis. You set up the plays and I follow orders."

"OK. I'll take a look inside."

There were plenty of trees around for me to choose from. I selected one of the sturdiest and scrambled up into the lower branches. From there I had a clear view into the room Zomor was using. It was only a few seconds before I dropped to the ground again.

"Zomor is still watching television," I reported to Bayliss. "The other dog is in the room with him. It looks pretty restless to me."

"So?"

"You try for Zomor through the window. As soon as the glass is broken, I'll deal with the other dog."

Although this wasn't exactly inspirational, it was the best I could manage. We had to have control of the villa and its grounds before Ramirez returned. It was no use hanging around, waiting for a better opportunity.

When we were on the verandah, I risked another quick glance through

the window. Zomor was still relaxed in his armchair, absorbed in the Norwegian version of "Upstairs, Downstairs." However, the dog was far from relaxed. It was on its feet, pacing restlessly and staring fixedly towards the window. I knew it couldn't have seen me but it was obviously aware that there was something wrong out in the garden. I was very glad that nobody had trained it to speak.

Bayliss had one of the 9mm Ingrams with the Sionic noise suppressor. It was the click of the second safety catch in front of the trigger guard which finally made up the dog's mind for it. A little thing like a closed window wasn't going to stand in the way of what it had been trained to do. I ducked back when I saw it start forward but there was no chance to warn Bayliss. Although the window frame was solid wood, it became instant matchsticks as soon as the Rottweiler hit it. A fraction of a second later it hit Bayliss as well and, as he went backwards, the verandah rail splintered under their combined weight. The tranquillizing dart I put into the rump of the Rottweiler was the best I could manage because the game plan had been drastically altered by the dog's intervention. Zomor had suddenly become my responsibility and, as I swung round, I discarded the shotgun in favour of my own Ingrams.

I was far too late. Hudson was still dominating the television screen but his audience had vanished. I went in through the window without giving myself an opportunity to think about what I was doing, aiming for the cover of the sofa. I could still hear Bayliss wrestling with the Rottweiler in the shrubbery but this was only of peripheral interest. The sound of footsteps running upstairs was of far more significance. Once my Ingrams was cocked, I came out from behind the sofa and monitored Zomor from the doorway. He appeared to have taken up a position on the first-floor landing, where he could command the stairs, and I was quite happy for him to stay there.

It was almost half a minute before Bayliss joined me and he was a lot slower coming through the window than I'd been. And the Rottweiler, come to that. His left arm was hanging limply at his side and blood was dripping from under the cuff of his jacket. His Rottweiler had had longer to work on him before the tranquillizer had taken effect than mine had done. We'd made a mistake trying to be humane. We should have killed both dogs and to hell with the RSPCA.

I indicated where I thought Zomor was and mimed what I intended to do. It was a pretty basic ploy but Bayliss nodded his agreement. First, though, I tried to talk the bodyguard down.

"Zomor," I called. "There's no need to get yourself killed. Just come downstairs with your hands on your head and we won't harm you."

Zomor did precisely what I'd have done in his place. He stayed where he was and kept quiet. He obviously didn't believe a word of what I'd said which all went to prove how sensible he was. Ramirez would be the only prisoner we took.

"Come on," I tried again. "We can't hang around all night."

But Zomor could. He was armed and he was ready to kill anybody who tried to go upstairs. This was why he was keeping quiet and refusing to give his exact position away.

Bayliss didn't need a cue from me. One-handed as he effectively was, he'd have had problems with most sub-machine guns but the Ingrams was only nine inches long and weighed under four pounds. It also had a cyclic rate of fire of 1,200 rounds a minute. It took Bayliss a little over a second to empty a 32-round clip through the ceiling and I went up the first flight of stairs in the same length of time. Zomor was taken completely by surprise. He'd been hit more than once by the hail of bullets from below and he only managed one wild shot from his automatic before he tried for the greater safety of one of the bedrooms. A short burst from my Ingrams cut him down while he was still only halfway there.

After I'd checked that the bodyguard was dead, I went downstairs to Bayliss. Although he wasn't complaining the way I would have been, he was obviously in considerable pain. I had to cut away the sleeve of his jacket and shirt before I could examine his arm. One quick look was all I needed. The Rottweiler had taken him just below the shoulder and the whole of his bicep was a hell of a mess. It brought home just how lucky I'd been out in the garden. Apart from the various lacerations and teeth marks, there was probably muscle damage as well. There was so much blood it was difficult to tell exactly how bad it was. It couldn't have been much fun discovering what it felt like to be inside a tin of Pedigree Chum.

"How is it?" I asked.

"The way it looks. Bloody terrible."

Coming from Bayliss, this was a serious complaint. It probably meant I'd have been on the floor screaming in agony.

"There must be a first-aid kit somewhere in the villa. We'd better hunt it up."

"Aren't you forgetting the dogs?" However much he might be hurting, Bayliss still had his mind on the job. "After what happened outside, I don't have much faith in the half-hour guarantee."

"OK. I'll deal with them. You start looking for the first-aid kit. The bathroom seems as good a place to start as any."

To be on the safe side, I gave both dogs a booster shot of Skelopane before I attempted to cart them to their pen. Although this kept them quiet, it didn't make them any easier to cart around. In the end I had to drag them one at a time and I made sure the gate of the pen was securely

locked before I returned to the house. When they recovered consciousness, we'd have two very angry dogs on our hands. I didn't want either of
them to chew me the way Bayliss had been.

He'd found himself a medical box and was sitting in the kitchen, dab-
bing away at his arm with cotton-wool and disinfectant. The way he was
bleeding, this was rather like trying to mop up the Thames with a sponge.
Although I did my best with sticking plaster and bandages, I was fighting a
losing battle. It would take a lot of stitches to stop the bleeding. By now it
was obvious that Bayliss was finished for the night. He was losing far too
much blood to sit around waiting for Ramirez to return home. Bayliss, of
course, disagreed.

"I'll be all right," he insisted, his face white with pain.

"Of course you will," I agreed. "A transfusion every hour on the hour
and you'll be as right as rain."

"It's not that bad."

"Maybe not but it's damn close. Besides," I added callously, "I'll have
more than enough on my plate without having to babysit you. All you'll be
is a liability."

The pain must have been really getting to Bayliss by now because he
didn't bother to argue any more.

"Are you fit enough to find your own way to the doctor?" I asked.

The Embassy had one standing by, ready for just such an emergency.

"If I have to," he answered. "I assume that means you'll be staying."

"Naturally. I've always been a hero at heart."

"There'll be two bodyguards as well as Ramirez."

"I'll manage. Come on. Let's get you out of here."

At least, I hoped I'd manage but this was something I could worry about
once I had Bayliss off my hands.

It would have been much easier to kill Ramirez with the bodyguards
because the Ingrams gave me all the firepower I needed. Their hired
Mercedes was a production model, without any armour-plating, and one
long, indiscriminate burst would have done the trick. Trying to keep
Ramirez intact might save on ammunition but it also meant a hell of a lot
of complications.

I thought about this a lot after I'd packed Bayliss off with all the equipment I no longer needed. If Ramona kept to schedule, I had at least two
hours to wait and I'd have liked to use the time to devise some brilliant
new strategy. Unfortunately, I bogged down at the point where I decided
one of me wasn't enough to handle everything that had to be done. With
Bayliss as my back-up it would have been relatively straightforward. On
my own I had problems unless every single break went in my favour and

fate hadn't been smiling on me since I'd been in Oslo. The sensible thing
to do would have been to leave with Bayliss but ingrained pride had
stopped me. This and the knowledge that I'd have Pawson to face afterwards. He took to failure as easily as kangaroos did to water.

There just wasn't any room for manoeuvre. The outer gates and those in
the chain-link dog fence were operated electronically from the house.
Although there were manual over-rides, they were useless for my purposes. I had to open both sets of gates from the villa to allow the Mercedes
into the grounds. Otherwise its passengers would know something had
happened to Zomor. This in turn meant that I'd have to try for them
when they stopped outside the house.

It was almost a quarter to one when the buzzer sounded to let me know
Ramirez was back from his night on the tiles. It took less than a minute to
operate the gates, then I picked up the Ingrams and went out into the
darkened hallway. Adrenalin should have been pumping through my
system but I felt sluggish and apprehensive. I couldn't escape the nagging
thought that the entire operation had been doomed ever since our arrival
in Oslo.

All the same, up until the moment the Mercedes parked at the bottom
of the steps everything went perfectly. With the door opened a crack, I
could see the outlines of the three men in the car, one in the front and two
in the back. They were no more than a few yards away from me. All I
needed now was for them to pile out of the Mercedes and start up the
steps towards where I was waiting for them. They didn't, though. They
stayed in the car and I was pretty sure I knew why. There were no
Rottweilers gambolling around the vehicle. There was no Zomor in the
doorway, ready to welcome them. I'd left the television on full blast in the
hope that it might reassure them but it wasn't sufficient to cancel out their
other doubts. Now was the time when I'd have liked to have Bayliss in the
garden so the Mercedes was bracketed between us.

The seconds stretched into a minute. The engine of the Mercedes was
still idling and I was willing somebody to get out because I couldn't
possibly allow them to drive off again. It was only when one of the front
doors eventually opened that I realised I'd been holding my breath. The
driver emerged very slowly. The interior light of the car showed the gun
in his hand and he was moving like someone who knew things were
seriously wrong. Ramirez and the other bodyguard remained where they
were, in the back seat, while the driver cautiously moved away from the
car.

"Zomor," he called from the bottom of the steps. "Where the hell are
you?"

At least, he must have said something like that. I didn't speak Arabic so I didn't know for sure and I didn't really care. All that concerned me was a simple matter of coordination. Right foot to hook the door of the villa wide open, right hand to toss the stun grenade into the Mercedes, left hand to control the burst from the Ingrams. Three very simple, basic moves but they had to be performed in one continuous movement and there was absolutely no margin for error.

As soon as the stun grenade had left my hand, I was swinging the Ingrams towards the driver. Although his reflexes were good, he'd thought the grenade was meant for him and he was diving to his right as he raised his automatic, a mistake which cost him precious microseconds. I'd stitched a line of 9mm bullets up his body before he'd hit the ground and as I stopped firing the stun grenade detonated in the front seat of the Mercedes. There was no time to check whether or not the driver was dead. I still held the initiative but only for the second or two it took the men inside the car to recover from the blast. And the remaining bodyguard was sitting on the far side of Ramirez which meant I couldn't risk going for him through the window.

While I was only halfway down the steps, I was aware of fate's final attempt to guarantee my failure. The explosion had rocked the whole car and the driving door was slowly swinging closed. It took no more than a moment to wrench it open again but moments meant the difference between life and death. The last bodyguard must have had exposure to stun grenades included in his training because he was recovering from the shock and he was very good indeed. As I dived into the car, the Ingrams held in front of me, he was already raising his own weapon, knowing that he was going to die but remembering that the unarmed Ramirez was still his responsibility. This was why the Markov was pointing across his body, aimed at Ramirez not me.

Although he only managed the one shot, this was enough because Ramirez suddenly slumped into the corner of the back seat and none of my bullets had gone near him. Wearily, I climbed out of the car again and pulled open the rear door, allowing Ramirez to tumble out in an untidy heap. The bullet must have hit his lung because I could hear the bubbling inside as he fought for breath. I only needed a quick glance to realise he was beyond my help.

"The bastard," Ramirez groaned, blood trickling from his mouth. "I didn't know he was going to do that."

"Like they say, you die and learn," I said callously, turning away from him.

There was nothing more I could do except watch him die. I'd failed and I knew it but there was one small compensation. The whole sorry operation was over now and I could pretend I'd never, ever heard of Ramirez.

There was nobody around to tell me this was simply the beginning and that a dead Ramirez was going to cause me far more problems than he had while he was alive.

LONDON, ENGLAND

Andrea decided to pack in the morning. Her train didn't leave until midday and Philis had told her the flat was hers for as long as she needed it. As he'd pointed out, she'd be stuck in London for several days and it didn't make sense to use a hotel when the flat was vacant. All Philis had asked in return was that she should do a little of the cleaning he'd been saving for a rainy day. As far as Andrea could see, the drought must have lasted for quite some time.

She'd been kept too busy at headquarters to do any real shopping and there wasn't a great deal to eat in the kitchen, not that she felt particularly hungry anyway. There were some eggs to scramble and the slight stale remains of a loaf of bread which would do for toast. Washed down with the last of the wine she'd bought the previous night, this would be more than sufficient. Before she ate, though, Andrea decided to shower. She put a tape on, turning it up loud so she'd be able to hear it above the sound of the water, undressed and went through into the bathroom. The hot water drumming down on her felt good, rinsing away the weariness and grime, and she took her time.

After she'd washed her hair, Andrea soaped her body, enjoying the slippery feel of the lather. Without really intending to, she was turning herself on and her hands moved slower and more lasciviously. Suddenly she wished Philis was there. Although Andrea tried to conjure up other images, it was Philis's which kept returning. She was honest enough with herself to know that it was partly because he'd never made the play she'd anticipated. And wanted, if she was being really truthful. Philis was definitely the one who'd got away.

The mood was still on her when she went back into the bedroom and walked across to stand in front of the full-length mirror. She'd always been proud of her body and she couldn't see any reason to change her mind now. It was a body which had excited a lot of men and, she promised herself, would excite a lot more in the future. Andrea couldn't understand why Philis hadn't reacted because, God knew, he'd had plenty of opportunity. Probably he was too obsessed with that other woman he'd taken to Oslo. Andrea wasn't exactly jealous but she was, she admitted to herself, more than mildly miffed. If their paths crossed again, Philis wouldn't escape so lightly. She'd make damn sure he made a play and then she'd take the greatest pleasure in slapping him down. Or maybe she wouldn't. Andrea was still considering this when the light suddenly went off in the living room.

"Blast."

Andrea snapped back to reality fast, hoping it was a bulb and not a fuse. The stereo was still going which was a hopeful sign.

The switch for the wall lights was over by the door. Andrea was halfway across the living room when the bedroom light went too, plunging her into total darkness. For the first time she felt frightened. Andrea tried telling herself it was simply imagination, that the darkness was playing tricks on her, but it didn't work. She still thought she could sense a presence in the room with her.

"Is anybody there?"

There was no answer and Andrea suddenly felt foolish. She was behaving like some hysterical, middle-aged spinster. She started moving forward again, slowly with her arms outstretched, until her fingers touched the wall. Now she had a point of reference, Andrea moved more confidently. She actually had one hand on the switch when the bedroom light came on again. Andrea could distinctly see the shadow of the man who was standing just inside the door and for an instant it was as though her heart had stopped.

"Who is it?" She didn't like the panic she could detect in her voice, or the sudden smell of fear. "What do you want?"

There was no reply from the bedroom but Andrea was aware of a movement behind her. Before she could react, a forearm had clamped brutally across her throat while a second snaked across her chest. The fingers gripping her breast were like steel claws gouging into the sensitive flesh and Andrea would have screamed if she'd been able to. When she started to struggle, the man behind her simply lifted Andrea bodily from the floor, increasing the pressure on her neck. It was only a few seconds before she stopped bucking and kicking. By then the second man was standing in the bedroom doorway.

"You haven't killed her, have you?"

He was speaking in Arabic.

"Of course not. I know what I'm doing."

"Well, bring her through here then. We have work to do." This was the last that either man said for quite some time.

Watson had just finished being sick when Pawson arrived. Pawson could understand why after he'd been through into the bedroom and seen the body. He could feel the bile rising in his own throat as he covered Andrea with the bloodstained sheet.

"Grisly, isn't it?"

The doctor had completed his initial examination and was repacking his instruments.

"You always were prone to understatement, Matthew." Pawson was irrationally pleased that his voice was so steady. "Can you approximate the time of death?"

"Not with any real accuracy."

"A guess will do."

"That's what it will have to be until I have the corpse back at the lab. I'd say she died somewhere between twenty-four and thirty-six hours ago."

"Cause?"

"Her neck was broken but that could have happened after she was dead. It wouldn't surprise me to learn she actually died of shock."

Pawson nodded and looked around the bedroom. There were no indications of a struggle.

"How do you read what happened? In simple, layman's language."

The doctor shrugged resignedly. His work relied on meticulous attention to detail but the first thing he was always asked to do was to speculate.

"You can see for yourself," he said. "She was mutilated."

"While she was still alive?"

"Oh yes." The doctor seemed surprised that Pawson had to ask. "Otherwise there wouldn't have been so much blood. The bastards took their time as well, several hours at least. They took a lot of care carving the letters on her abdomen."

"Letters? I didn't see them."

Pawson reached down to pull back the sheet again.

"It looked like a name to me," the doctor said. "Jan-Carl Ramirez. Does that ring a bell?"

There was no answer because Pawson was already moving towards the door. He had no idea how the Libyans had managed to catch up so fast but this wasn't immediately important. There was an urgent message to dispatch to Cairo. Otherwise Andrea Montgomery wouldn't be the department's only casualty.

CHAPTER FIVE

I was standing on the northern tip of Rawdah Island, watching the Nile flow sullenly past on either side. To my left I could see, and hear, the bustle of traffic on the Corniche which ran along the bank of the river between me and the Coptic Mu'allagah church. Immediately to my right was the Nilometer, over a thousand years old and a reminder of the city's glorious past. At my feet was a reminder of Cairo's limited future, the bloated corpse of a dog bobbing aimlessly on the murky waters. Yousuf Aweis, who was standing beside me, was equally bloated but he was definitely alive. The cologne he was wearing made him smell considerably better as well.

"Pretty, isn't it?"

He spoke in English which was just as well as my Arabic was restricted to a few of the choicer expletives.

"Like a picture postcard," I agreed. "All this with Gyppo belly and bilharzia thrown in."

"You're too cynical, my friend. You have no respect for the past. This is Misr, Umm al-Dunyah, the mother of the world."

"That's simply a polite way of saying Cairo was a whore. As far as I'm concerned, it hasn't changed very much."

Yousuf laughed.

"He who hath not seen Cairo hath not seen the world," he intoned mockingly. "Her soil is gold, Her Nile is a marvel."

"I know, I know." This was a game we'd played before, on the last occasion I'd been unfortunate enough to be stuck in Egypt. "And I suppose that's one of the bright-eyed houris of Paradise."

I nodded in the direction of the black-clad crone who was relieving herself in the gutter a few yards away, her urine making intricate patterns among the dust and filth. Yousuf laughed again.

"Hardly, Philis," he admitted. "You have to go out to Sahara City to find them nowadays. And if they're bright-eyed, that probably means they're on cocaine."

"Thanks for the tip. Do you have anything important to say or did you drag me out here to swap platitudes?"

"No, my friend, I didn't."

His tone was serious now and I turned to face him. If size had been a measure for respect, people would have prostrated themselves at Yousuf's feet. He might not be particularly tall but he was the widest man I'd ever met, side to side and front to back. When you were walking round him, it was wise to take provisions.

"How was it in Oslo?" he inquired.

"Oslo? What the hell are you talking about now?"

I hoped there was nothing in my voice to reveal my sudden panic. Oslo was supposed to be my secret. I'd even been prepared to endure three months' purgatory in Cairo to keep it that way. Now Yousuf was talking about it as though it was common knowledge.

"Oslo," Yousuf repeated patiently. "The capital city of Norway. Where that butcher Jan-Carl Ramirez was killed."

"Thanks for the geography lesson but I know where Oslo is. You can find it by looking for the bloody great rainclouds but I haven't been there for years. And what has Ramirez got to do with anything?"

"I didn't come here to play games, Philis."

"I'm glad of that. Nor did I."

"In that case we're both wasting our time."

Now was a good time for me to have second thoughts. Officially Yousuf held down a senior post at the Egyptian Ministry of the Interior. In reality he was the linkman between the Mukhabarat, the external intelligence agency, and the Mabahes, Egypt's counter-espionage unit. Although Yousuf obviously had something important to tell me, he wasn't handing it away for free. If the price was a minor concession, it seemed sensible to go along with him.

"OK, Yousuf. Just for argument's sake, let's pretend I have been in Oslo recently. What exactly would you have to say to me then?"

"Congratulations. You'd have done society a great service by disposing of vermin like Ramirez."

"And?"

"I'd advise you to leave Cairo as soon as possible."

"Is that official advice?"

This time I made no attempt to hide my surprise. I was in Cairo as an official liaison officer with the Mukhabarat. Everything was up front, I even had the documentation to prove it, and there was no reason I could think of for the Egyptians to object. If they didn't want me, they'd had plenty of time to say so before my arrival.

"I'm thinking purely of your health, my friend. I wouldn't want anything unpleasant to happen to you while you were a guest in my country."

"That almost sounds like a threat."

It didn't but I was desperately buying myself time to think.

"Don't be so obtuse, Philis. You know you have nothing to fear from me."

Although this was very nice to know, it didn't take us very far forward. I'd never been much good at riddles.

"Is it Ramirez we're talking about?"

"Not quite. I'm talking about the man who arranged to have him killed. That's you, my friend."

"What makes you so sure?"

If our conversation continued much longer, I'd have to copy the crone and relieve myself in the gutter. Either that or change my underwear. There was no Egyptian spy network in Norway. How the hell did Yousuf know so much?

"Simple deduction," he went on. "My contacts in Tripoli assure me that an assassination squad is already in Cairo. You, my friend, are its only target."

"Oh shit," I said.

There was plenty of this in the Nile. I hoped that wasn't where I was destined to end up.

Yousuf had done all he could to help me. He'd passed on the warning and playing at wet-nurse wasn't a part of his job. He repeated his advice about leaving Egypt and then waddled off to where his car was parked. As soon as he'd driven off, I flagged down a taxi. It helped considerably to discover that the driver spoke some English.

"This is for you." The banknote was excessive by any standards but I was never mean when the Philis life might be at stake. "Do as I say and there'll be another like it when I leave you."

Perhaps I'd overestimated the driver's linguistic ability because there was an uncomprehending expression on his face. All the same, the language of money was international, and I'd bought myself his unswerving devotion. He probably prayed to Allah for rich foreign fares like me.

"Take the Gizah bridge," I told him, speaking more slowly now. "Then turn right along the Shari al-Nil. Don't dawdle but remember the speed limit."

"OK, sir. OK. England number one, sir."

Either he wasn't too sure of his numbers or he hadn't read a newspaper since the middle of the nineteenth century but he did manage to follow my instructions.

I began checking for tags the moment we were across the Nile. The odds against having anybody on my tail at this stage were probably several thousand to one but this didn't encourage me to be complacent.

Complacent agents quickly became dead agents. They started telling themselves they were safe, they neglected elementary precautions and bang, they became entries in an obituary file. It was the ones who jumped at every shadow like me who lived to receive a telegram from the Queen. At least, I hoped this was the way it worked.

It wasn't until we'd driven along the back of the Zoo and done a complete circuit of the parkland surrounding the Ministry of Agriculture that I was satisfied we were clean. Then I had the taxi take me across the Tahrir Bridge on to Gezirah. When he left me, the driver was one of the happiest men in Cairo. He probably couldn't wait to tell his friends about the crazy Englishman who had travelled in ever diminishing circles, scattering Egyptian pounds in his wake, until he arrived at the expected destination.

In actual fact, I'd had him drop me at the Cairo Tower. Built back in 1957, the 600-foot latticed tower stood next to the exclusive preserve of the Gezirah Sporting Club. After I'd paid off the taxi, I took the lift to the revolving restaurant at the top of the tower. It came as no great surprise to discover that the restaurant wasn't revolving at all. Cynics, of whom there were plenty in Cairo, likened it to the so-called Egyptian revolution. The restaurant had taken one turn and then ground to a dead halt.

Nevertheless, there was no denying the view and, as always in Cairo, there was a marked contrast between the old and the new. Immediately below me on the river was one of the streamlined pleasure cruisers. It was packed with camera-festooned tourists and could have been transported direct from Paris, Amsterdam or Venice. Only a few hundred yards downstream were three triangular sailed feluccas, the traditional Nile riverboats whose design hadn't changed since the days when Cleopatra was being bitten on the asp by Mark Antony.

It was the same when I looked across to the east bank of the Nile. The downtown commercial area hugging the river's bank could have been anywhere. The concrete and glass jungle of office blocks, apartment buildings and hotels was standard twentieth-century design. Similar buildings sprouted up in any major city, no matter where it was. It was only when I looked further east, beneath the escarpment of the Muqattam Hills, that I could see the real Cairo. The Old City was a teeming warren, a maze of tortuous alleyways, mud-brick houses and antique mosques. The TV aerials and telephone lines were there, of course, but it was the ornate minarets which dominated the skyline.

It was the new Cairo which interested me at the moment because this was where my immediate dilemma lay. And it was the hotel where I was staying, the Nile Hilton, which interested me most. I could distinguish it from where I was sitting, a totally anonymous modern block apart from its multi-coloured mosaics. It stood on the Corniche, virtually next door to the Egyptian Museum, and what I had to decide was whether or not it was safe to return there.

By the time I'd finished my meal, I'd assessed all the various risks and decided they didn't make much difference. I didn't have any real choice and the same went for the phone call I made. Croker was my only reliable pipeline into the Embassy so he was the person I had to use. I noted the caution in his voice as soon as I'd identified myself. The various inter-departmental rivalries didn't make for a spirit of willing cooperation. The Military Intelligence mob considered SR(2) as being only slightly less dangerous than the KGB.

"What do you want, Philis?"

"I need accommodation. The Hilton isn't safe any longer."

"It always amazes me how quickly your lot manage to make friends." Croker was beginning to enjoy himself. It had probably made his day to discover I was in trouble. "There's no chance of getting you inside the Embassy, you know."

"I don't want to be. I'm looking for somewhere quiet, unobtrusive and untraceable. I also need it fast."

"How fast is fast?"

"Any time in the next half an hour will do. It's an emergency."

"Isn't it always with you chaps. You really shouldn't be allowed out to play on your own."

I overlooked the snide remarks and gave him the number of the restaurant. I needed his assistance far more than I needed any hassle.

"Is there anything else?"

Now Croker's tone was long-suffering.

"Just one thing more. I'll have a message for you to relay to London when you phone back. It will have a priority prefix."

"That will please Communications. I suppose you'd like me to check to see if any messages have come through for you while I'm about it."

"I'd appreciate that."

"Think nothing of it. After all, why should I waste time doing the work I'm paid for when I can have so much fun running around after you?"

"I knew you'd see it like that. It's nice to know there's still a few of you who haven't defected to Moscow yet."

I hung up and set about encoding my message to Pawson. This only took a couple of minutes because, when it came right down to it, I didn't have a great deal to say. The entire Oslo operation had blown sky-high and there was no point in being verbose about it. If the Egyptians and Libyans knew what had happened already, the details were probably being serialised in *Woman's Own*.

After I'd finished the message, I sipped a cup of coffee which was as muddy as the Nile below and went back to admiring the view. A couple of tables behind me, a loudmouthed English tourist was telling anybody who cared to listen that he could just distinguish the pyramids at Saqqarah some twenty miles to the south. I didn't need to check to know that he was the victim of wishful thinking. Either that or he was a close relation of the Six Million Dollar Man.

In any case, my own interest was still focussed much closer to hand. Yousuf hadn't been able to give me a precise timetable for the Libyan hit team but his source suggested that they couldn't have been in Cairo for more than twenty-four hours. They should still be settling in which meant the hotel was probably still safe. It was the "probably" which stuck in my craw. There had to be some sane Libyans but I certainly hadn't met any of them. It was always safest to remember that they were ruled by Gaddaffi, not convention.

Even so, I had to return to the Hilton some time and the sooner I did it the better. Quite apart from my own things, there was stuff in my room which Pawson wouldn't want me to leave behind and I was the only person who could collect it. It wasn't something I could ask Croker to do for me. He was only likely to involve his men after I'd been fished out of the Nile with a knife between my shoulder-blades. Even then he might not bother. He'd probably thank his lucky stars I wasn't around to pester him any more.

To give him his due, though, he did manage to cut the half an hour I'd suggested to twenty-five minutes. As if this wasn't warning enough in itself, he actually sounded solicitous.

"Come on," I said. "What is it?"

"It's bad news from London, I'm afraid."

Croker hesitated. He was milking the melodrama for all it was worth. "Well?"

"It's your girlfriend, Philis. She's been killed."

The overwhelming sense of loss caught me by surprise. I'd already admitted to myself that Ramona was special. Until now, though, when it was too late, I hadn't realised quite how special she'd been.

"How did it happen?"

My voice was very flat and controlled.

"She was murdered, Philis. I don't have any of the details but Pawson sent a warning for you to be careful. He seems to think you may be the next target. Does that make sense to you?"

"Some of it does." But there was an awful lot which didn't. Even if I'd been tied in with Ramirez's death, Ramona should have been in the clear. I'd deliberately set it up this way. "Was there anything else?"

"Not a lot. The message says she was killed at your flat but that's about it."

"At my flat?"

"That's what it says here."

"Do you have a name for the victim?"

"Hang on a sec." I could hear the rustle of paper. "Montgomery. Andrea Montgomery."

There were times when I didn't like myself a lot and this was one of them. There'd been nothing I could do about the sudden surge of relief when I realised Ramona was all right. It was probably a human reaction but Andrea had deserved better and it made me feel shabby. It took a conscious effort to force myself back to practicalities.

"How about the accommodation I wanted?" I inquired. "Have you managed to fix it?"

"It's all arranged. I'm giving you our safe house in Muski, just off the Shari Port Said. It's no luxury apartment but it's the best I could do at such short notice."

"It sounds fine. You'd better give me the address."

After I'd jotted it down, I reeled off my message for London. In the light of the information Croker had given me, there were additions to make. I asked for more detail about Andrea's death and said I'd be in direct contact as soon as possible. I left this part in clear because I wasn't saying anything I objected to Croker's people hearing. Pawson had already given them most of it with his message to me.

"Is there anything else, Philis?"

Croker was still acting out of character, putting himself out to be helpful.

"Not for the moment. If something does crop up, I know where to contact you."

"Do that, Philis. I'm always glad to be of assistance." Croker paused while he wondered exactly how to phrase what he wanted to say next. "I'm sorry I had to be the bearer of such bad news," he went on. "I must say, though, you've taken it remarkably well."

"Sure." However he phrased himself, the criticism was still implied. Croker thought I should have been wailing and gnashing my teeth. "Haven't you heard? I'm the man who invented the stiff upper lip."

As I hung up, I wasn't so sure I didn't agree with Croker. I'd have liked myself a lot more if I still hadn't been relieved that it was Andrea, not Ramona.

I walked back to the Hilton across the Tahrir Bridge, working my way along the crowded pavements. By now I'd pushed both Andrea and

Ramona out of my mind as dangerous distractions. It wouldn't help anybody if I was killed as well.

This was why I approached the hotel from the rear and used one of the
service entrances. The Hilton might already be under surveillance and I
didn't want to advertise my return. For the same reason, I used the stairs
rather than the lift. My biggest disadvantage was that the hit team knew
precisely who they were looking for. They had my name and they'd have
my photograph. I wouldn't be able to identify any of them until they
made their move. Until then they'd simply be an anonymous part of the
crowd. I'd have been a lot happier if I'd brought a gun into Egypt with
me, but even this was no answer. Provided the hit team knew their job, I
wouldn't be allowed the opportunity to use any kind of weapon.

The instant I opened the door of my room I knew my precautions had
been wasted. With my back against the wood of the door, I tried to pin
down exactly what had sounded the alarm bells. My first visual check
didn't provide me with any clues. The room looked out over the Nile and
there was more than enough light coming through the windows for my
examination. My suitcases were still on the stand, the top one open. My
dirty shirt was still lying on the bed where I'd discarded it. The sliding
doors of the wardrobe gaped wide, just the way I'd left them. It all seemed
normal enough. There was no alien smell of tobacco or perfume. I
couldn't hear anything to alarm me, no creaking or shuffling. The only
obtrusive sounds were of a vacuum cleaner being used down the corridor
and the ticking of my travelling alarm by the bed. All the incoming data
was comfortingly negative and I wasn't comforted at all. Instinct still
insisted that there was something wrong.

When I ran a second check, I managed to identify the source of my
unease. The bathroom door was closed and I'd left it open. At least, I
thought I had. A quick mental replay of my movements before I'd gone to
meet Yousuf still left the door ajar. And my room had been cleaned before
I'd gone out. Suddenly my mouth was dry. There were several quite
innocent explanations for the closed bathroom door and I didn't believe
any of them. Instinct and paranoia both insisted that there was somebody
inside.

Now I did need a weapon. The metal bedside lamp looked as promising
as any and I was halfway towards it when the bathroom door stopped
being closed. The Libyan who'd been inside didn't behave like somebody
who had dropped in to wash his hands or empty his bladder. At least, I
assumed he was a Libyan for want of a normal introduction. He came at
me like a thunderbolt and there was no question of meeting his charge
upright. I simply dropped to the carpet and chopped upwards at the only
target which presented itself.

If I'd landed properly, the blow would have broken his knee. Even mistimed it brought him down with a screech of pain. I immediately threw myself on his back, scrabbling for a neck hold. This lasted for as long as it took the Libyan to butt the back of his head into my face. Then he was free and I had to kick him on the back of his undamaged knee to bring him down to my level again. For the next few seconds we rolled around on the floor, struggling for an advantage. Apart from messing up our clothes, we were too close to do each other a great deal of damage. It might have lasted until we both collapsed from exhaustion if the Libyan hadn't allowed one of his ears too close to my teeth. Although he didn't taste very nice and the stink of cheap hair oil made me feel sick, it seemed as good a way as any to break the deadlock.

The Libyan had a surprisingly high pain threshold. Although he did groan a bit to show his appreciation, he didn't immediately release his hold on my wrists. I was behind him still, even if he was on top, and he knew as well as I did that once my hands were free, he was finished. This no longer seemed quite so important to him after I'd managed to roll him over. I was pulling back now with all the strength in my neck muscles, as well as biting and chewing, and he was faced with a straight choice. Either he released one of my wrists or I'd liberate one of his ears. In the end, pain and vanity triumphed. He only let go of one hand, stabbing back with stiffened fingers at my eyes, but this was all I needed. Once I had a grip on his throat, I could forget about the ear. I spat blood out of my mouth and concentrated on the arteries in his neck.

The temptation to kill him was very strong. I kept hold of his throat after he'd stopped struggling, feeling the vulnerable larynx beneath my palm. Or I could simply keep the supply of blood to his brain cut off for a few more seconds. It took a conscious effort to make me unclamp my fingers. Despite what had happened to Andrea, I could think of too many good reasons why I needed the Libyan alive.

The first thing I did was go into the bathroom to wash out my mouth, rinsing and spitting until I no longer had a taste of him. I'd have made a lousy cannibal. I had my first proper look at the intruder when I returned to the bedroom, massaging the cramped muscles of my right hand. He was in his early twenties with thin, foxy features which his moustache did nothing to improve. The jacket he was wearing suggested he was an employee of the hotel. The Makarov automatic he had in one pocket suggested otherwise.

This was about all he did have in his pockets and I thoughtfully balanced the weapon in my hand. A blow by blow, or bite by bite, replay of the struggle only served to nurture the germ of an idea which had taken root with my discovery of the pistol. Perhaps I hadn't been fighting to preserve the priceless Philis hide. Perhaps the Libyan had been fighting to escape from the room. If he was a Libyan, although this still seemed the most likely bet. In any case, the next step was an obvious one and I used the telephone beside the bed. Yousuf didn't appear to be at all surprised to hear from me so soon.

"Well, Philis, my friend," he said. "What can I do for you now?"

"You can tell me whether you sent one of your men to search my room."

There was only a momentary hesitation before Yousuf answered. He would have had my room searched as a matter of routine.

"If I had," he said carefully, "you wouldn't know anything about it. One of my men wouldn't leave any traces behind."

"You're sure of that?"

"I'm positive."

"In that case, I have a present for you. I seem to have acquired one slightly damaged Libyan. He's lying on my carpet right now."

"And you want me to take him off your hands?"

"That's up to you but it might be more rewarding to let him run. He's all yours anyway because I'm leaving now. You have about twenty minutes before he'll be fit to move."

"Is he alone?"

"I doubt it. He must have somebody down in the lobby and there's probably more support out in the street."

They were Yousuf's problem because I'd no intention of trying to pinpoint them for him. I was still intent on avoiding trouble.

"All right, Philis. I'd better get moving. Where can I contact you?"

"You can't. If I need you, I'll be in touch."

I'd hung up before Yousuf had a chance to protest.

TRIPOLI, LIBYA

Zaleski was experiencing the greatest difficulty in containing his irritation. The Libyans seemed to be obsessed with petty revenge. In their minds, this took precedence over an intricately planned operation which had been designed to cripple vital sectors of Western industry for months to come. They all seemed to believe the ridiculous image Gaddaffi and the media had managed to build up between them. None of them appeared to realise that Ramirez had been a thug, a psychopath who would work for anybody who was prepared to subsidise his slaughter.

"So the woman didn't talk."

"No."

The Russian's obvious displeasure made Major Khadduri uneasy. Trying to serve two different masters was no simple matter.

"Did your men actually question her before she was killed?"

"Of course." This was Khadduri's first direct lie and he was aware of the sheen of sweat on his forehead. "She confirmed that the man Philis was in charge in Oslo."

"And that's all?"

Khadduri nodded unhappily, aware that the Russian didn't believe him. Zaleski stifled a sigh and looked out over the bay, not really aware of the view. He still hoped that the Ramirez incident was simply a coincidence. So far there was nothing to suggest otherwise but there was too much at stake for the threat to be ignored. He had to be sure one way or the other.

"How about Philis?" he asked. "Have you located him again?"

"Not yet but it should only be a matter of hours."

"Your men have been instructed what to do?"

"Philis will be taken alive. We'll find out everything he knows about Operation Dove."

Zaleski was shaking his head before Khadduri had finished. When he spoke his tone was sharp.

"No. Your men pick Philis up and that's all. Once they have him, I'll send somebody in to handle the interrogation. There are to be no more mistakes."

"As you wish but I think you're worrying unnecessarily. Operation Dove has already begun. The FNLC troops should be moving into Kolwezi within the next forty-eight hours. There's nothing anybody can do to stop them now."

"I'm paid to worry," Zaleski told him, rising to his feet to signify that the interview was at an end.

He couldn't tell the Libyan that Operation Dove was doomed to failure, that it was no more than a smokescreen. The French and Belgians would never allow the FNLC rebels to establish themselves in Shaba. The real significance of the invasion lay elsewhere and this was why Philis had to be interrogated. If London or Washington had finally realised what was happening, Zaleski needed to know what counter-measures they were taking.

CHAPTER SIX

The cockroaches clearly loved the apartment Croker had found for me but I wasn't nearly so keen. It was small, dark and noisy and although the flat was probably ideal for Croker's Egyptian operatives, it was no permanent answer for me. The tenement housing it was lower middle-class and Egyptian, without another European in the block. I stuck out like the proverbial sore thumb and I doubted whether it would take Yousuf more than forty-eight hours to track me down. Come to that, I couldn't see the Libyans being much slower.

All the noise came from outside the apartment. From the small balcony I had a bird's-eye view of one of the busiest intersections in Cairo, where the Shari Port Said and the Shari al-Gaysh met. Bedlam and Dante's Inferno must have been peaceful by comparison. Cars, lorries, buses, street vendors and even the occasional camel all made their individual contributions but it was the trams which really added to property values. They came by at what seemed to be thirty-second intervals and each one made the building shake on its foundations.

During the first twenty-four hours I only ventured out of the apartment once. I bought myself a few essential provisions and made another phone call to Croker. He had the details I'd asked him for and they were just the fuel my growing anger needed. Every report and psychological profile since I'd been working for SR(2) had made some mention of my lack of detachment. This was intended as a criticism but I'd always found it reassuring, proof that I remained human. I didn't want to be an automaton like Bayliss. Besides, Andrea Montgomery had been tortured and killed in my apartment because she'd been with me in Oslo. The Libyan hit team out there in the streets of Cairo wanted to kill me, not some anonymous representative of the department. If this didn't make it personal, I didn't know what did.

All the same, I didn't allow my emotions to dominate my brain. Realistically, there were three options open to me. The most obvious, and probably the most sensible, was to do the British thing and run like hell. Leave Cairo, drop out of sight and cower in safety until the Libyans had forgotten me. They made so many enemies, they couldn't hope to keep them all in the frame at the same time. Its greatest virtue was that this was a course of action which didn't have to be acted on immediately. A couple of phone calls and I could be on my way out of the country any time I chose. It was this factor which enabled me to give serious consideration to the other options.

Option number two only really appealed to the vengeful part of me. It was feasible because I knew of at least two people who'd used the ploy and were still alive. On the debit side, I knew of several others who'd tried it and now resided in pine boxes. What I'd have to do in this scenario was turn the tables on the hit team, create a situation where I became the hunter and the Libyans the prey. The macho Clint Eastwood part of me loved the idea. The sensible part of me dismissed it out of hand.

Fortunately, there was a much easier course open to me. Yousuf wanted the Libyans almost as much as I did myself. Come to that, he might already have them, although I very much doubted this. There had been nothing on television about it and Yousuf wasn't famous for hiding his light under a bushel. Anyway, this was something I have to check before I put my suggestion to him.

It was early evening when I left the apartment and going down on to the Shari Port Said was like descending into another world. It was the Cairo rush hour which meant the street was kerb to kerb vehicles with every driver intent on proving what a quiet, unemotional race the Egyptians really were. Horns blared incessantly, unsilenced engines revved frantically and hundreds of car radios were turned to full volume, each of them tuned to a different station. Then there was the smell, a pungent aroma of rotting garbage, third-grade petrol fumes and smoke from the roadside kebab stalls. It was an all-out assault on the senses which made me feel a very long way from home.

Allowing for all this, it was the constantly moving sea of humanity on the pavements which bothered me most. You were never really alone in Cairo and a street like the Port Said was the Arab world in microcosm. Of course, a lot of the pedestrians were minor civil servants and businessmen on their way home from work, wearing the short-sleeved safari suits which seemed to be the standard uniform. There were even a few women in Western dress but you didn't have to look far to spot the exotica. There were thin, hawk-faced men from the desert in their turbans and galabiyahs. Young, wide-eyed girls, fresh from the country, paraded their colourful print dresses and headscarves. Old crones, dressed from head to foot in black, squatted on the kerb, occasionally spitting into the gutter. It was all a bit like Shepherds Bush on a busy Saturday afternoon.

With so many people around, it was impossible to tell whether or not I was being followed, and after the first few yards I stopped checking. I had to assume I was still in the clear. If I wasn't, nobody would have any difficulty tagging me. I was the oddity on the street. It was my clean cut, English features which were attracting all the attention. Even a camel, reclining gracefully in the back of a truck while it chewed the cud, spared the time to give me a curious glance. I preferred the camel's attention to that of the street urchins. They were out in force and to them a European meant money. Although I only had a couple of hundred yards to walk, I must have been solicited by at least a dozen children on the way. None of them offered me anything as interesting as a sister but they did try me with everything else from plastic combs to chewing gum.

The telephone I'd found on my previous sortie was in a sweetmeat shop. The owner nodded to me as I came in, gave his right buttock a vigorous scratch and then continued with what he was doing, dribbling flour on to a circular hotplate. What with the general standard of hygiene in his establishment, it looked as though he was trying to corner the market in the local version of Montezuma's revenge. Even the swarm of flies buzzing around his head looked distinctly unhealthy.

Although the temperature inside the shop must have been well over a hundred, it was a veritable oasis of peace after the street outside. I flicked sweat from my forehead, batted away a squadron of flies and headed for the telephone in the corner. Yousuf wasn't at his office but I had better luck with his home number.

"Well?" I inquired. "How did it go?"

"Badly."

I could almost hear his shrug.

"What went wrong? Didn't you make the Hilton in time?"

"It wasn't that. My men were in position in plenty of time and they spotted your visitor when he left."

"So what was the problem?"

"He'd been well trained. He knew he was no further use after you'd seen him. He went directly to the airport and booked himself on a flight to Algiers."

"There were documents and money waiting for him?"

"Yes. In a baggage locker."

"But you didn't allow him to fly off into the wide, blue yonder."

"Of course not. Unfortunately, he was prepared for arrest as well. The bastard had a cyanide capsule. We didn't discover it in time."

I waited to see whether Yousuf had anything else to offer but he obviously hadn't.

"So that's that. Do you have any other leads?"

"None at all." Yousuf sounded resigned. "It's much easier for Libyans to found Kalashnikovs, machine-guns and mortars any aid to their sex life. Although plenty of Western tourists stopped off in Sahara City after a visit to the Gizah pyramids down the road, it was Arab money which kept the complex going. Compared with the other Muslim countries, Egypt was relaxed and sophisticated. It offered the kind of lewd, lascivious entertainment the oil-rich Saudis, Libyans and Kuwaitis couldn't buy at home. Just like everywhere else, they were the really big spenders. This was why the performer on stage at La Parisienne was doing a belly-dance, not the can-can.

Although she was good, entertainment was the last thing on my mind. The course of action I'd proposed to Yousuf depended on my going public. I had to show myself somewhere I'd be noticed in the right places. We also needed somewhere Yousuf's men could cover easily and La Parisienne scored highly on both counts. With all the action in Sahara City, Yousuf could have moved all the Egyptian security forces into the area without anybody being the wiser. And, more important, the Palestinian owner of the club wasn't everything he purported to be. According to Yousuf, he was the paymaster for Libyan intelligence in the Cairo area. As such, he should know all about me. My only reservation was that we might be overdoing it. Mixing the odd metaphor or two, I felt like a gift horse in the lion's den.

When my meal arrived, I ate slowly, not really enjoying the Arab cuisine. Even if I hadn't been nervous, I probably wouldn't have enjoyed the food. You could hardly expect a people who lived in areas where the main crops were oil and sand to come up with much to tantalise the palate. If sheep's eyes and goat's testicles were the delicacies, the ordinary fare wasn't likely to set the saliva flowing. During the rest of the cabaret I drank sparingly and equally slowly. I had to allow the opposition plenty of time and I was grateful when one of the waiters provided me with an excuse for staying longer.

"You like company?" he asked after he'd cleared away the last of the dishes.

"Company?"

"We have house girls. Very nice. You buy drinks, they make conversation. Very nice indeed."

The programme said that one of the belly dancers was a sociology student at Cairo University so the waiter was probably an English graduate but this was the way he chose to speak. I was surprised he didn't throw in the odd effendi or memsahib for good measure. Perhaps he thought this was the way I expected an ignorant wog to speak. Whatever the reason, I did what he expected a lonely Englishman to do and allowed myself to be persuaded.

lose themselves in Cairo than it is for an Englishman. If you don't mind n repeating myself, I'd feel much happier with you out of Egypt. I dor want your blood on my conscience."

Nor did I. I wanted it to stay neatly packaged inside my skin.

"Tell me something, Yousuf. How do you feel about Libyan assassin working your territory?"

Yousuf responded with something obscene about Libyans in genera and the hit team in particular. From this I deduced that he wasn't over happy about the suggestion.

"We could work together," I suggested. "Provide me with plenty o cover and you can use me as bait."

"It's far too risky, my friend." The speed with which Yousuf answered said that this was an option he'd already considered. "It doesn't matter how much cover you have. We still wouldn't know who we were looking for until the Libyans made their move. By then you'd probably be dead."

"I'm not volunteering to be a hero. The Libyans might not be after a straightforward kill. My friend at the hotel had a gun and he had plenty of opportunity to use it if he'd wanted to."

"Maybe he panicked."

"Maybe, but that wasn't the way I read it. I think the Libyans want to take me alive."

Yousuf didn't answer immediately. Although I knew he must be sorely tempted, he was probably thinking of all the flak which would be heading his way if things should go wrong.

"It's still too risky, Philis. If we sit around and wait for the Libyans to come to us, we leave them with the initiative. When they've located you, they can afford to take their time. They'll check to see what cover you have. Once they've spotted it, they may decide they'd rather have you dead after all."

"OK, but why don't we take the initiative away from them? Why don' we rush them and set it up on ground of our own choosing?"

As I explained, Yousuf became more enthusiastic. By the followir morning, when I phoned him again, he'd come up with the ideal place f our purposes.

The enormous neon sign which welcomed visitors to Sahara City saic all. The sheer tastelessness of it summed up the entertainment on offer the complex of nightclubs beyond. It certainly wasn't the kind of trib any self-respecting Pharoah would have wanted next door to his tor

Before the Lebanese had started trying to kill each other off, Beirut been the undisputed fleshpot of the Middle East. Now Cairo was slo taking over because there was a strictly limited number of people

Basman, the hostess he provided, was far more Westernised. Her face, dominated by the large, liquid eyes, was unmistakably Egyptian but her cosmetics and dress were Western and her English colloquial. The only real evidence of her upbringing was in her behaviour. Although she had all the trappings of a bar girl in any club the world over, her restraint was Middle Eastern. There was no rubbing of thighs, no contrived glimpses down her considerable cleavage. The champagne she was drinking bought conversation and nothing more.

Converse was precisely what we did, talking to each other from opposite sides of the table. Most of what we said was inevitably stilted, a succession of questions and answers. As Basman was the one with a vested interest in what we were saying most of the questions came from her. I responded with all the appropriate lies and wondered whether there was more to her than met the eye. Not that it really mattered. The important thing was that she gave me an acceptable reason for staying and helped the time to go a little faster than it would have done if I'd been on my own.

The arrangement with Yousuf was that I'd leave at about two in the morning and at a quarter to I asked for my bill. Basman's pout was the first sign of real animation she'd displayed all night. Once again, I couldn't be sure whether this was professional pique or something more.

"Why are you leaving so early?" she demanded. "Don't you like me?"

"I like you a lot."

"Then why leave? I finish here in an hour. We could go on somewhere else."

Now she'd thrown in the first hint of sexual promise.

"It's a nice thought," I told her, "but I can't manage it tonight."

I'd deliberately left the door open. I wasn't going anywhere with Basman unless I'd checked with Yousuf first but if it was her brief to bring me back to La Parisienne for another visit, I was open to persuasion. She didn't bother to try, and while I was saying goodnight, her eyes were already wandering. Presumably she was looking for another lonely tourist who could afford the price of a bottle of champagne.

I'd always known that if anything was going to happen, it was likely to be after I'd left the club. This was why my nerves were crawling as I stepped into the cool, night air. The entire evening had been based on the assumption that I was wanted alive. If this was wrong, it would only take one bullet from a rifle to prove how vulnerable I was. There were still plenty of people around and I distrusted them all. However, the only person who seemed at all interested in me was the doorman who called my cab. I tipped him, instructed the driver to take me to Tahrir Square and sank back into the cushions of the back seat. When we drove off, I resisted the temptation to peer out of the window at the road behind us.

They weren't there in any case. They were waiting at the junction with the main Cairo road, where the taxi had to stop to give way. The first I knew of it was when a hand came through the open window beside me. It was a large, steady hand and it was holding a gun to my head. I sat very still while I watched the other back door open and the second Libyan clamber in. He was holding a knife with a wicked, six-inch blade. This was enough of a deterrent to keep me quiet while his companion with the gun joined us in the back seat. From start to finish, it must have taken all of three seconds and I hoped Yousuf's men were as good as he'd promised. If they were, our trap had worked. If they weren't, I was in way, way over my head.

It only took them a few seconds to find the Makarov. If I'd had any other weapons in my possession, they'd have gone almost as quickly. Although it wasn't easy to conduct a thorough body search in the back seat of a moving car, the man to my left was depressingly competent. He wasn't the slightest bit concerned with my personal comfort and he didn't stop until he was satisfied I was clean. The search was followed by a rapid-fire exchange in Arabic which included the driver as well as the men in the back. I couldn't even begin to understand what was being said apart from plucking some names out of the conversation.

We were driving fast but so did all Egyptians and none of my captors seemed at all worried by the possibility of pursuit. A couple of casual glances out of the back window was the sum total of their concern. I took this as a hopeful sign. We were on the main Gizah road and, now that my initial panic had subsided, cautious optimism was taking over. Yousuf's men wouldn't be very far behind.

There was nothing I could do except take stock of the men with me. It hadn't taken me very long to appreciate that the Libyan hit team was Libyan in origin only. Ibrahim, the driver, could have been Libyan but I doubted it. Even from behind, he didn't have an Arab look about him and I guessed he might be Iranian. Ahmat, or Ahmed, the man who'd searched me, definitely was an Arab, probably Palestinian. He was in his mid-thirties with bushy eyebrows and thinning hair. His thin, hollow-cheeked face had a mean look to it and I wouldn't have been surprised to discover he was on drugs. I decided I'd think very seriously before I took any liberties with him.

There was no doubt at all about Luitz, the third of my captors. He was unmistakably German and considerably older than either of his companions. Although his leather jacket was scuffed and he obviously hadn't shaved for a couple of days, his greying hair was neatly groomed. It wasn't too difficult to imagine a cleaned-up version in a business suit. I placed him as the leader of the group, something he confirmed when he addressed me in faultless English.

"Now, Mr. Philis," he said. "Precisely what back-up do you have?"

"Back-up?" There were times when I could make a parrot jealous. "What do you mean?"

Suddenly I was very frightened because Luitz hadn't sounded at all like somebody who'd walked blindly into a trap. He'd sounded far more like somebody who'd taken the trap for granted and was confident he could spring it. My sagging morale sagged a bit further when he jabbed his knife into my side. I yelped in appreciation as I felt the blood trickling down over my hip. We seemed to be deviating from the prepared script.

"Whether you die now or live a little longer is a matter of total indifference to me. For you, I assume, it's different. You have to buy any extra time I allow you. Do you understand?"

"Perfectly."

Luitz had sounded awfully convincing.

"Excellent. In that case, let's try once more. What back-up have you and that fat slug Aweis arranged?"

"There were men inside and outside La Parisienne." This time I hadn't even hesitated. "I don't know exactly how many."

"But there are mobile units?"

"Obviously."

There was very little point in denying things which were self-evident. Ibrahim and the German conducted another brief conversation in Arabic. This didn't make Ibrahim drive any faster but he did pay more attention to his driving mirror. The report he gave Luitz must have been negative.

"Presumably we're supposed to lead Aweis back to our base."

"That was the general idea, yes."

Luitz nodded. He elected to do his thinking out loud.

"Aweis is renowned for his caution. Loose surveillance wouldn't be enough to satisfy him. After all, he knows your life is at stake."

I kept quiet. So far Luitz hadn't made any mistakes that I'd noticed and I didn't think he was about to start now. Teutonic efficiency had always given me a pain. So did his bloody knife when he jabbed it another couple of millimetres into my flesh.

"Well, Mr. Philis?"

"The tie-pin," I told him.

Whatever it was that Luitz said, it was definitely a reprimand and Ahmat was angry as he tugged the tie-pin free. He handed it across to the German who examined it for a second or two.

"It's a simple homing device?"

"Yes."

Luitz grunted with satisfaction and I sunk deeper into the slough of despond. Even when he took some of the pressure off the knife in my side, I didn't cheer up. The German had made no attempt to destroy the homer. He was still holding it in his hand and it was no good pretending that its discovery had come as a surprise. He'd come prepared for every contingency and I was no longer counting on Yousuf for any help.

We were well into Gizah before the pattern changed. Luitz signalled this when he leaned forward to say something to Ibrahim. When he'd finished, he casually tossed the homer out of the window and, almost at the same moment, Ibrahim swung the taxi off the main road.

Now there was no longer any doubt about what we were trying to do. We were losing Yousuf's mobile units and this was obviously the type of manoeuvre Ibrahim had been practising. He'd lost me within the first minute and I was there sitting in the car with him. Admittedly, the maze of sidestreets could have been designed for his benefit but he careered through them with a joyous abandon which displayed a total disregard for the safety of anybody, or anything, which happened to be in his way. If the late night pedestrians we encountered hadn't had agility training, we'd have left a string of dead or maimed Cairenes in the streets behind us.

Almost from the moment we'd left the main road, I'd no real idea where we were. The map of Cairo I carried in my head was a generalised one, with only a few focal points accurately charted. It certainly didn't include the tangle of sidestreets we were in now. I thought we were probably heading towards the river but this was no more than a guess until suddenly the Nile was there ahead of us, the headlights glinting off the muddy water.

The sight acted as a kind of trigger. If I was going to do something to save myself, it had to be soon. This wasn't a conscious thought but it had been there at the back of my mind ever since we'd left the main road. Now I could see the glimmer of an opportunity, I reacted immediately. I far preferred taking my chances in the river to tamely allowing myself to be driven to my captor's base.

There was no doubt about what I had to do. Ibrahim was driving as fast as ever, there was a T junction no more than two hundred yards ahead and I was desperate enough not to mind a crash. My left hand went across my body, forcing the knife away from my side, and my right elbow went back and up into Luitz's face. Then I was lunging forward, my right arm hooking around Ibrahim's neck.

Nobody, not even the Mario Andrettis of this world, drove too well when they were being throttled and for a glorious moment I had him. The crook of my elbow was locked across his throat, I was pulling his head back

towards me and I could feel the taxi slipping out of control. At the speed
we were going the river was no more than three seconds away. Then
Ahmat had to spoil it, clouting me on the head with his gun. It was only a
glancing blow and I managed to hang on to Ibrahim but when he tried
again Ahmat was far more accurate. For all I knew, he might have hit me a
third and fourth time as well. I was already unconscious.

GUERRILLAS INVADE SOUTHERN ZAIRE

Kinshasa—Unconfirmed reports from the provincial capital of
Lumbumbashi suggest that secessionist guerrillas of the Congo National Liberation Front (FNLC) have invaded Zaire's southeastern
Shaba province. The Belgian pilot of a light plane was attempting to
land at Kolwezi airport when he was driven off by heavy ground fire.
He saw several aircraft burning, including Italian-built Macchi jet
trainers and some helicopters. An important mining centre, Kolwezi
was the target of an FNLC attack in March last year. Then the rebels
were only driven out with the help of Moroccan troops.—Reuter.

CHAPTER SEVEN

We were on a boat. Despite the nausea and the pain, I knew this immediately. The distinctive movement, the thudding of the engine and the various other shipboard noises had all registered in the twilight zone before full consciousness returned. Although my head was complaining mightily about the treatment it had received, there didn't seem to be much wrong with my memory because I could remember everything that had happened right up to the moment Ahmat had started bouncing his gun off my cranium. This was why I woke up frightened.

For a few seconds I kept my eyes closed, feeding in all the available data. None of it was particularly encouraging. I was laying on a hard mattress of some description, my left wrist was manacled, there was somebody nearby smoking a cigarette and this was about it. The somebody was Luitz as I discovered when I opened my eyes. He was sitting at a table in the centre of the large cabin, a brooding expression on his face as he watched me. His nose was red and puffy and he looked tired. Somehow I couldn't generate a great deal of sympathy for him.

The big surprise was the size of the cabin. I was on a wide double-bunk built into the wall. This placed me at least six feet from the table and there was another six feet of floor before you reached the matching bunk on the far side. I clearly wasn't aboard any holiday cruiser. I was a guest on a floating home, one of the flat-bottomed houseboats which were a feature of the Nile.

And this one had been constructed on a palatial scale. Even with cupboards, wardrobes, a chest of drawers and a sofa, the cabin wasn't overfurnished. Above the bunks was a row of windows, each with its own chintz curtains. There were two doors. The one behind my head was ajar and led into the galley. The other, which presumably led out on deck, was on the opposite wall at the end of the bunk.

"Do you like it?" Luitz inquired.

"Sure. It's like a home from home."

"How's the head?"

"Not too bad."

It was but I was cast in the heroic mould. Luitz stubbed out his cigarette and raised a hand to his own face.

"My nose hurts like hell," he said. "I think you've broken it."

"Bloody good show. I hope you don't expect me to apologise."

"No." The German managed a faint smile. "I suppose your only regret is that you didn't succeed in killing us all."

"I did do my best."

While Luitz lit himself another cigarette, I took a closer look at the chain manacled to my left wrist. It was about two feet long and bolted into the bulkhead above my head. If I'd had a week to spare and a bag of tools, I'd have had no problems freeing myself. As it was, there was no question of forcing the links or pulling the chain free of the wood. Unless somebody presented me with a key, I wouldn't be moving very far from the bunk.

"You could save yourself a lot of unnecessary suffering, you know." Luitz was feeling talkative again.

"How?"

"You cooperate. You tell us what we want to know voluntarily."

"What's on offer in exchange? My life?"

"No." Luitz knew I wouldn't have believed him if he'd said otherwise. "That was forfeit the moment Jan-Carl was killed. What I can offer you is a chance to die with dignity."

However much it hurt, I couldn't prevent myself from laughing.

"Balls to dignity," I said. "That's the least of my worries."

"You don't know what you're saying, Philis." The German was leaning forward now, stabbing with his cigarette for emphasis. "Ahmat and Mahomed enjoy inflicting pain. They're little better than animals. In the end, they're bound to make you talk so why not be sensible. All I'm after is the names of your companions in Oslo. Most of all, though, I want the name of the man who actually killed Jan-Carl."

"I'll think about it," I promised.

Mostly, though, I thought about other things. I thought about Mahomed, who was a new name to me. Unless Ibrahim had dropped out of the picture or I'd made a mistake with my maths, this meant there were at least four men on board with me. For the time being anyway, I was completely in their power. So why was Luitz trying to negotiate with me when there was no need for it? This was a conundrum which was still puzzling me when I drifted off to sleep.

The table-top seemed to be coming up towards me in slow motion, and there was plenty of opportunity to observe it in fine detail. I admired the grain of the wood, a cigarette burn, the spots of fresh blood. At the very last instant, my neck muscles responded to the frantic messages from my brain and I turned my head so my cheek struck first, not my nose. I dribbled blood from my mouth until Ahmat or Mahomed grabbed hold of my hair, pulling me upright again. Then Mahomed or Ahmat started hitting me. Luitz had been right. They were animals, brutal and stupid.

My eyes had slipped out of focus and sight wasn't the only faculty to suffer. Although I could hear the sound of the blows landing, I wasn't really feeling them any more. After a minute or so the Arabs' arms must have grown tired. Or perhaps I was bruising their fists with my face. Whatever the reason, they stopped hitting me. I was vaguely aware that Luitz was talking to me but I'd ceased listening to his questions some time ago. He'd repeated them so often I almost knew them by heart. Besides, they'd lost all relevance once I'd decided I wasn't going to answer any of them.

For a moment, when Luitz switched to Arabic, I thought my ears were playing tricks. It took a second or so before I realised he was being answered in the same language, which meant it couldn't be me speaking. I slumped further down in the chair and fought to keep awake. Unconsciousness was a luxury I couldn't really afford.

Some time later I felt rough hands undoing the straps around my wrists. The same hands went under my armpits. They were lifting and carrying me, moving me back towards the bunk. I tried to summon my legs into action but they refused to function. They preferred to hang down limply beneath me, my toes dragging across the floor. Being dumped on the bunk was like returning home. Even with the steel bracelet in place again, the mattress seemed like the ultimate in luxury.

All I really wanted to do was sleep and I had to struggle to keep my eyes open. The decision couldn't be delayed much longer. Either I found a way out or I killed myself before I was forced to talk. There just weren't any other alternatives. I cheered myself up by thinking about this for a while without coming close to a decision. It was all rather academic anyway. I didn't have the faintest idea how to escape and I was far too weak to kill myself even if I'd had the inclination.

Returning sensation was helping to keep me awake. I was hurting again and the thin mattress no longer seemed nearly so luxurious. When I attempted to make myself more comfortable, a sudden sharp pain in my ribs made me groan out loud. This was sufficient to alert Luitz. He'd stayed behind when the other two had left, sitting in his customary position at the table.

"Why not be sensible, Philis?" We were straight back to the same old theme. "There's no need for all this."

"You can stop whenever you like. I promise not to complain."

My mouth was swollen and talking was as painful as everything else.

The best I could manage was a mumble but it was in my own best interests to keep the dialogue going. Luitz was the key to everything. If I was going to escape, it would have to be while the two of us were alone in the cabin. I had to persuade him that the time he was spending with me wasn't completely wasted.

"Just give me one name," he urged. "That would be enough."

"I can't."

I didn't have to act at sounding disappointed.

"Of course you can. It's not as though you'd be betraying anybody. Eventually we're going to piece it all together anyway."

"In that case, why bother with me? Why not leave me in peace?"

Luitz wasn't really listening to me. He was intent on pressing home the advantage he thought he had.

"It just doesn't make sense," he forged on. "You'll only be able to stand so much before you talk. Today was merely the beginning."

We were entering areas I didn't want to explore too thoroughly so I changed the subject.

"May I have a cigarette, please?"

"You don't smoke."

Luitz was instantly suspicious.

"I used to have a sixty a day habit. It seems a bit pointless to worry about my health when you intend to kill me anyway."

Luitz considered my request carefully before he decided it was to his advantage to humour me. I wasn't really surprised when, instead of bringing the cigarettes and matches across, he threw them to me from where he was sitting. To date he hadn't been within an arm's length of the bunk while we were alone in the cabin. I'd have liked to believe this was no more than coincidence but I wasn't deluding myself. He knew that human beings were rather like wild animals. Caged or chained, they could still be dangerous.

"Does it taste good?"

"Wonderful."

The cigarette tasted vile. It made me feel giddy and rather light-headed and the acrid smoke was making the cuts on my lips sting. All the same, I'd always considered my vices to be worth suffering for.

Luitz tried a bit longer to make me see the error of my ways and then he gave up. This was fine by me because it allowed me an opportunity to think. For a start, there were so many inconsistencies in his approach, I felt I must be missing something. There had to be some element in the equation I knew nothing about. OK, I hadn't been killed on sight because I possessed information Luitz wanted. This, at least, made some kind of sense. Against this, Luitz knew that Yousuf and half the Egyptian security forces were looking for him. Every second he wasted was an added danger yet he was still playing silly buggers. Even the interrogation had been curiously half-hearted. I might not enjoy being knocked around but this was something I could live with. I wouldn't be nearly so brave if somebody threatened to start hacking off fingers or experiment with how well my tackle conducted electricity.

My captors weren't really doing one thing or the other. They hadn't killed me and there'd been no determined effort to make me talk. The only explanation I could manage was that Luitz might be awaiting further orders. This might be wishful thinking on my part but it was the best I could come up with. If I was right, I might still have a few hours' grace and this was precisely what I needed. Unless I escaped in the next few hours, I'd never escape at all.

The houseboat was still heading upstream, battling against the current. I'd been aboard for about twelve hours now and, apart from one brief stop, we'd been on the move all the time. Although the chain on my left wrist wasn't long enough for me to look out through one of the curtained windows, there was no impression of speed. Houseboats weren't generally streamlined and I doubted whether we were travelling at more than two or three miles an hour. This meant we should still be inside the net Yousuf would have thrown around Cairo. Unfortunately, so were about ten million other people and I didn't have any illusions about a dramatic rescue. It was self-help or nothing. Realistically, I knew I didn't have a chance but this wasn't something I intended to dwell on. Positive thinking was the order of the day. I'd take it step by step, dealing with one difficulty at a time, and step one was to rid myself of the manacle.

For this I needed a weapon and they were very thin on the ground. If I'd been in the SAS, I'd have had a knife in my sock and a bazooka in my jock-strap. As I wasn't, all I had was my belt. Pointing it at Luitz and saying "Hands up" wouldn't do much good unless he died laughing but the belt did have other uses. It had taken me almost an hour to remove it, easing it off a little at a time when I was sure I wasn't being observed. Fashioning the loop had been considerably easier, although I'd had to work beneath my body. The real problem would be persuading Luitz close enough to the bunk for me to use it. By now I'd smoked half-a-dozen of his cigarettes, establishing a routine, and he remained as careful as ever.

OK. It was time to put the mighty Philis brain to work because there had to be some way to bring him over to the bunk. For example, I could deliberately throw short when I was returning the cigarettes and matches. Or I could send him a telegram, announcing my intentions in advance. Luitz was no fool and if I made him suspicious I was finished. He'd be more determined than ever not to come near the bunk.

Think again. How about the psychological approach? Assuming that Luitz had a normal boiling point, it should be easy enough to make him angry. Unfortunately, this wasn't enough. I'd have to make him lose control to the extent that he launched a physical attack on me and I just couldn't see this happening. Even if Luitz had the temper for it, I'd no idea which were the right buttons to push. For all I knew, he'd simply laugh at my mother and camel cracks.

The old ways were the best. For some unknown reason, it was important to Luitz that I stayed alive. This was something I ought to capitalise on. Faking appendicitis or a heart attack was no answer but I was supposed to be a secret agent. At least, this was how Luitz saw me and I could try living up to the popular image. After all, the Libyan I'd collared at the Hilton had preferred death to dishonour. I didn't but this was beside the point. He'd carried a cyanide capsule with him so why shouldn't I?

"Tell me something," I said, breaking a long silence. "Is there any way I can save my life?"

"You already know the answer. I could lie, I suppose, but I won't insult you."

"How are you going to do it?"

I was doing my best to sound resigned and fatalistic.

"Do what?"

"Kill me."

By now Luitz was watching me very closely. He knew I was up to something but he wasn't quite sure what.

"I don't know, to be honest. I haven't really thought about it."

"I have. I've thought about it a lot. I suppose it will be Ahmat."

"Maybe."

I still had Luitz's undivided attention and I adjusted my position on the bunk. He couldn't have failed to notice me fiddling with my shirt-button and I hoped I wasn't overdoing it. I'd have liked a clearer idea of the lay-out of the boat, the same way I'd have liked to know where the others were, but it was now or never. The button made a nice, ripping sound as it came loose. I popped it straight into my mouth and bit down hard.

"What are you doing?"

Although Luitz hadn't moved yet, there was a note of alarm in his voice. I made a gargling sound at the back of my throat and arched my body convulsively, supporting myself on my heels and the back of my head. This might have been bloody uncomfortable, but it was impressive enough to convince Luitz. He thought I was committing suicide in front of his very eyes and I heard his chair topple over as he pushed himself to his feet. Then he was bending over me, hands reaching out to unclamp my jaws.

The loop of the belt went over his head before Luitz had any idea what was happening. When he did, Luitz would have very much liked to shout for assistance but I'd already pulled the loop tight. The trouble was, I couldn't kill him. The chain kept getting in my way, my hands were slippery with sweat and, worst of all, Luitz just didn't want to be killed. Even with the thin belt cutting deep into the flesh of his neck, he was fighting back, desperately trying to break my grip on the belt. Although he wasn't winning, I wasn't either. I simply couldn't pull the belt tight enough to finish him off. I might be slowly throttling him but slow wasn't good enough. I was too weak to keep going very long.

It was easier once I finally brought Luitz down to his knees beside the bunk. Then I could twist my body and hook one leg round him. Although this didn't give me much extra leverage, it was sufficient. The German's resistance became progressively weaker and it was only now, when it was too late, that he remembered his gun. I responded by hooking closer to the side of the bunk with my leg and pulling even tighter on the belt. His face was turning a blackish purple now, his tongue was out of his mouth and he was simply flopping about. Even so, it was another minute before he stopped twitching completely and I could relax my grip.

As far as I could tell, nobody else on board had been aware of the struggle. Everything appeared to be proceeding as normal and the only unusual sounds were my ragged breathing and the pounding of my heart. Although there was no guarantee that the door wouldn't open at any moment, this was down to chance. Step one was complete and, now that I'd liberated Luitz's Walther, any visitors would receive a warm welcome.

Step two should have been straightforward but it wasn't. I discovered this when I went through the German's pockets, taking care not to look too closely at his face. The key to the manacle wasn't there, not even after I'd been through Luitz's pockets a second time. It looked as though I'd killed him for nothing.

This would have been a very good moment for me to panic but I couldn't spare the time. It was no longer a question of being killed at some indeterminate moment in the future. I'd committed myself and there was no turning back. Either I finished what I'd started or I was finished myself. Unless I could free myself from the damned bunk, my life expectancy could probably be measured in minutes.

It was the kind of incentive I always responded to. The thing was, I knew for a fact that Luitz had had the key. I could even have described the ring it was attached to. And the ring had definitely been in his pocket.

Despite the urgency, I forced myself to slow down while I went through his clothes once more, turning each pocket inside out after I'd finished with it. There were still no keys and now was an even better time to panic.

When I thought it through again, Luitz was still the man who should have had the key. If it wasn't on his person, there was only one other place it could be, on the table. At first I thought it wasn't there either until I spotted the keyring, half-hidden by the copy of *al-Ahram* that Luitz had been reading.

There was only one minor snag—there was no way I could reach the table. And it wouldn't be long before one of the others came in for a coffee or something. I was going to look pretty silly unless I'd escaped from the bunk by then. A few seconds were wasted while I examined alternative means of ridding myself of the manacle but there was no way I could pull it free of the bulkhead and I didn't have anything to work on the lock with. Using the gun to shoot myself free would have been far too noisy.

A couple of seconds more told me that using the gun to capture the first man through the door wasn't much more promising. Apart from being certified maniacs, the men recruited by the Libyans had one other thing in common. They were prepared to die for their cause, which was one of the prerequisites for becoming a certified maniac. Somehow or other I had to reach the table.

I climbed off the bunk, took in all the slack in the chain and worked myself across the floor on my back. It was no go. When I'd finished, the toes of my right foot were a few, tantalizing inches short of the nearest table leg. So stretch yourself, Philis, I told myself. Otherwise you're going to die. I thought tall and I stretched and my foot was suddenly touching the wood of the table-leg. This still wasn't good enough. My foot had to hook around behind it. I was losing enough sweat to fill a bucket and my contortions were racking my whole body with pain but it didn't occur to me to give in. Do that and I might as well shoot myself with Luitz's automatic.

Wincing in anticipation, I pulled even harder against the chain. The top half of my body was being held clear of the floor and it was my left shoulder which was taking most of the strain, the tendons stretched almost to breaking point. My left wrist was suffering as well, where the steel manacle was gouging into my flesh. It was probably the blood and sweat acting as a lubricant which gave me the last couple of inches I needed to hook my toes behind the table-leg. All I had to do now was pull the table towards me and I couldn't. The bloody thing was too heavy. I tried thinking negatively. I conjured up graphic images of what was likely to happen to me if I didn't succeed and suddenly the table was moving.

Although it only moved an inch or two to start with, every inch closer to me meant more of my foot behind the table-leg. I must have managed six whole inches before I was forced to rest. It hadn't occurred to me that a table could be so heavy. I didn't rest for very long and my second attempt shifted the table another six inches. This was the good news. The bad news was that no matter how hard I pulled, the table wouldn't come any closer. One of the floorboards was warped and unless I could physically lift the table there was nothing more I could do.

It was back to the drawing-board time, and I leaned back against the bunk while I massaged my left shoulder. Although I'd completely lost track of how long it had been since I'd attacked Luitz, I knew it was too long. Worse still, the beating had taken far more out of me than I'd realised and I was rapidly reaching the end of my tether.

This was why my first try for the key-ring was the easy way. After it was unfastened from Luitz's neck, I used my belt again, casting it like a fishing-line, but it was no good. The belt wasn't quite long enough, a refrain which seemed to be coming my theme song. The only alternative was going to be very noisy. Before I began I checked that the safety on the Walther was off and laid it close to hand on the floor beside me. Then I stretched out on my back again.

Now the table was closer, it was much easier to reach and I managed to get quite a good grip with my ankles near the top of the table-leg. Unfortunately, it was virtually impossible to control what I was doing. Although I had enough strength in my legs to tip the table over, it was far too heavy for me to hold once it started to topple. If I wanted the keys, the whole table had to go over and it wouldn't be a gentle landing because I'd have to make sure my legs were well clear. I had enough problems already without a couple of broken legs thrown in.

The crash seemed to rock the entire boat. It was so monstrously loud that I didn't even bother to check where the keys had ended up. I simply snatched up the Walther and prepared to shoot anybody who entered the cabin. Nobody came. After a full minute had gone by, I finally allowed myself to believe that the engine must have drowned the noise. With the keys in my hand, it seemed as though the first round had gone to me. All I had to do now was deal with three armed killers and I'd be home free.

The shore was a hell of a long way away. When I padded across the cabin and tried the windows on either side, the opposite bank wasn't any closer. At a rough guess, it was almost a quarter of a mile to the white, flat-topped houses lining the river. Another guess, based on the way I felt, made this approximately four hundred yards further than I was capable of swimming. All the same, on balance I preferred swimming to waging war. If I was weak enough to have doubts about reaching the shore, it would be sheer madness to attempt a takeover of the boat. I'd already stretched my luck as far as it would go. Now was the time to get out, while I had the chance.

First, though, I had to reach the water. Now that I'd looked out of the windows, I knew it was only two paces to the rail. Because the houseboat floated so low in the water, there should be virtually no splash when I went overboard. Even if I couldn't swim all the way to the bank, I could always float. However, there was no point in going overboard unless I could do so unobserved. Bobbing around in the Nile while Ahmat and company took potshots at me from the boat wasn't my idea of a fun afternoon.

The door leading out on deck was at the front of the cabin, which placed it about three feet behind the wheelhouse. At least, I was 99.9 per cent certain this was where the wheelhouse would be. It certainly wasn't above the cabin and there wasn't anywhere else it could be.

Wheelhouse or not, I was 100 percent certain about at least two of my captors being there. With my ear pressed against the wood of the bulkhead, I could hear the faint murmur of their voices. This left me with the problem of the third man. He might not be any Harry Lime or Kim Philby but he worried me. I hoped he was in the wheelhouse with his two companions. Failing this, I'd like him to be in the crew's quarters, which I placed at the rear of the boat. I didn't even mind if he was up above, provided he was fast asleep. What I didn't want was for him to be right outside the cabin, waiting to say "Surprise, surprise."

I pulled the door towards me an inch at a time. Once there was sufficient space for my head, I stopped pulling and forced myself to suck some oxygen into my lungs. The wheelhouse was where I'd expected it to be, the sliding door leading inside right beside me. I only examined it long enough to see that the door was open. Then I ducked back inside the cabin to wipe the sweat from my brow.

The door to the wheelhouse didn't bother me nearly as much as the missing man but I now knew as much as I was likely to until I made my try for the river. I had it all planned in my mind. I'd half-open the door, creep a few feet away from the wheelhouse in the shadow of the cabin wall and roll under the rail. After this, it would all be down to luck.

It was a truly terrible plan and I could speak with the authority of an expert in the field. The best I could hope for, assuming that everything went my way, was that I might not drown. Every other projection left me dead, maimed or recaptured. I went to one of the windows again, looking across to the bank. It was as far away as ever and I knew I'd been deluding myself. I'd been opting out, going for the line of least resistance. The only way to be safe was to make sure I didn't leave any enemies behind, enemies who could fire live ammunition at my back. Somehow or other I had to secure control of the houseboat. Either that or I had to destroy it.

Until I went through into the galley, it hadn't occurred to me that I might be able to scuttle the houseboat. It had vaguely occurred to me that there might be a bloody great plug somewhere but this was never a serious consideration. After I'd spotted the cylinder of propane gas, my attitude changed dramatically. In fact there were two cylinders but one of them, attached to the stove, was nearly empty. However, the other was full and I knew just how to use it. The idea had instant appeal for the vandal in me.

I carried the heavy cylinder across the cabin and put it down against the wooden bulkhead separating the cabin from the wheelhouse. The table weighed too much to lift and I had to drag it, minimising the noise as much as possible. Tipped over on its side, it neatly blocked the doorway from the galley to the cabin. It wasn't going to be a controlled explosion and blasting myself into several small pieces wasn't part of the master plan. I'd need protection and the table seemed solid enough for my purposes.

The only real problem was detonation. I couldn't risk turning the tap on and flicking burning matches across the cabin. Putting a bullet or two into the cylinder might be sufficient to detonate the gas. On the other hand, it might not and this was another risk I didn't want to take. I tied a couple of knots in Luitz's handkerchief, then lit it with his matches. This wasn't a great success. The linen simply smouldered for a few seconds and then went out. Once I'd soaked it in liberal quantities of cooking oil, it burned much better. I dropped the blazing handkerchief on the floor beside the gas cylinder and ran back across the cabin, no longer concerned about the noise I made. If my big bang theory was correct, I was about to make a noise which would be heard over most of northern Egypt.

And it was a big bang because theory converted into practice far, far better than I dared hope. I put two bullets into the cylinder, aiming just above the burning handkerchief, before I ducked down behind the table. I was still ducking when my version of Armageddon arrived. In the confined space, the explosion was awesome and if I hadn't had my mouth open, I'd have lost both eardrums. Even with a solid tabletop in front of me, the blast lifted me bodily and threw me back into the galley. All the air in the cabin and galley seemed to have been sucked into the explosion and I was gasping for breath, blood trickling from my mouth and nostrils. If the pain was anything to go by, it was gushing from my ears as well.

All the same, I was the lucky one. Even through the smoke and flames, I could see there were no longer any windows in the cabin. Nor was there much of the roof left, especially at the far end. As for the wheelhouse, it no longer existed. The gas cylinder appeared to have gone straight through the bulkhead, across the wheelhouse and out at the front, destroying everything in its path. Through the eddying smoke, I could clearly see the river ahead.

Somewhere in the debris, one of the hit team was screaming hideously, a keening wail which set my teeth on edge, but I didn't stay to listen to him. The entire cabin was ablaze and the heat was already scorching my hair and eyebrows. I was more worried about the second cylinder of propane and I went through the remains of the galley window without any ceremony, banking on the billowing smoke to conceal me.

The entire front half of the houseboat appeared to be ablaze, the flames shooting twenty feet or more into the air. The air was hot enough to roast me and this determined which way I headed. I'd had another look at the river and it still didn't tempt me, especially as a couple of feluccas were already sailing in our direction. It made more sense to go to the stern and await developments. I didn't know how many of my captors were still alive but I should be able to delay going overboard until there was a boat within easy swimming distance.

There was no shortage of hiding places in the stern. A pile of packing cases was stacked there, with plenty of room to spare between the cases and the rail. Once I'd squeezed myself into the space, it was time to take stock. Although there was far too much smoke for me to see the bow, it was fairly easy to piece together what was happening. A lot of frantic shouting in Arabic had replaced the screaming. While there was no way of telling what condition they might be in, at least two of my captors were still in the land of the living. Before very long they'd be wondering what had happened to their prisoner and they wouldn't have much difficulty guessing where I was. They could search the whole of the boat in a matter of minutes.

This was the bad news. On the credit side, I must have demolished the steering gear along with the wheelhouse. Although the engine still seemed to be chugging away, the boat had started to swing across stream. As far as I could tell, we'd begun to travel in a wide circle. Combined with the fire, this was bound to attract a lot of attention. I could see several other boats coming in our direction, rapidly closing the gap. The nearest of them was barely a hundred yards away, its two-man crew straining to see what was happening.

When the leading felucca came within hailing distance, it sailed parallel to us, one man steering while the other stood in the bow. He could obviously see somebody at the front of the houseboat and the verbal exchange was both brief and one-sided. It was terminated by a burst of gunfire from the bow of our craft. It only needed a few bullets ripping into its taut sail and the felucca was pulling away from us again. The kamikaze spirit was alive and flourishing on the Nile. Having the boat destroyed beneath them wasn't going to deter my remaining captors from completing what they'd set out to do.

I nestled in amongst the packing cases and gloomily waited for what had to come next. Although I was out of the worst of it, the smoke was much thicker now and my eyes were watering badly. This was the only excuse I could think of for not killing the figure which suddenly emerged from the smoke. I hit Mahomed all right, somewhere up by the right shoulder, but it definitely wasn't a fatal wound. Dead men weren't too clever at firing PPS sub-machine-guns and this was precisely what Mahomed was doing as he disappeared back into the smoke.

Almost immediately, a second gun opened up to my right, from the far side of the superstructure. I huddled lower and allowed them to waste ammunition. Apart from a fluke ricochet, I was fairly safe but I wasn't exactly comfortable. Sooner or later it would occur to them to try shooting down at me from the top of the superstructure and when that happened I wouldn't have any choice. I'd be forced to go overboard and take my chances in the river. Schistosomiasis was a much better bet than lead poisoning.

Ahmat and Mahomed must have realised they were wasting their time because the gunfire ceased, to be replaced by a shouted exchange. It would have been nice to know exactly what they were plotting. About all I could be certain of was that it definitely wouldn't be to my benefit.

I was as surprised as anybody when a third voice joined in the conversation, a voice distorted by a megaphone. I was even more surprised when I realised whom the voice belonged to. The police launch had been closing in from behind without my noticing it and there was no mistaking Yousuf's massive bulk in the bow. I suddenly felt very, very fond of him. One of the surest ways to my heart was to help keep it beating.

"Are you all right, Philis?" His bellow was loud enough to wake the odd Pharaoh or two. "Wave your hand if you are."

I waved briefly and then turned back to the front. The local cavalry might have arrived but I couldn't see any white flags fluttering aboard the houseboat. I was still right up the creek and I merely had to look at the turgid, brown water to realise what it was full of.

"How many are there on board with you?"

I raised two fingers, hoping Yousuf would realise I wasn't trying to insult him.

"OK, my friend. Stay where you are and keep your head down. It won't be long now."

By now the fire on board was spreading and the entire boat rocked as the second cylinder of propane gas exploded. The resulting billow of smoke was thicker than ever but if it was bothering Ahmat and Mahomed, it certainly hadn't affected their lungs. They'd started shouting at each other again and this time it didn't take very long to discover what they'd been discussing. Ahmat began hosing the packing cases with bullets and Mahomed materialised from the smoke again, charging directly at my position. I could have handled him on my own but there was no need. It was the opportunity the policeman manning the machine-gun in the launch had been waiting for. So many of the heavy-calibre bullets hit Mahomed, he seemed to disintegrate in front of me, jerking around like a demented puppet before he flopped to the deck. Ahmat must have had as good a view as I'd had because he stopped firing at once. He was out-gunned and if he was going to commit suicide, he wanted to make damn sure he took me with him.

"Now there's only one," Yousuf shouted cheerfully over the megaphone. "Can you swim, Philis? If so, I suggest you slip over the stern while we cover you."

There was no need for a second invitation. Some people willingly spent a small fortune for a cruise up the Nile but I'd had a bellyful of it.

The water was warm and oily. It was like swimming in soup and, despite the urgency, I couldn't manage more than a geriatric dog paddle. I tried telling myself that Ahmat might start shooting at any moment and even this didn't make me swim any faster. The adrenalin had finally run dry and my body was fed up with the demands I kept making of it. It would get me to the launch all right but it would do so in its own sweet time.

Although there was only about twenty-five yards to swim, it seemed to take forever. I was wallowing, shipping the filthy water through my mouth, and Yousuf could see I was having difficulties. He was leaning out over the side of the launch, yelling what were meant to be words of inspiration and encouragement. If he leaned far enough, he might fall into the river himself and then he could inspire and encourage himself. Halfway to the launch I stopped for a breather, treading water while I looked back at the houseboat. At least half of it was burning now, sending its column of smoke high into the air, and I wondered what Ahmat was doing.

About thirty seconds later I found out. One of the policemen was holding out a boathook and I was actually stretching for it when Ahmat's hands grasped my ankles. The attack was totally unexpected. I was several feet down before I started to kick, not that this did me a lot of good anyway. I was still going down and I hadn't had a chance to fill my lungs with air. The only thing that saved me was that Ahmat needed air as well because he'd swum underwater from the boathouse.

After he'd released my ankles, we both kicked for the surface. For a moment or two our heads were side by side, far too close for anybody to risk a shot from the launch. I was vaguely aware of Yousuf shouting more useless advice but I was too busy coughing up water to pay much attention to him. Before I could replace the water with a refill of air, Ahmat had ducked down under the water again, taking me with him.

This time we went even deeper. Although I was struggling, I was too weak and too starved for oxygen to be very effective. I might have gained a foot or two but then consciousness started to ebb away and Ahmat wasn't slow to sense his advantage. He was clambering up my body now and there was nothing I could do to stop him, not even when his fingers clamped around my throat. Although I was hitting out at him with all my strength, this didn't seem to bother Ahmat at all. He simply clasped his legs around my waist and squeezed harder with his hands. I was dying. My arms fell limply to my sides, my mouth was full of water and I could actually feel the life drain out of me. I no longer minded very much. I just felt sad, and a little disappointed.

Somebody was hurting me. When I tried to complain, sour, vomit-tainted water came gushing out of my mouth and nose. The hands pressed brutally down on my back again, pushing me harder against the rough planking, and more water dribbled out. The process was repeated another three times before I was strong enough to groan. Another twice and I managed to roll over on my side.

At first the faces looking down at me were simply unidentifiable blurs. Then my vision cleared a little and I recognised Yousuf. Several policemen were grouped around him and all of them looked appropriately concerned.

"Ahmat?" I croaked.

Yousuf didn't understand and his features creased in perplexity.

"Ahmat?" I repeated.

This time Yousuf realised what I was talking about.

"Over there."

Nobody had bothered too much about covering the body properly as both feet and one arm were sticking out from beneath the tarpaulin. A small pool of blood and water was forming on the deck beside him and two of the policemen, out of uniform, were dripping wet. I assumed they'd come into the river to rescue me.

"Satisfied?" Yousuf inquired.

"Very." I was feeling better by the moment. "What now?"

"We have a doctor on board." Yousuf was waving a fat hand in the direction of the burly man who'd administered artificial respiration. "If we go into the cabin, he can examine you properly."

Under the circumstances, the doctor was very thorough. He had the time for it because the launch was heading back downstream instead of making for the nearest portion of bank. The only limiting factor was that of language. As the doctor spoke no English, the only way for him to discover where I hurt was to keep prodding me until I yelled.

When the doctor had finished, it was left to Yousuf to give me a resume of what he'd discovered. To my relief, nothing was broken and there were no apparent internal injuries. A few days' rest would allow the bruises to fade and should see me as good as new.

"I owe you an apology, my friend," Yousuf announced once we were alone.

"Too bloody right you do," I agreed.

"I let you down badly, Philis." Yousuf seemed genuinely contrite but this didn't necessarily mean a thing. "You've no idea how I felt when you went missing last night."

"I wasn't exactly shouting with joy."

"I can imagine. I feel quite ashamed."

"So you should but I went into this with my eyes open. I knew the risks."

"It was still my responsibility."

He seemed determined to shoulder the guilts of the world and I wasn't in a mood to argue. After all, it had been pretty sloppy.

"Have it your own way," I said. "Just explain one thing, though. If you'd lost me, how did you manage to be cruising down the river just now?"

"I was afraid you'd never ask, Philis." Suddenly Yousuf was all smiles. "That was one thing I did do right. The doorman at La Parisienne was one of my men. He attached a transmitter to your taxi."

"In that case, why did it take so long for you to catch up? Did you all have a late breakfast or something?"

Yousuf shrugged, sending small ripples up and down his body.

"It took time to discover which boat you were on but that's something we can discuss later. We seem to have arrived."

I'd felt the launch bump against the jetty but looking out of a porthole did nothing to tell me where we were. It was simply one of those anonymous small towns which lined the Nile. The only features which were at all out of the ordinary were the number of policemen waiting for us and the large black Cadillac.

"Where do we go now?" I inquired.

"Back to Cairo. You're going to be my guest for a couple of days. That way I can be sure you follow the doctor's orders."

"And after that?"

"I shall come and wave goodbye to you at the airport, my friend. Next time around we might not be so lucky."

And there would be a next time if I stayed in Cairo. This was why I wasn't arguing with Yousuf any more.

REBELS ATTACK MINING TOWN IN ZAIRE

Kinshasa—On Thursday night about 4,000 rebels attacked Kolwezi, a large copper mining town in Zaire's southeastern Shaba province. According to Foreign Ministry sources almost the entire town is in rebel hands. Today there was a further attack on the railway centre of Mutshatsa. The Zaire News Agency stated that there was fierce fighting before the rebels were driven off.

The attack on Kolwezi was carried out by former Katangese gendarmes based in Angola. They had previously invaded Shaba in March of last year. It is said that the rebel forces include several "whites," positively identified as being Cuban.

Unofficial sources say the rebels control all strategic points in the town of Kolwezi, including the airport where several aircraft have been destroyed. Concern is being expressed about the fate of the several thousand Europeans, mostly Belgians, who live in Kolwezi.

The Zaire News Agency has accused the Soviet Union, Cuba, Libya and Algeria of supporting the invasion. Both Libya and Algeria had formed commandos for the rebels and their base camps were situated in Angola. The rebels were careful to arrive in Shaba from Zambia so that Angola would not be directly involved in the invasion.—Reuter.

CHAPTER EIGHT

"Are you all right, Philis?"

Although her English was atrocious, there was no mistaking Fatima's concern. I'd stopped so suddenly on the top step that she'd bumped into me. I wasn't entirely certain whether the hand she put out was to steady herself or me. Knowing Fatima, it was probably me. Generations of Egyptian women had been taught that their primary function was to serve their menfolk and Fatima was a traditionalist.

"I'm fine," I assured her.

"Are you sure? I don't think you should be leaving so soon. You still don't look well to me."

I doubted if I ever would. Yousuf's wife was a large, cuddly woman with all the instincts of a born nurse. For the past thirty-six hours she'd been spoiling me outrageously and I'd enjoyed every moment of it.

"The only thing I'm suffering from is too much rich food. If I stayed much longer, I'd end up the same size as Yousuf. I'm not used to being treated so well."

Yousuf smirked proprietorially and Fatima blushed. She blushed even more when I kissed her on the cheek.

"Thanks again," I said. "You've been absolutely marvelous."

"You're forgetting me, Philis." Yousuf was doing his best to look hurt. "Fatima might do all the work but I pay the bills."

"What do I have to thank you for? You've spent the past two days telling me it was all your fault I was hurt in the first place."

Yousuf laughed.

"That doesn't mean you have to agree with me. You could at least make some effort to salve my conscience."

It was all very friendly and it was another five minutes before I finally managed to tear myself away. The car had been sent by the Embassy and it was the sight of the man behind the wheel which had made me stop so suddenly. I'd already known that Pawson was coming to Cairo and this was ominous enough. Seeing Bayliss there as well definitely spelled trouble.

"How's the arm?" I asked.

"Not too bad." Bayliss flexed his bicep to reassure himself. "I gather you're on the mend too."

"So the doctor says."

I turned round in my seat to wave to Yousuf and Fatima. Both of them stayed on the steps until we'd pulled out of the drive. One of the few nice things about my job was that I made friends in the most unlikely places. Unfortunately, the same was true of enemies.

"I didn't expect to see you in Cairo," I said.

"I wasn't expecting to be here either."

"So what brings you here? You're not my personal bodyguard by any chance."

"Hardly. I'm just passing through."

"Sure."

As it was obvious that Bayliss didn't intend to tell me anything, I stopped trying to pump him. I didn't stop worrying, though. With a bit of effort, I'd managed to think of several innocuous reasons why Pawson might need to come to Cairo but there was nothing at all innocuous about Bayliss, no matter where he might be.

Pawson didn't do a thing to make me feel any better. By now I'd learned to read most of his moods and he was far too cheerful and friendly for my liking. Besides, Bayliss had stayed with us after he'd ushered me into my master's presence. Both of us were blunt instruments and if we were going to be working in tandem again, whatever Pawson had lined up for us wouldn't be a rest cure.

To begin with, though, we were living in the past. Pawson debriefed me about what exactly had been happening in Cairo and, in return, gave me a more detailed account of how Andrea had been killed. This was sufficient to bring all the old anger back to the surface. Nobody deserved to die the way Andrea had.

"You say she was mutilated. Was that simply for kicks or was she tortured for information?"

"There's no real way of telling."

"But you can make an informed guess."

"In that case, I'd say the manner of her death was intended as a lesson."

I walked across to the window and looked out. There wasn't much to see apart from one of the Embassy's interior courtyards. Suddenly, I was very glad about what I'd done on the houseboat.

"How are negotiations going with the Mad Mullah in Tripoli?" I asked.

"Slowly, I'm afraid."

One of the Embassy secretaries was crossing the courtyard below me, a pretty blond in a flowered skirt. She was walking with the self-conscious swing of the hips of a woman who knew there were a dozen windows overlooking her.

"Have the Libyans made a try for anybody else yet?"

"Not so far but they'll be coming after you again, Philis. You do know that, don't you?"

"Thanks for reminding me. I needed cheering up." I'd turned away from the window so I could watch Pawson's face. The old fox was up to something and I didn't want him to think he was fooling me. "Where do I hide now?"

"We could always bury you somewhere." Pawson made this sound like a serious suggestion but it wasn't what he wanted. Otherwise he wouldn't have been in Cairo with Bayliss. "We could hide you in a safe house until it's all blown over."

"Fine. I'll buy that."

I failed to see why I should make it easy for him.

"Of course, there is an alternative." Pawson's expression hadn't changed. Nor had his tone of voice. "As it happens, I have something on the boil which would keep you well out of the Libyans' way."

"It's OK. I'll settle for the safe house."

"This is important, Philis."

"When isn't it?"

"All right." Pawson acknowledged the point with a faint smile. "Let's say this is very important."

"You do that."

I still wasn't feeling cooperative.

"It's also urgent. Either the operation takes off in the next few hours or it doesn't take off at all. You and Bayliss are all I have. It would take too long to pull somebody else off an assignment."

This still wasn't enough. Pawson must have realised this because he pressed on before I had a chance to reply.

"I can't order you, Philis, and I'm not going to try. I'm asking you. If you like, I'm appealing to your loyalty. I'm calling in any favours you owe me."

"Are there any?"

"There must be one or two."

There were as well. Besides, Pawson had pre-empted me, neatly out-flanking any possible objections. The least I could do was give him a hearing.

"That's a dirty trick," I said.

"What else did you expect." Now Pawson was smiling at me. "A leopard can't change his spots."

"Go on then. Let's have it."

"I'll explain on the way to the airport."

"What about my luggage?"

"It's already on its way."

Hard as I tried, I couldn't stop myself from matching his smile with one of my own. However much I might resent the way Pawson ran rings around me, at least he did it with a degree of style.

Even before I knew the three of us were booked on a flight to Kinshasa, I'd already worked out that it had to be connected with the invasion of southern Zaire. The prospect of becoming involved in a real shooting war didn't exactly thrill me but Pawson's presence on the Air Zaire Boeing worried me almost as much. Although he'd admitted that it was a rush job, I hadn't realised he was cutting this close to the bone. It was a reaction operation with Pawson patching it together as he went along, slotting each piece into the jigsaw as it became available. It was painfully obvious that the timing of the FNLC invasion had caught everybody on the hop. When I'd been in Oslo the invasion hadn't been expected for several more months and now that it had actually happened, panic buttons were being pushed all over the place.

On the way to the airport, Pawson gave me a résumé of the military situation which wasn't very different from what I'd been reading in the newspapers. So far the FNLC rebels had attained almost all their objectives, aided by yet another shameful performance by the Zairian forces. The FAZ had caved in on virtually every front, leaving the rebels firmly in control of Kolwezi and a large swathe of Shaba province.

"It all seems straightforward enough," I commented. By now we were aboard the aeroplane. "Bayliss and I simply swan down to Kolwezi and drive the rebels out. They'll probably surrender as soon as they realise the calibre of the opposition."

Pawson laughed and even Bayliss managed a smile of sorts.

"That's not quite the scenario I had in mind, Philis."

"So why the hell are we on our way to Kolwezi?"

"Cobalt, Philis," Pawson answered succinctly. "Cobalt."

"Of course," I said. "That explains everything."

Pawson did his best but he wasn't much happier delivering a technical briefing than I was at understanding it. He was simply passing on material which had been fed to him and which he'd had no opportunity to digest. This meant there were sizeable gaps in his knowledge, as I soon discovered when I tested him with a question or two. He wasn't even certain whether cobalt ore was mined as such or recovered as a by-product in the processing of other ores such as copper. It would have been laughable if my life hadn't been one of those on the line.

Fortunately, the technical side didn't matter too much because the picture Pawson painted was graphic enough anyway. Total world production of cobalt was between twenty and thirty thousand metric tons a year. In any given year as much as 60 per cent of this cobalt came from Zaire and 85 per cent of Zairian production centred on the mines in the Kolwezi area. My math might not be very good but it didn't take me long to calculate that approximately half of the world's output of cobalt was currently in the hands of Communist-backed FNLC rebels. And cobalt was vitally important in equally vital sectors of Western industry. For centuries it had simply been used as a decoration, giving a bluish tinge to glazes and ceramics. Nowadays, however, far more significant use was made of the metal's special properties.

"Such as?" I inquired.

"For a start, there are only three elements which are magnetic at room temperatures. Cobalt is one of them. More important, it retains its magnetism to a far higher temperature than any other known metal."

"Bully for cobalt." Pawson had sounded like a highly-trained parrot as he reeled off the gobbledygook. "What exactly does that mean?"

Apparently it meant that one of the most important applications for cobalt was in the production of permanently magnetic materials. Pawson made this sound of the greatest significance although the information didn't do a great deal to set my pulse racing. There were, of course, plenty of other uses. A radioactive form of cobalt, Radioisotope 60, was used a lot in medicine and nuclear engineering. It was also used in industry for the inspection of materials to find flaws or foreign objects in the internal structure. Other uses were found for cobalt in ceramics, electroplating and, for God's sake, dentistry.

"I see it all now," I said. "It's a communist plot to destroy our teeth. None of us will be able to eat and we'll starve to death."

"There are times," Bayliss commented, "when I'm very glad I don't have a sense of humour."

"I know precisely what you mean," Pawson agreed.

"OK, OK." In the face of their mutual admiration, I conceded the point. "I apologise for being facetious but do we have to take the long way round? All I want to know is why cobalt is so bloody important."

Of course, it was its strength. Its toughness and durability made cobalt an essential element in the production of cemented carbides which were used for machine tools, drill bits, dies and saws. It was an equally essential ingredient in the production of steel-alloys, which were required to maintain their strength at high temperatures, because cobalt was one of the few metals which could withstand heat, flame and corrosion stresses. These alloys were needed in the automobile and oil refining industries. In aerospace, they were required for turbines, burners, exhaust systems and thermal shields. Even to a moron like me, the military applications were obvious.

There were, of course, alternatives to cobalt. High temperature alloys could use nickel instead but the results just weren't as effective. In certain areas of military and space hardware, there simply weren't any acceptable substitutes for cobalt. Similarly, although satisfactory permanent magnets could be made utilising samarium, without cobalt you couldn't make the soft magnetic alloys needed in precision electrical equipment and electronic devices. Once again, the military applications were only too apparent. As far as cemented carbide cutting tools were concerned, the basis of the machine tool industry, there just wasn't any known substitute for cobalt.

Apparently it was not the accepted opinion of the various intelligence chiefs that control of the cobalt producing area was the factor which had made the Russians so eager to sponsor Operation Dove. Political chaos in Zaire could only be to their advantage. The overthrow or assassination of President Mobutu would be even better but these were now believed to have been purely secondary considerations. The real prizes were economic. It didn't matter whether or not the invasion succeeded in the long term because the rebels would still be in a position to cripple an important sector of Western industry, a sector which was largely militarily orientated. Although there were small, strategic stockpiles of cobalt in the West, hoarded away for a rainy day, the amounts involved were relatively insignificant. It was difficult to amass stockpiles when the demands for cobalt already outstripped production.

In any case, the Russians believed in doing things properly and an important part of their strategy had been to create an artificial shortage. Cobalt was sold on the Commodities Market and for several months mysterious buyers had been snapping up any cobalt available. This hadn't been unusual enough to attract a great deal of attention at the time but, with the benefit of hindsight, the transactions could now be seen in quite a different light. It was generally assumed that the buyers had been agents acting on behalf of the Soviet Union.

"And none of the geniuses at the top worked this out until now?" Pawson had paused for breath and I was eager to seize the opportunity. "They knew there was going to be an invasion, they knew the cobalt was produced in the Kolwezi area and yet they've only just pieced it together?"

"Of course not, Philis." For the first time Pawson sounded irritable. "Cobalt is a strategic material and it was one of the first considerations. Unfortunately, the timing of the invasion caught everybody by surprise. That was why it was so important to capture Ramirez."

"What difference would that have made? Forbes told me in Oslo that there'd be a military response anyway."

Pawson was nodding his agreement.

"It's been on the drawing boards for months. The Americans are keeping out of it but the French and Belgians will handle it between them. They'll be sending in troops within the next few days."

"In that case the FNLC rebels will be driven out of Kolwezi and that will be the end of the cobalt crisis."

I hadn't thought I was being naive but the others apparently did. Bayliss was smiling cynically to himself and Pawson was shaking his head vigorously.

"On the contrary, Philis. Even if the rebels don't use explosives to destroy them, the cobalt mines are likely to be out of action for at least six months. The FNLC cut off the electricity supply, the pumps stop working and the mines will flood."

"And if they do use explosives?"

"Then it might be years before the mines are back to full production again. It all depends on how thorough a job they do."

Now, for the first time, I thought I had an idea of what Pawson was going to ask me to do. I didn't like it one little bit.

"I'm no explosives expert," I pointed out. "Nor is Bayliss."

"You won't need to be because I'm not sending you anywhere near the mines. They're the Belgians' problem."

"So what exactly do you want us to do?"

"We're going to hijack a train, Philis," Bayliss answered for Pawson. "And then we're going to drive it out through rebel-held territory. Won't that be jolly?"

I didn't need to answer because my expression must have said it all. I'd never, ever wanted to be a train driver, not even when I was a kid, and I didn't want to be one now.

NEAR KOLWEZI, ZAIRE

Marie Dessault was in the kitchen at the rear of the farmhouse when she heard her uncle slam the front door. She was a tall, slim girl with blond hair and the white of her shorts showed off just how tanned her legs had become during her stay. So had the rest of her but she buttoned the top of her workshirt before she transferred the bacon and eggs from the pan to the plates. Good old Uncle Pierre had been a bit free with his hands the last few days. She didn't want to do anything to encourage him.

"Breakfast is ready," she called.

"I'm on my way."

The door to the living room opened behind her and Marie wasn't quick enough to move away from the stove. There was nothing to object to about his peck on the cheek, apart from the smell of stale whiskey. It was the way his hand had slid up from her waist to rest against the underside of her breast. Marie knew this was no accident. Unless she did something, she'd have to start locking her bedroom door at night. Before she'd left Brussels, somebody should have warned her about what happened to middle-aged men who spent too long alone in the bush. Then she wouldn't have been fighting to preserve her virtue on the remotest farm in Africa.

"Any luck with the radio?" Pierre asked.

They'd seated themselves at opposite ends of the long, wooden table.

"It's worse than ever. I still can't get anything except static."

"Bloody thing."

Pierre forked bacon into his mouth. He was a heavy-built, grey-haired man in his mid-forties. Apart from his annual trips to Brussels and a few months after independence, he'd spent all his adult life in Katanga. The government in Kinshasa might refer to it as Shaba province now but it would always be Katanga for him.

"Are you still planning to drive into Kolwezi today?" he inquired.

"I was hoping to." It was five days since Marie had last had any outside contacts and it seemed like as many years. "Will you be coming with me?"

"I can't. The irrigation ditches need clearing. You'll be all right on your own, won't you?"

"I don't see why not."

Marie had barely managed to conceal her relief. It would be nice to get away on her own for a few hours.

"Fine. You can buy some spares for the radio while you're in town. I'll give you a list before you leave."

He scrawled it down for her as soon as he'd finished breakfast, then left to start work. Marie didn't bother to clear away or wash up—the black housekeeper would see to that. She went upstairs to shower and change instead, already planning the day in her head.

When the bedroom door opened some five minutes later, it was the final straw. Marie lifted her hands to cover her bare breasts and swung round angrily. It was high time she put Uncle Pierre straight, explained to him that the *droit de seigneur* didn't apply to her. But it wasn't Uncle

Pierre. Instead, there were two black men in the doorway, dressed in dirty, tiger-striped combat fatigues and carrying automatic rifles. The angry words died stillborn on Marie's lips. Suddenly she was very, very frightened, more frightened than she'd ever been in her young life.

CHAPTER NINE

We were still more than twenty miles from Kolwezi when we ran into the roadblock. I assumed it must be manned by government troops but Jofre had no such illusions. Apart from knowing how to drive, he was a Belgian who'd spent most of his life in Shaba.

"It's the FNLC," he announced cheerfully. "I didn't realise the bastards had come this far."

Not for the first time, I was wishing I hadn't injured my leg. Then I could have parachuted in with Bayliss.

"What do we do?" I asked.

"We stop like the man says."

One of the soldiers had stepped into the road and was flagging us down. The carbine he was carrying endowed him with a certain authority.

"Is that wise?"

"I think we're safe enough. Our sources say the rebel troops are under strict orders not to harm Europeans."

These were the same sources which had promised us that the Suba road was clear but by now we were too close to turn tail and run. Apart from the one in the road, I could see another five soldiers grouped around the camouflaged truck. None of them looked particularly friendly, or as though they paid much attention to orders.

"The worst that can happen is that they'll turn us back." Jofre was still happy in cloud cuckoo land. "Then we'll have to find another route into Kolwezi."

We'd slowed to a crawl and Jofre had started to wind down his window. I could see past the truck now, round the bend in the road. The burned-out Peugeot, and the two bodies beside it, were another triumph for Jofre's sources.

He saw the wreck at the same moment I did and his reaction was instant. His foot floored the accelerator and we were surging forward again, aiming for the narrow gap between the truck and the deep gulley at the side of the road. The solid thump as we hit the FNLC soldier in front of us was followed by the scream of tortured metal as the Land

Rover scraped along the side of the truck. Then we were in the clear, accelerating into the bend.

"Hold tight, Philis."

The mad bastard was actually smiling at me as we bounced back on to the road. It was a smile which was still in place when the hail of bullets from the two FNLC men on the far side of the truck shattered the windscreen and blew off the top half of his head. I ducked and grabbed for the steering wheel, fighting to keep the Land Rover on the road. More automatic fire hammered into the bodywork and the windscreen, showering me with splinters of glass. I popped my head up above the level of the dashboard, taking a quick look at the road ahead before I ducked down again. More automatic weapons were firing now, most of them from behind me, and when they hit the rear tyres there was no holding the Land Rover any longer. It was veering to the right, towards the gulley, no matter how hard I tugged at the wheel. The best I could manage was to kick the passenger door beside me open and roll myself clear as the vehicle left the road.

I only hit the ground twice as I somersaulted to the bottom of the gulley and if it hadn't been for the thick, reddish mud left by the previous night's rain, I'd probably have broken my neck. For a second or two I was too stunned to move, then my instinct for survival took over. The nearest of the FNLC soldiers were less than two hundred yards away, just around the corner. I could already hear the shouting as they started to run towards me and the gulley was a death-trap, offering me no cover at all. Unless I wanted to end up like Jofre, I had to be out of it before they came into sight. Otherwise I'd have as much chance as a target in a shooting gallery.

Falling into the gulley had been a hell of a lot easier than climbing out proved to be. The same thick mud which had saved the priceless Philis neck had now become an enemy. My first attempt took me halfway up the slope before I slid back and my second try wasn't much of an improvement. It would have been a case of third time unlucky as well if I hadn't managed to grab hold of a thorny bush some six feet below the lip of the gulley. It was an extremely thorny bush, the kind which made roses seem under-protected, and it gouged strips of flesh from the palm of my left hand but it did give me the extra traction I needed. With its help I was able to haul myself up the last, slippery stretch and over the rim of the gulley.

Although all this seemed to have taken me for ever, the FNLC men still weren't in view. What I desperately needed now was somewhere to go to ground and the shallow, bush-shrouded depression in front of me was tailor-made for my purposes. I dived into it just as the first rebel soldiers arrived round the bend.

When they halted at the point where the Land Rover had left the road, they were no more than twenty-five yards away from me. Unless they were blind, they couldn't miss the tracks I'd made wallowing in the gulley. Even if they did, they had more than enough fingers among them to work out that there was only one dead body in the wreck. I pressed myself deeper into the mud and looked over my shoulder at the trees behind me. They were twice as far away as the four FNLC men and, apart from the odd shrub, I'd be out in the open all the way. I'd be blasted into pieces before I was halfway there, which seemed a compelling reason for remaining where I was. While I remained, I hoped the rebel soldiers were feeling lazy and wouldn't want to waste their day chasing me through the jungle.

For a minute or two it looked as though I might be in luck. The soldiers had had plenty of time to examine the gulley and none of them were anxious to get mud all over their uniforms. They might have left me in peace if a fifth figure hadn't appeared at the crown of the bend, one of the bossy types you encountered in any army. He shouted something to the soldiers on the far side of the gulley and one of them shouted something back. As they weren't using French, I couldn't translate but there was no real need for an interpreter. When the shouting had finished, three of the FNLC men slid down into the gulley. The fourth stayed where he was to provide them with covering fire.

I took another look over my shoulder but the trees hadn't moved any closer. The ground was rough and slippery and even without a limp it would have been too far to run with an automatic weapon threatening my back. Back in Kinshasa, I hadn't been too pleased when I'd been issued the 9mm Browning Hi-Power. I'd never really trusted automatics and it weighed so much I walked like Quasimodo. Now I was glad to have its stopping power. Both shots I fired hit the soldier on the far side of the gulley somewhere in the chest and they knocked him halfway across the road. I didn't hang around to see whether or not the parabellums kept him down. I was already up and running, zig-zagging towards the trees and praying that I wouldn't twist an ankle.

There was a lot of excited shouting from the bottom of the gulley but I far preferred this to shooting. Apparently, the soldiers weren't any better at climbing slippery slopes than I was. Once I was safely among the trees, I stopped briefly to reassess the situation. The men in the gulley were still down there. Two other rebel soldiers were running towards their stricken comrade in the road but there were definite grounds for cautious optimism. Although I'd virtually guaranteed that the FNLC men would come after me, I now had the headstart I'd wanted. I didn't think they were likely to catch me among the trees.

Unfortunately, there just weren't enough trees. I'd had some vague idea that I was running into a forest which covered most of central Africa but it wasn't like that at all. The trees were in a narrow belt parallel to the road and it didn't take me more than a couple of minutes to run right through them. The ground on the far side offered even less cover than there'd been beside the road and for the time being I elected to keep to the edge of the trees. The big question was how well the FNLC men knew the local topography.

A quarter of an hour later I had my answer. They weren't simply chasing aimlessly after me; they were systematically beating the woods with men both behind and ahead of me. Worse still, they'd sent a couple of soldiers right through the trees to patrol the scrubland, just in case I was fool enough to make a break for it. I picked one of the biggest trees and climbed as high as I could. Although the leaves and branches effectively screened me from view, this was no permanent solution. I had an appointment to keep in Kolwezi. Bayliss had parachuted in with most of our equipment and the time schedule Pawson had us working to didn't leave much scope for delay. We had to have the train out of Kolwezi before the French Foreign Legion and the Belgian paras moved in.

After an hour or so all sounds of the search had died away. By then I was certain that the men I'd seen on the road were only a small element of the FNLC contingent manning the roadblock. There had been at least a dozen men looking for me in the trees. Some of them were still lurking there, waiting for me to make my next move. I was strongly tempted to stay where I was.

Up above the storm clouds were gathering and there was the occasional roll of thunder. I'd been waiting for the rain to start for the past thirty minutes but I couldn't afford to delay any longer. I had to get to Kolwezi and I had to be there before the following morning. Although Bayliss and I did have a back-up rendezvous, leaving it that long really would turn the whole affair into Mission Impossible.

As soon as I was moving again, I was at a disadvantage. Every shadow appeared to conceal an enemy and I kept the Browning in my hand. In the first few yards I nearly shot two trees and a bush. No matter how careful I was, it was impossible to see further than the next tree.

It was the sudden rasp of a match which saved me. The man with the cigarette was unnervingly close and I melted into the shadows while I tried to pinpoint him. Even with the smell of burning tobacco to assist me, I couldn't see him but this wasn't really the point. Where there was one man, others would be close to hand. I'd have to work my way around him and hope my luck held.

I was still hoping when I stood on the dead branch. If the unexpected crack sounded deafening, it was nothing compared with the burst of gunfire which followed. Obviously, I wasn't the only person in the trees with my nerves on edge. Although the soldier doing the shooting came frighteningly close, he was aiming by guesswork. Besides, there were far too many trees between us for him to be any real threat. The main danger came from the other men, the ones who were calling out excitedly, trying to discover what was happening.

I moved much faster now, heading away from the excitement, but I could hear the sounds of pursuit behind me. Judging by the voices, there were at least four of them. They might only have a rough idea of where I was but they all seemed to be coming in the right direction. The best I could do was keep ahead of them.

It was only a few minutes before I'd been forced right to the edge of the belt of trees again. Ahead of me was a football-pitch-sized area of elephant grass, thick and coarse and prickly. There was no time for any proper evaluation. All I knew was that the woods behind me seemed to be full of shouting, armed men. And that the grass didn't look like the kind of place where any sane man would want to hide.

I went into the grass on my hands and knees. As I'd hoped, the grass was coarse enough to spring upright again after I'd taken my weight off it and I didn't think I was leaving a trail. On the other hand, there was nothing I could do about the wave effect on the tops of the sharp blades. This was why I only allowed myself forty-five seconds hard crawling. Then I stopped and rolled over on my back. The die was cast and there was nothing further I could do. Either I was caught or I wasn't. It was in the lap of the gods.

There were a lot of ants about, large, black and inquisitive. Although they seemed intent on exploring the most intimate recesses of my body, it could have been far worse. At least they weren't testing me for flavour with their mandibles. I reciprocated and left them in peace, apart from those few which ventured on to my face. Up above, framed by the screen of grass, the storm clouds were still gathering, sullen and lowering. Despite the almost constant thunder, it hadn't yet started to rain.

As far as I could gather, the rebel soldiers were grouped a few yards away at the edge of the trees. I didn't need to understand their language to know they were discussing tactics. This in itself was a relief. It meant my hiding place wasn't too obvious.

After a minute or so the group began to disperse. At first it was difficult to tell in which directions they were headed but it wasn't long before I knew exactly where one of them was going. He was wading into the elephant grass and it sounded as though he was coming directly towards me.

It was no good reminding myself that it was a large patch of grass. He appeared to be on a collision course and even a near miss would lead to my undoing. The grass just wasn't thick enough to pass anything approaching close scrutiny. I slipped off the safety catch of the Browning and held it across my chest. Since I'd shot the FNLC man at the roadside, surrender had been out of the question.

The first large drop of rain landed on my forehead as I caught a glimpse of the soldier's legs. The rain had come too late because he was little more than five yards away. He was almost certain to see me and the moment he did, I'd shoot him dead. Then I'd have to run like I'd never run before.

The FNLC man hadn't really expected me to be there in the grass. For an instant, when he saw me laying there, he was frozen by surprise. This was when I shot him. If I hadn't been able to see it, still clutched in my hand, I'd have believed the Browning had exploded. The clap of thunder was so loud it completely drowned the sound of the shot. The very earth itself seemed to shake. A second later, I was drowning too. The rebel soldier was still toppling to the ground when the heavens opened and the rain came down, descending in a solid sheet. Perhaps it hadn't arrived too late after all.

The farm complex was unnaturally quiet. Judging by the number of buildings, it was the centre for quite a sizable operation but there was no sign of life. There wasn't even a dog basking in the afternoon sun. I rested behind the tree, with the last of the steam rising from my clothes, and thought it through. Although I'd no precise idea of my position, I knew I couldn't be more than twenty-five miles from Kolwezi. Admittedly, I'd done a lot of dodging around in the rain while I was losing the soldiers but I hadn't done too much back-tracking. I might even be closer to my destination than I'd been when the Land Rover was forced off the road. In this case it was possible that the owners of the farm had simply moved out for the duration of the hostilities.

There was only one way to find out. I moved in closer, making the best use possible of the available cover, and it was almost ten minutes before I reached the first of the outbuildings. The silence was beginning to get on my nerves. The body just outside the sliding doors did nothing to steady them. He was an African, presumably one of the farmworkers, and the front of his shirt was soaked with blood where he'd been hit by several bullets. I stepped over him and peered round the corner at the main building.

It looked as deserted as everywhere else but all my instincts were telling me this wasn't somewhere I wanted to be. On the other hand, I desperately needed transport if I hoped to keep my rendezvous with Bayliss. Walking into Kolwezi would take at least six hours and I reasoned that such a big farm was bound to have vehicles.

I covered the distance to the verandah in a crouching run, half-expecting to be cut down by a burst of automatic fire. None came and I peered inside through the nearest window. There was another body on the floor, a white man this time. So much for the rebel directive about not harming Europeans.

The front door of the house wasn't locked and once I was inside the unmistakable signs of looting were all around me. Drawers hung open while broken glass and china littered the floor. In one way this was encouraging. The mess suggested that a group of FNLC soldiers had popped in for a quick social call. They'd butchered anybody who was in their way, grabbed anything they wanted and then moved on. I spared a few precious moments to examine the dead man on the floor. He was heavily built and in his mid-forties with grey hair where it wasn't stained with blood. He'd been battered to death with what I guessed to be a rifle butt and he was far beyond any help I could give him.

I left him to the flies and moved on. The garage was at the rear of the house and I exited through the kitchen. It was in as much of a mess as the other room and I'd have passed straight through if it hadn't been for the blood on the floor. It was only a couple of spots but the blood was fresh, not coagulated like the blood I'd seen around the two bodies.

I was still looking down at it when I sensed the sudden movement behind me and I swung round with the Browning in my hand. The girl was over in the far corner of the kitchen, huddled between a cupboard and the wall. She was naked and I only had to see the bruises and the scratches and the blood trickling down her thighs to guess what must have happened. When I moved towards her she huddled into an even tighter ball and brought her hands up over her eyes.

"It's all right," I said. "I'm not going to hurt you."

If she understood me, it certainly didn't show. She was a foetus, safe back in her mother's womb where nobody and nothing could hurt her any more. At least, that's what a psychiatrist might have said. To me she was simply a frightened girl who'd been terrorised and brutalised and I had to make contact with her.

"It's all over. I'm a friend."

I tried French this time but it might have been Serbo-Croat for all the difference it made. The girl remained where she was and I knew precisely what I ought to do. I should leave the girl where she lay, appropriate a vehicle and drive off for my rendezvous with Bayliss. The girl hadn't suffered any serious physical injuries that I could see and I couldn't afford to collect any waifs and strays. I had a job which was difficult enough without any distractions. I knew all this but I also knew there was no way I could turn my back and walk away, not if I wanted to live with myself afterwards.

The first saucepanful of water didn't have any effect. The second had her spluttering, though, and the third dousing had her hands away from her face. There was a crazed look in her eyes which encouraged me to back off warily but after a second they cleared and she shook her head, spraying water like a dog. It was as if she was seeing me for the first time.

"Who are you?" she asked in French.

"Philis. I'm English."

"Philis." She tested the name in her mouth as though it was a new food. "My name is Marie. I was raped."

"I know."

Her voice had a lifeless quality to it which showed how deep the shock had gone. She was much too calm as she surveyed the wreckage of the kitchen.

"Where's Uncle Pierre? Is he dead?"

"Yes."

I assumed she must be referring to the middle-aged man in the living room.

"I thought he was."

Although she managed a brief shudder, this was Marie's only reaction.

"We have to get out of here," I told her. "It's not safe to stay. Do you want me to get you some clothes?"

"I can manage."

She'd used the cupboard to pull herself to her feet and she seemed steady enough.

"I'll come with you if you like."

"It's all right."

A minute or so after she'd gone upstairs, I heard the sound of the shower being turned on. It seemed to go on for an awful long time before it stopped.

KOLWEZI, SHABA PROVINCE, ZAIRE

Bayliss was becoming cramped and he adjusted his position slightly without taking the binoculars from his eyes. By now, after three hours of observation, he was positive that there were no guards posted. Although there were plenty of soldiers in the station itself and small groups occasionally wandered through into the marshalling yard, these movements appeared to be random. Quite possibly the rebels had no idea of the treasure within their grasp and they wouldn't know an electrolytically refined cathode from a hole in the road. Until a few days previously, Bayliss would have had difficulty spotting the difference himself.

Even without guards or regular patrols, the approach would obviously have to be made after dark. If Pawson's information was correct, it would be at least three days before the Foreign Legion and the Belgian paratroopers arrived so there was no point in taking unnecessary risks.

For the next half an hour Bayliss was busy working out the route he and Philis would have to take. He already knew which train he wanted. He'd been instructed to look for 1-ton wooden packing cases marked for delivery in Belgium and the rebels had made his job easier for him. The doors of the closed trucks had been opened and there was no mistaking his target.

Although Bayliss wasn't underestimating the problems involved, it was beginning to look as if the operation might be feasible after all. If everything worked out, he and Philis really might be able to drive off with 2,000 tons of cobalt cathodes. They might be able to steal almost 10 per cent of the world's annual supply of cobalt from under the very noses of the FNLC.

CHAPTER TEN

Marie was still with me when I met up with Bayliss. I'd originally intended to drop her off as quickly as possible, somewhere she could be looked after properly. What I hadn't allowed for was that she might be almost as much of a stranger in Zaire as myself. By the time I discovered that Marie didn't really know anybody in the area apart from a few acquaintances in Kolwezi itself, it was too late because I was already lumbered. Whatever the temptations, I couldn't simply stop the pick-up and leave her by the side of the road. Bayliss might have managed it but I couldn't.

Because of the danger of roadblocks, we abandoned the pick-up and walked the last five miles with me in the lead and Marie tagging along behind. Even so, we arrived at the rendezvous almost an hour before the deadline and Bayliss should have been pleased to see me. He clearly wasn't as he indicated when he immediately led me out of earshot of Marie.

"Who's the girl?" he demanded brusquely.

"Marie Dessault. She's a lame duck I picked up along the way. And before you say anything, I wouldn't have brought her with me unless I'd had to. There wasn't any choice."

"Of course you had a choice, Philis." Bayliss was as angry as I'd ever seen him and I wasn't sure I didn't sympathise with him. "We can't afford lame ducks or camp followers. We have enough on our plate as it is."

"I know that."

I had intended to say more but Bayliss wasn't in a mood to allow me to finish.

"I'm glad we both agree. In that case we get rid of her now."

"No." I'd had a long, trying day and I didn't bother to be polite. "We'll get rid of her as soon as we find a safe place to leave her. Until then she stays."

"Why?" Bayliss was calm again and he was trying to persuade me by logic. "What we're trying to do is far more important than the well-being of an individual. You know that as well as I do."

"We need her. She has contacts here in Kolwezi and we don't."

"But we do have Jofre to provide them for us."

"Not any longer we don't. Jofre is dead."

Bayliss had assumed that the Belgian had gone on ahead into Kolwezi to find us a safe base and for a moment he was stunned into silence. I glanced across to where the girl was standing. She was where I'd left her, waiting for us to reach a decision.

"How did it happen?"

"We ran into a roadblock. Jofre was shot."

"Christ. That really does upset the apple cart."

It did as well because Jofre had had far more than local knowledge to offer. He was the only one of us who knew how to drive a train. By unspoken mutual consent, this was a problem we put aside until later.

"You've been into town," I said. "What's it like in Kolwezi?"

"Eerie. It's like a ghost gown. All the Europeans have been rounded up or are in hiding and the native population is in hiding as well. Apart from the FNLC patrols and a lot of bodies, there isn't anybody around. There's one thing in our favour, though. The electricity supply is out so there won't be any street lights."

"What about the train? Is it there?"

"It is. We'll go and take a look at it in a couple of hours. Until then we'd better find somewhere safe to hide ourselves."

Bayliss started walking off almost as soon as he'd finished speaking, leaving me to collect Marie. It was his way of telling me that he still didn't want her along.

The most significant fact to emerge from our expedition to the railway sidings was that the FNLC evidently did know about the cobalt. We went right down to the train and we discovered that demolition charges had been placed in all the trucks. If the rebels were forced to retreat, they didn't intend to leave 2,000 tons of cobalt behind.

However, this was only a relatively minor snag, one we could deal with when we were ready to leave. If, that is, we were ever ready to leave. This was the problem Bayliss and I sat down to discuss once we were safely back at our base, a house in the European section of Kolwezi. The mess inside suggested that the FNLC rebels had already come visiting and the former occupants had either fled or been captured.

"What do you know about driving a train, Philis?" Bayliss inquired.

"I had a toy one when I was a kid but I don't think that qualifies me as an expert. I wouldn't even know how to wind up one of the big ones."

"It can't be that difficult. I mean there's no steering problem once you have the locomotive started."

Bayliss didn't really believe what he was saying. At least, I hoped he didn't because I didn't want to be stuck in Kolwezi with an idiot.

"It can't be that easy either," I pointed out. "Otherwise British Rail wouldn't spend so much time training its drivers. Besides, there are a lot of soldiers around the station. We won't have much time to experiment."

"So what do you suggest?"

"We find ourselves another driver. Either that or we abandon the mission."

"We can't abort."

The very thought seemed to offend Bayliss, which was a shame. I still hadn't managed to get very worked up about the cobalt.

"In that case, Pawson will have to dig up a replacement driver bloody fast. The rebels are going to blow up the train the moment they hear the Foreign Legion is on its way."

I wasn't going to play at engine drivers under any circumstances. Quite apart from the difficulties I'd already mentioned, there was no guarantee we could head the locomotive in the right direction even if we could get the thing started. We'd look damn silly if we delivered the cobalt to Benguela in Angola. Do that and the FNLC would probably award us medals.

"I know somebody who drives trains."

These were almost the first words Marie had uttered since we'd returned from our reconnaissance and they were enough to grab our undivided attention. I hadn't even realised that she understood English.

"Here in Kolwezi?"

"Yes. He's Belgian like me. My uncle introduced him to me."

By now we were talking in French. There was too much at stake for us to risk a misunderstanding.

"Do you know where he lives?"

"It's quite near here I think. I've only been to his house once."

"But you're sure he drives trains?"

"Well . . ." For the first time, Marie hesitated. "I know he works for the railway because we were talking about it. I think he's a supervisor or something."

This was good enough for us. At the very least he'd know far more about controlling a diesel electric locomotive than either Bayliss or myself. Once we'd caught up on some sleep, we'd pay a visit to René Durand. If we were very lucky, we might not have to call on Pawson for a replacement after all.

"He must be mad," Bayliss breathed in my ear.

"Can't we do anything to help?" Marie asked from the other side.

I shook my head and gestured for Marie to keep quiet. Most of the FNLC patrol appeared to be drunk and their boisterous, tuneless singing had given us plenty of warning of their approach. The house we'd dived into was deserted, like so many others in the European sector, and we'd intended to stay there until the patrol had passed by. For the moment, though, it wasn't going anywhere. The eight rebel soldiers had found themselves a victim and they were enjoying themselves, grouped around the Peugeot they'd flagged down. I couldn't understand how any European could be stupid enough to be out driving the streets of Kolwezi. Or why he should be even more stupid and allow himself to be stopped by a bunch of drunken FNLC soldiers.

Although we were too far away to hear what was being said, we were ideally situated to watch the tragedy unfold. There was nothing we could do to help without compromising our mission and there was an awful inevitability to what happened, made more chilling by the casual joviality of the soldiers. There was no real malice or hostility behind what they did. They were simply having a bit of fun.

The driver of the Peugeot was bespectacled and middle-aged and he tried very hard to be dignified when he was hauled from the car, something which became considerably more difficult when he was forced to strip. In the process he lost his wallet and watch as well as his dignity. The horseplay which followed was rough and equally humiliating and the victim was crying when the soldiers eventually tired of their games. One moment the soldiers were pushing him around between them. The next their ranks had parted and he was walking off down the road, his shoes and socks incongruous in contrast with the nudity of the rest of his body.

He'd gone about fifty yards, followed by the jeers of the soldiers, when one of the rebels casually lifted his carbine and fired a short burst at his back. The soldiers didn't even bother to check to see whether their victim was dead or not. They simply crammed themselves into the Peugeot and drove off, shouting happily as they passed the bottle around. Behind them they left a crumpled body and several articles of clothing scattered untidily across the road.

"They're animals." Marie was sobbing. "Filthy, disgusting animals."

This wasn't an assessment either Bayliss or I was prepared to argue about. We waited another few minutes, partly to allow Marie time to calm down, partly to make sure the patrol didn't return. Then we moved out again, keeping to the gardens as much as possible because the streets weren't safe in daylight. We'd known this before but the incident we'd just witnessed encouraged us to be more careful than ever.

It took us almost three quarters of an hour to reach the Durands' house. On the way we passed several more bodies littering the road, all of them black and some in the early stages of decomposition. When we did reach our destination, it seemed as though our journey might have been a waste of time. Several of the windows had been broken, the front door hung open and the house appeared to be deserted. Either the Durands had been rounded up by the FNLC or they'd gone into hiding.

Once we were inside, we discovered that the house hadn't simply been looted. It looked as though a squad of soldiers had used it as a temporary bivouac. Most of the furniture which hadn't been removed was smashed, and FNLC toilet training wasn't much better than their self-discipline because there was excrement everywhere. Bayliss and I left Marie on guard in the lounge, where she could observe the street, while we went through the rest of the house. By the time we rejoined her we knew the Durands were no longer in residence. We also knew we'd have to contact Pawson, although we weren't quite sure how this could be done. Bayliss had brought in a couple of the Israeli PRC-601 palm-held transceivers but they only had a range of 15 kilometres. The rest of our radio equipment had been in the Land-Rover.

"There must be a lot of radio hams in a town like Kolwezi," Bayliss suggested.

I nodded my agreement. I'd noticed the aerials on several of the houses.

"There's one minor problem," I said. "How many of the radios are likely to be intact? The rebels have been through the area like a dose of salts. You've seen the state this place is in."

"There must be some radios they've missed and it's up to us to find one. If the worst comes to the worst, we'll have to liberate one from the FNLC."

Bayliss made it all sound too easy but I didn't voice my reservations because I could only think of one other alternative. And after my experiences at the roadblock, I didn't fancy another trip along the Suba road.

The noise from upstairs stopped us dead in our tracks. Most buildings had their built-in creaks but this was different, it was the definite sound of movement. Although it wasn't much of a noise, all three of us had appreciated its significance.

"There's somebody . . ."

Marie didn't finish because I'd clamped a hand over her mouth. I didn't feel threatened; I simply wanted to listen because the noise had definitely come from upstairs and we'd checked all the rooms. The sound wasn't repeated and after a second Bayliss started for the stairs with me right behind him. Now that we knew there was somebody else in the house with us, we were more cautious and I made sure I was in a position to cover Bayliss if necessary. We also searched more thoroughly and there still wasn't anybody upstairs.

This left just the one possible hiding place. We'd both noticed the hatch leading to the attic during our previous search and dismissed it at once. There was a counter-balanced loft ladder inside the hatch and it hadn't occurred to us that anybody would be able to close it behind them. Now we knew better and opened the hatch again but when we tried to pull the ladder down, it wouldn't budge. Although it could conceivably have been jammed, I was sure there was somebody up above hanging on to the ladder for grim life.

"Monsieur Durand," I called in French. "We're friends. We don't mean you any harm."

There was no reply. Either the attic was empty or there was somebody up there with a suspicious nature. I left Bayliss stationed underneath the hatch while I went downstairs to fetch Marie. She knew the Durands so perhaps she'd have better luck. Besides, she spoke French the way it should be spoken, not with an English grammar school accent.

"It's Marie Dessault," she said. "I came to your house before with my Uncle Pierre. The men with me are English. They want to help you."

For a moment I didn't think she'd have any more luck than I'd had. Then, to my surprise, a woman's voice answered Marie. She was frightened and hesitant but at least she was talking.

"Is that really you, Marie?"

"Can't you see me?"

Marie moved to stand directly beneath the hatch and her reward came when the loft ladder started to descend. The first person to emerge was a little boy who could have been no more than eight. Another boy, only slightly older, followed him. The last to appear was a thin, blond woman in her late thirties who I assumed was Madame Durand. Judging by the grime on her clothes and face, and on the children, they must have spent some considerable time in the attic.

Over the next few minutes, Madame Durand's story came out in bits and pieces without a great deal of continuity. Apparently, she and the two boys had been hiding in the attic for several days, including one terrifying episode of almost twenty-four hours with rebel troops camping in the house below. Fortunately, the FNLC men had been more intent on looting and destruction than a thorough search and somehow she'd managed to keep the boys quiet. There'd also been a couple of other occasions when she'd thought she'd heard people in the house but she couldn't be sure.

Although this would have made a great human interest story and I sympathised with what must have been a harrowing ordeal, Madame Durand hadn't touched on the only point which really interested us. Even Bayliss was becoming impatient and he was about to intervene when Marie saved him the trouble.

"What about René?" she inquired. "Isn't he with you?"

"No." For the first time Madame Durand started to cry, the tears leaving white streaks down her cheeks. "I haven't seen him since the invasion started and I don't know where he is. I hope he's still at the hospital."

"Is he hurt then?"

The question was much blunter than I'd intended but René's health was very important to me. If he'd been wounded, we were back at square one.

"I don't think so."

It seemed that Durand had been on duty at the station when the FNLC had launched its attack. Madame Durand had heard the shooting down in the town but she hadn't really known what was happening until one of the doctors at the hospital had phoned her. He'd told her about the FNLC invasion and explained that René was one of the Europeans who'd been captured and brought to the hospital. Although René was unharmed, he was likely to be held there for the duration of the hostilities. René's message for her had been to take some provisions and hide in the attic until the fighting was over. This was precisely what she'd been doing until we'd come along.

"And you haven't heard anything from René since?" I asked.

"No. We've been in the attic all the time."

"The telephones aren't working anyway," Bayliss chipped in.

This was the sort of thing he would have checked. He really was very thorough.

"What was the name of the doctor who contacted you?"

"Paul. Paul Delacroix. He's an old friend of the family."

"Does he usually work at the hospital?"

"Yes. He's one of the surgeons there."

"Fine." I looked across at Bayliss. "I think we leave Marie here, don't you?"

"That's the best idea. We'll come back after we've been to the hospital."

"You're going to see René?"

Now Madame Durand was really animated.

"We're going to try to," Bayliss told her, damping her enthusiasm down.

So far it hadn't occurred to her to ask what we wanted with her husband and this wasn't information we were about to volunteer. She had more than enough worries already without us adding to them.

It was mid-afternoon before we reached a position where we could observe the hospital. There'd been the sounds of heavy firing from the north of the city while we'd been travelling across town and we'd assumed that the Zairian forces must be mounting a counter-attack. This certainly seemed to be borne out by the number of wounded being brought into the hospital. It also seemed that the attack must have failed because everything had been quiet for the past hour or so.

Our observation post was on the top floor of a looted supermarket which afforded us a good view of the front of the modern hospital and there was a lot of activity outside. Trucks were bringing in the wounded, rebel troops were lolling about on the steps and grass and there was little hope of getting inside without being seen. However, this wasn't necessarily a drawback. We saw several white-smocked Europeans, presumably members of the hospital staff, and there didn't seem to be any restrictions on their movements. One of them had even driven off in his car, although he'd only travelled as far as an accommodation block a few hundred yards down the road.

"What do you think?" I asked.

"One of us has to take the risk, Philis."

I nodded and raised my binoculars to my eyes again. What I saw didn't fill me with any particular enthusiasm.

"This is becoming bloody ridiculous."

"It is a little silly," Bayliss agreed.

"I don't want to get myself killed looking for a train driver in a dump like Kolwezi."

"It isn't one of my ambitions either."

"There has to be a cut-off point," I said, warming to my theme. "A point where we agree it just can't be done."

"It might come to that."

Bayliss was simply being polite and humouring me because he wasn't taking my griping very seriously. Nor was I, come to that. Action was easy because it didn't usually give you time to think. A ludicrous situation like the present one allowed all the doubts plenty of time to surface.

"Which of us is going to play doctor?" I asked.

"We could toss for it."

"I haven't brought my double-headed coin with me."

"OK, Philis. You find me a doctor's smock and I'll try my luck inside the hospital."

"That's exceedingly generous of you."

"I thought so myself."

The cowardly part of me wanted to grab at Bayliss's offer and the other 5 per cent wouldn't have minded either. Creeping around Kolwezi had been fraught enough. Strolling into a building which was packed with rebel troops scared the pants off me, especially as I'd already witnessed just how unpredictable they could be. Unfortunately it was a job for a coward, somebody who was totally dedicated to survival. Nobility and patriotism and loyalty wouldn't count for a damn inside the hospital. The person most likely to come out again was somebody who'd cheat and lie and all the other things which were likely to save his skin. Hard as I tried I could only think of one of us who fitted the bill.

"Your French is better than mine," I said, trying to argue myself out of my decision.

"I'd noticed."

"On the other hand, you stand out in a crowd. I don't."

Bayliss considered this for a moment.

"Now you mention it, I suppose that's true."

"I think it's better if I go."

"You're the boss, Philis."

Bayliss was actually smiling at me. He knew the real reason as well as I did.

"What took you so long?"

Bayliss had gone looking for a doctor's smock in the accommodation block and he'd been far longer than I'd expected.

"Getting lonely, were you?" Bayliss was actually grinning at me. It was hard to tell with him but I guessed he might be beginning to like me a little. "I thought I might as well dig up some hard information while I was on the prowl."

"And?"

"The situation at the hospital is pretty well what we expected. The FNLC have suffered a lot of casualties and they didn't bring enough medics of their own. That means they can't afford to interfere too much with the doctors and nurses at the hospital. In theory, they're allowed to go home when they're not on duty. In practice, all the European staff are staying around the hospital buildings. They know how safe it is for whites on the streets."

I nodded.

"Any idea where I'm likely to find Dr. Delacroix?"

"None whatsoever. I do know where the European hostages are being held, though. There's about a couple of dozen of them cooped up in the isolation ward. That's at the far end of the main hospital block."

"Is Durand definitely there?"

"That I don't know. The nurse I spoke to at the hostel didn't recognise the name so we'll have to act on the assumption he hasn't been moved."

By this time I'd put on the doctor's smock. It was a bit roomy but I thought it would do.

"How do I look?" I asked.

"I wouldn't want you to operate on me but you should pass muster. Are you going in now?"

"I might as well."

There was no real advantage in waiting until dark. The hospital must have its own electricity supply so there'd be no shadows for me to hide in once I was inside.

"Be lucky," Bayliss said.

"I'll try. If I'm not, you'll have to shift the train on your own."

There wouldn't be any dramatic rescue attempts by Bayliss. If I wasn't lucky, we'd both be on our own.

I knew the young FNLC man meant trouble. He was only one of a group of soldiers on the steps of the hospital and none of the others were paying any particular attention to me but this wasn't going to cut any ice with the young African with the broken nose. He was young and he was bored and when our eyes had locked for an instant there had been a flash of mutual hostility. Both of us had only needed the one glance to know we could never be friends. Although I'd deliberately avoided looking at him since, I knew he must be the one who, at the very edge of my vision, was pushing himself to his feet.

"Halt," he commanded.

For a dangerous second I toyed with the idea of walking on, pretending I hadn't realised that he was talking to me. Then common sense prevailed. I stopped halfway up the steps and turned to face him.

"Where are you going?"

"Into the hospital. I'm a doctor."

"I haven't seen you here before."

"And I don't remember seeing you, citizen."

The *"citoyen"* was a calculated gamble because it was the term of address used by the Mobutu regime and I knew the effect it would probably have. All the same, this was much, much better than being asked for the identification I didn't have. At least, this was what I thought until the young rebel's face suffused with anger and his rifle swung up. Then I wasn't nearly so sure.

"Comrade," he shouted. "You call me comrade, not citizen. That's all dead now."

"As you wish, comrade. If you'll excuse me, there are patients waiting, patients who are comrades of yours."

I could feel the sweat trickling down my body as I turned and continued up the steps. There was no order to halt again, no burst of shooting and I kept myself walking until I was inside the swing. Only then did I pause, leaning against the wall while I shook like a badly set jelly. They'd been a nasty few seconds and they were probably only the first of many. I hoped I stayed alive long enough to have nightmares about the experience.

Although there were an awful lot of men in FNLC combat fatigues
wandering the corridors, the hospital appeared to be functioning fairly
normally. Nobody was paying me any particular attention and I was
beginning to gain confidence. It was simply a matter of looking as though I
belonged until I managed to catch one of the staff on their own. My
opportunity came when I saw an African nurse carrying an armful of bed
linen. She must have known I wasn't one of the medical staff but she
didn't comment when I stopped her. There'd probably been too many
upsets in her recent life for a bogus doctor to worry her unduly.

"I'm looking for Dr. Delacroix," I explained. "Do you have any idea
where I can find him?"

"If he's not operating, he's probably in the maternity ward. The doctors
are using it as a rest room."

"And where's the maternity ward?"

The question earned me another curious glance but the nurse answered readily enough.

"You follow the corridor to the end, then it's the third door on the left.
It's clearly marked so you can't miss it."

The nurse obviously wouldn't miss me either because she hurried off on
her way as soon as she'd given me directions. She recognised me as
trouble and wanted to stay well clear.

There wasn't a single pregnant woman or squalling baby in sight in the
maternity ward. Of the five male occupants, only one of them was awake
and he was lying flat on his back, staring up at the cracks in the ceiling
while he smoked a cigarette. Judging by the purplish smudges beneath his
eyes, he should have been asleep too.

"Is Dr. Delacroix here?" I inquired.

"What's that to you?"

He didn't sound rude or offensive. His voice simply sounded as tired as
the rest of him looked.

"I have to speak to him."

"Can't it wait? The poor bastard has been on the go nonstop for the past
thirty-six hours."

"It's very urgent, I'm afraid."

"In that case, he's the one with the beard in the end bed."

"Thanks."

My gratitude didn't appear to impress him unduly because he'd already
resumed his contemplation of the ceiling. Like the nurse, he didn't seem
to have any curiosity left.

Delacroix was sleeping the sleep of total exhaustion, not so much snor-
ing as bubbling air out through his mouth. He hadn't bothered to undress
before he'd thrown himself down on the bed and, even in the dim light of

the ward, I could see that his face was grey with fatigue. All the same, behind the beard it was a good face, a sensitive, caring face which went well with his job. It was a face most patients would respond to.

Waking him wasn't easy and at first he resisted my efforts to rouse him. It took several seconds hard shaking to bring him to and he spent another couple of minutes with his head in a washbasin, splashing cold water on to his face, before he was ready to talk to me. If I hadn't had so many problems of my own, I'd have felt guilty about disturbing him.

"You're English, aren't you?"

He was towelling his face as he spoke and I could see that the cold water hadn't done anything for his bloodshot eyes. Give him a set of fangs and some wings and Dracula would have had to look to his laurels.

"How did you guess?"

"Nobody else speaks French quite so badly." Tired as he was, Delacroix managed a smile which removed any possible offence from his remark. "What are you doing here? Or is it better not to know?"

"It's better not to know."

"As you wish." Perhaps lack of curiosity was a primary qualification for becoming a doctor in Belgium. Or perhaps the staff at the hospital had been through so much in the past few days that it had all been leached out of them. Whatever the reason, Delacroix made no attempt to press the point. "What can I do for you before I go back to sleep?"

"I'm hoping you can take me to see René Durand."

"René Durand?" Now the doctor was registering mild surprise. "How did you know he was here?"

"I spoke to his wife. She told me he was here."

"You've seen Alice?"

"This morning. She's fine."

"And the boys?"

"They're all right too."

"That is good news."

Although I didn't doubt Delacroix for a moment, his expression didn't match the words. There was a sadness about him which made me wonder about the circumstances of his own family but I didn't ask. I was afraid to. Since I'd arrived in Kolwezi, I'd already used up all the sympathy I could spare.

There were a couple of heavily armed FNLC soldiers standing outside the swing doors which led to the Isolation Ward. Even before we reached them, it was obvious that they'd no intention of moving out of our way to let us past. I hung back a little, allowing Delacroix to take the lead, and cowardice didn't come into it. It was the doctor who'd have to do the talking. And if talking wasn't good enough, I'd need room for manoeuvre.

"Where do you think you're going?"

The guard who'd spoken had his sub-machine-gun pointing uncompromisingly at Delacroix's chest. He might simply have been a good actor but he didn't seem pleased to see us.

"Inside." Delacroix didn't allow any shadow of doubt enter his voice. "The people in there are my patients. I want to check that they're all right."

"There's no need to bother. They're fine."

"That's right," the second guard agreed. "We've been taking very good care of them."

This made both men laugh. They were ugly laughs and this was what frightened me most about Kolwezi because it was a long time since I'd last been somewhere the violence was quite so close to the surface. When, and if, the killing started, there wouldn't have to be any rhyme or reason for it. If Delacroix was aware of my misgivings, he didn't appear to be sharing them. He was projecting authority and confidence.

"Out of my way," he said impatiently. "I don't have time to play childish games."

"Our orders are not to allow anybody inside."

The guard wasn't as convincing as Delacroix. The first elements of doubt had entered his voice.

"Well, I'm not anybody. I'm Dr. Delacroix and this is my assistant. For the past forty-eight hours we've been tending to the needs of your wounded comrades."

When Delacroix started forward again, he gave the guards a straight choice. Either they moved out of his way or they shot him and, in the event, they moved. As I followed Delacroix through the swing doors, I found myself wondering how many of these little confrontations the doctors had had to face each day since the occupation began. If they were a regular occurrence, it was hardly surprising that the medical staff all looked so exhausted.

There were a couple of dozen people inside the ward, including five or six women. Several of them already knew Delacroix and they surged forward to greet him, eager for news of the outside world. None of them were interested in me and I moved to one side, choosing a position where I could look out of the barred window. It overlooked a sizable parking bay. Normally it would have been reserved for ambulances but all the vehicles there now were trucks. One encouraging sign was that in contrast to the front of the hospital, there were no FNLC troopers hanging around. If only there'd been some way down from the window, it would have made a good escape route.

I'd been standing on my own for a couple of minutes when one of the men broke away from the group around the doctor. He was short and stocky and could have been almost any age between thirty and fifty. He also had that air of calm competence which was so common among men who'd elected to live their lives outside their native country. Unlike most of the other male prisoners, he was clean-shaven and his shirt and slacks were remarkably clean considering how long he must have lived in them. As I'd been shown his photograph earlier in the day, I'd already identified him as René Durand. This was just as well because he didn't waste time on introductions.

"How are Alice and the kids?" he demanded. "Paul said you saw them earlier today."

"They're concerned about you. Otherwise they seem to be in pretty good shape."

"Have they been hiding in the attic?"

Durand had a score of questions to ask and I gave him all the details I could. I even threw in a few reassuring lies for good measure. While I was busy with this, Delacroix had started examining some of the prisoners at the far end of the ward. Several of the captives were elderly and were clearly finding the uncertainties of their imprisonment an ordeal.

After I'd finished with the family details, Durand didn't waste time beating around the bush. He didn't need to ask what I wanted with him because he already seemed to know.

"Paul told me you wanted to ask me something," he said. "It's about the big cobalt shipment, isn't it?"

"How did you know?"

I was surprised and there was no point in hiding it. Durand's answering shrug of the shoulders was genuine, not done for effect.

"It was fairly obvious. You've risked putting yourself in the lion's den coming here to see me and the only thing I know about is railways. Unless you're here on a sabotage mission, that big shipment of cobalt is the only thing you could be interested in."

"A shipment that size is unusual, then?"

"I'll say. There've been a lot of labour disputes up at the mines during the past few months. Then there was a dispute with the drivers at the refinery. They've had to stockpile the cobalt until they could shift it out."

This was something I'd intended to ask Pawson about and hadn't. Two thousand tons had seemed a hell of a lot of cobalt to ship in one go.

"Anyway," Durand continued. "I can tell you exactly where the cobalt is in the yards. I can even draw you a diagram, if you like. There is one thing I ought to warn you about, though. The FNLC has put demolition charges in all of the trucks. They'd started doing it before I was brought to the hospital."

"I know. I've already been to take a look."

"You have?" It hadn't occurred to Durand that he might have more to offer than information. For the first time he was slightly off-balance. "In that case, what do you need me for?"

"We were rather hoping you'd drive the train out for us."

The silence which followed my announcement was lengthy and rather uncomfortable. At least, it was for me. Although I'd always maintained that people should think before they spoke, the Belgian was taking the principle to extremes. Besides, I didn't like the way he was looking at me. I hadn't really anticipated enthusiasm but the cold speculation I could read in his eyes was totally unexpected.

"Explain something to me." When Durand spoke, it was as slowly and precisely as he'd thought. "Unless I've misread your motives, you came to Kolwezi specifically to drive off with the cobalt."

"That's correct."

"In that case, wouldn't it have made sense to bring your own train-driver with you?"

"It would and I did. Unfortunately, there are roadblocks on the way into Kolwezi. Our driver was killed at one of them."

"I see."

I could almost hear Durand's brain ticking over as he assessed the situation and he was making me increasingly nervous. Perhaps there was something to be said after all for people who operated on a purely emotional level. At least, emotions could be manipulated and I was no longer sure this held true for Durand. He had the look of somebody who had every intention of manipulating what was going on, something he proved with his next question.

"Why exactly would I want to drive the train for you?" he asked.

"Because it's of vital importance both to your country and mine."

I'd had to try the patriotic appeal because there was no other answer but Durand evidently didn't enjoy flag-waving any more than I did.

"It's only important in the short term." He really had thought it through, God rot his soul. "If the mines themselves are destroyed, a trainload of cobalt will simply be a drop in the ocean. If the mines are left intact, production will be back to normal within six months."

"In industrial and military terms six months can be a hell of a long time."

"I suppose so."

Durand conceded the point with a nod of his head but he was still thinking. At this stage we were interrupted briefly by Delacroix coming across to tell me that we'd have to leave soon. However, he didn't argue about allowing me the extra few minutes I asked for.

"The FNLC won't simply sit back and allow us to drive the train away," Durand said as soon as we were alone again.

"I didn't pretend it would be easy." Now I was encouraged. For the first time Durand had sounded as though he might be willing to do as I'd asked. "There's one thing in our favour, though. The rebels don't appear to be mounting any regular patrols in the marshalling yards."

"There's bound to be hordes of the bastards in the station itself and that's not very far away."

"There'll be diversions on the big night," I told him. "Just say how long you'll need to get the train clear of the station and we'll see you have it."

Durand nodded his head again. At long last, it seemed as though we were making progress.

"You keep saying 'we' so you're obviously not on your own. What kind of back-up do you have?"

"At the moment I don't think that's any concern of yours."

"I disagree. I think it's very much my concern. More to the point, I don't think you can afford to keep any secrets from me."

Nor did I when he phrased himself like that. He was wasted working on the railway.

"There's just me and one other man."

"You must be very good."

"We like to think so but our boss wouldn't necessarily agree with us."

Durand's sudden smile was completely unexpected, warm, dependable and suggesting a strong sense of the ridiculous. I didn't trust it for a moment.

"OK," Durand said. "I'll drive your bloody train for you since you've asked so nicely."

"But?" I prompted.

"I'd heard that Englishmen were all cynical." Durand's smile had widened. "What makes you think there are any 'buts'?"

"A lifetime of dealing with devious foreigners like you."

"As it happens, you're right. There is one condition. Alice and the kids come with us."

"If that's what you want. You know the dangers they'll be facing."

I'd only hesitated for an instant before I'd agreed. Although it wasn't a development I welcomed, I wasn't in a position to bargain.

"And so do the rest of the prisoners here at the hospital."

"What?"

I was experiencing great difficulty in believing my ears.

"You heard but I'll say it again anyway. All the prisoners in this room go with us too."

"That's absolutely impossible."

This time I didn't hesitate at all because what Durand was asking was totally out of the question. I hadn't come to Kolwezi to stage a remake of *The Great Escape*.

"In that case, I suggest you start looking around for another train driver."

Durand was still smiling but he wasn't bluffing. I knew this the way I knew socks came in pairs. Either I accepted the Belgian's terms or I did as he'd suggested. Not for the first time, I wondered how on earth I'd allowed Pawson to persuade me to come to Kolwezi.

LUANDA, ANGOLA

Physically, Zaleski wasn't at all impressive and he had no personal charisma. He'd have no problems blending in with any crowd. However, he did represent power, awesome, ruthless power, and this was more than sufficient to outweigh any deficiencies of physique. It was his knowledge of what Zaleski stood for which made Agostinho so uneasy now. He knew that the mistake couldn't be laid at his door but he wasn't entirely sure that the Russian agreed with him.

"Let's recapitulate." Behind the thick lenses of his spectacles, Zaleski's eyes were very cold. "From the very beginning I made it perfectly clear that our support for Operation Dove was conditional. I stressed repeatedly that our interests were economic, not military. Isn't that so?"

"Yes, Your Excellency."

"In that case you should remember our primary condition. We stipulated that the mines at Kolwezi should be rendered inoperative. Do you recall that?"

"Yes, Your Excellency."

"Yes, Your Excellency." Suddenly Zaleski was shouting and when his hand slammed down on the table, Agostinho couldn't stop himself from taking a step backwards. "Why hasn't it been done then? Why haven't the mines been destroyed as we agreed?"

"I don't know." Agostinho wasn't simply sweating. He could actually smell his own fear. "I'll find out for you the moment communications are re-established."

Although he hadn't dared to say so, Agostinho already knew the answer. The commanders in the field had been carried away by their early successes. They'd thought they could hold on to what they'd won and if they did, the mines would be vital to the survival of an independent Shaba. Worse still, now the French and Belgians were on their way, it was too late to rectify the mistake. The communications link was out and within a few hours they'd be fighting for survival.

"You do that." Zaleski had reverted to a normal tone of voice again but Agostinho was uncomfortably aware that this was a dangerous calm. "What about the electricity supply to the mines? Has that been cut?"

Zaleski nodded, reflecting that this at least was some small consolation. Without electricity, the pumps couldn't work. Without pumps, there would be flooding. It should be several months before production returned to normal.

"And the train? What arrangements have been made there?"

"The demolition charges are already in position. They'll be detonated before any withdrawal."

"Make sure that they are. I shall be holding you directly responsible."

"Yes, Your Excellency."

As Agostinho turned to leave, Zaleski decided that the operation wouldn't be a total disaster. It might not be the triumph he'd aimed for but, provided the train was destroyed, there was no way his masters could deem it a failure.

CHAPTER ELEVEN

"I don't believe it, Philis."

Neither had I when Durand had made his demand so I didn't bother to argue with Bayliss. Besides, I was deriving a certain perverse satisfaction from the situation. The strain must have been getting to him because I'd never seen Bayliss quite so wound up before. It was quite refreshing to see him display the same human characteristics as the rest of us mere mortals.

"Who does Durand think we are anyway? Pied bloody Pipers? The way we're going, we'll end up with more camp followers than the FNLC."

"They do say there's strength in numbers."

While I wasn't particularly amused by the Belgian's demands myself, I couldn't resist the temptation to wind Bayliss up a bit more. The man was disintegrating before my very eyes. After a mere couple of days crawling around in a war-zone, his shirt was already rumpled and, unless it was my imagination, he'd even missed a small patch under his nose when he'd shaved. It made me feel a bit better about my own mud-spattered clothing and the thick stubble covering my face.

"It just can't be done, Philis. It's impossible."

"That's the line I tried with Durand but he had a much better argument. What alternative do we have? Have you bumped into any other engine-drivers while we've been wandering around Kolwezi?"

We were way past the point where we could call on Pawson for a replacement because it would only be a matter of hours before the French Legionnaires and Belgian paras came dropping in. Once that happened there wouldn't be a train for us to drive away. It was most unfortunate for us that Durand had realized just how strong his bargaining position was.

"I simply can't understand the man." Bayliss had started again. "The prisoners are safe enough at the hospital. They're certainly safer there than they will be on the train with us. Durand must be crazy."

"Don't you believe it." I didn't want Bayliss to get hold of the wrong end of the stick. However much inconvenience he might have caused us, Durand had impressed me a lot. "He knows exactly what he's doing. His main worry is what's likely to happen here in Kolwezi once the counter-attack begins. According to Durand, and the doctor backs him up, at least 100 Europeans have been killed so far."

"There are bound to be civilian casualties in any war."

"Maybe, but Durand is talking massacre. If we have any doubts, he suggests we visit a government rest-house down the road. The FNLC rounded up about three dozen Europeans there, including women and children, and then machine-gunned the lot. After the incident we witnessed this morning, I don't think he's exaggerating. And it isn't just the killing either because there are some nasty rumours flying around about what's happening at the Impala Hotel. The FNLC detachment stationed there has rounded up as many white women as it could find and turned the place into a brothel. Apart from the obvious, the women are being forced to perform nude discos on the stage."

"I'd no idea things were that bad."

"They might not be but they're getting that way. Being a European in Kolwezi is definitely a high-risk occupation."

"OK, but you say the prisoners actually in the hospital are being treated reasonably well. Surely Durand can see they'll be safer there than coming with us."

"Not necessarily. It seems the rebels have already heard that the Legion is on its way and they're getting edgy. According to Dr. Delacroix, some of the FNLC men are saying that if they're forced out of Kolwezi, the prisoners from the hospital will be going with them. They'll be used as hostages to cover the retreat. Once they've been taken across the Angolan or Zambian frontiers, I wouldn't give much for their chances of survival."

Bayliss stood up and walked across to the window. It was nearly dusk and although the rest of the town remained dark, the lights were beginning to come on in the hospital.

"So what do you think, Philis? Honestly."

"I think I'd get a hell of a sight more satisfaction out of saving the lives of those poor bastards in the hospital than I would from salvaging a million tons of cobalt."

"Philis the humanitarian. That's a new angle." Even in the dim light, I could see that Bayliss was smiling at me. "Putting sentiment to one side, though, answer me one question. Can it be done?"

"Yes."

My answer was unequivocal.

"But can it be managed without prejudicing what Pawson sent us here to do?"

"No." This was equally unequivocal. "Unfortunately, it's something we're stuck with, however you might feel about it. We need Durand and he only comes in company with the other prisoners. There's no way around it."

Bayliss nodded resignedly. His emotion was a thing of the past and he was back to practicalities again. It was a time for considering ways and means.

"I still don't like the idea of all those people going on the train. There are a lot of troops around those marshalling yards."

"They won't be on the train—I won one for us there. After I'd explained the situation to Durand, he agreed that we'd deliver the prisoners to his house and leave them there. Then he'd come with us to the station."

"We shift them by truck?"

"We'll have to but that shouldn't be too much of a problem. The FNLC have got plenty of trucks standing around at the hospital. There are several in the parking bay directly outside the Isolation Ward. Better still, they aren't guarded."

"That's something but it doesn't leave us with much time. Tomorrow night is the deadline."

"That's what I told Durand. He'll be expecting us just after nightfall."

"OK." Bayliss was sounding thoughtful. "We're going to be awfully short-handed, though. Apart from anything else, we'll have to take out the hospital generator. If the lights stay on, there are too many troops around for a European to have any hope of driving out unnoticed."

"I discussed that with Durand as well. He says we're going to need an African driver."

"Jesus Christ, Philis." Suddenly the emotional Bayliss was back on display. "We've had enough problems finding somebody to drive the bloody train without going into the market for a black truck driver. What are we supposed to do? Put an advertisement in the *FNLC Gazette?*"

"Not quite." Now it was my turn to grin because the new Bayliss was somebody I quite liked. The warts and blemishes improved him a lot. "Durand gave me the name and address of a man who'll help."

Bayliss's disgusted snort wasn't intended to be encouraging.

"If your remember, Philis, we had a name and an address for Durand and look what's happened there. We'll probably find this African of his will only drive the truck if we agree to take his entire bloody tribe with us."

I nearly said something about lightning not striking twice in the same place but I managed to stop myself in time. This would have been a bit too much like tempting providence.

"Don't do it, Antoine," she said. "It's madness."

"Hush, woman." For such a big man, Antoine had a surprisingly soft voice. "Let the man have his say."

"I've heard more than enough already."

At least, I assumed that this had to be the gist of their discussion. To keep what they were saying private, Antoine's wife had switched from French to Swahili. Or it could have been Kiluba because I couldn't tell the difference. As I'd said my piece, I sat back and left them to it. I was dog-tired, a deep-seated fatigue which even encompassed my bones. Somehow or other I'd have to squeeze in several hours of uninterrupted, dreamless sleep before the following night.

Despite the language problem, I was aware that Antoine was gradually winning the verbal battle. His contributions were becoming longer and more authoritative while his wife's counter-attacks became briefer and less assured. I knew the victory had been won when she abruptly stood up and went into the tiny kitchen. The way she slammed the coffeepot down on the stove suggested she might not be a gracious loser but this was none of my concern.

"I'm sorry about that," Antoine told me, reverting to French. "You know what wives are like."

I nodded sagely. This was a lot easier than admitting I was a confirmed bachelor.

"You say Monsieur Durand recommended me especially?"

"That's why I'm here. He told me you were somebody we could rely on."

The piece of information appeared to please Antoine.

"We've worked together for a long time," he explained. "I owe him a lot."

"That isn't the way René put it. He made it sound as though you were a team."

There was nothing like a little flattery to keep things going smoothly.

"I suppose we are." Now Antoine was more pleased than ever. "You say he and his family are all well?"

"They were when I saw them an hour or two ago."

"That's good. I've been worrying about them. A lot of Europeans have been killed in the last few days."

"So I've heard."

We were interrupted by his wife coming through and serving us with our coffee. She still didn't seem very happy and I tended to sympathise with her. I was asking a lot of her husband.

"How far will I have to drive the truck?" Antoine asked.

"Only from the hospital to the Durand house."

"And you have the truck already?"

"In a way. We'll pick one up at the hospital."

"Will it be very dangerous?"

The question came from the African's wife and I made sure I was looking her directly in the eye when I answered.

"There'll be risks, yes. You know what's been happening here in Kolwezi better than I do. Every time you step out on to the street, you take your life in your hands."

"But this will be especially dangerous?"

"It will be if we're caught, although that's something we hope to avoid. There's one thing I promise, though. If anything should go wrong, I and my friends will swear that Antoine wasn't helping us from choice. I'll say I held a gun to his head."

"And that will be all? You won't ask Antoine to do more than drive the truck?"

"You have my word on it."

For a few seconds she said nothing, examining me closely while she weighed up exactly how much my word was worth. Luckily she didn't know me very well.

"Thank you," she said. "I'm sorry I was so inhospitable earlier. I'd like Antoine to help Monsieur Durand but I was worried for his safety. Now I feel better about it. I can see you're a good man."

I couldn't remember the last time I'd blushed but I could feel myself reddening now. Although I'd been called a hell of a lot of different things in my life, nobody else had been quite so wide of the mark. It was Antoine who broke the embarrassed silence by pushing himself out of his chair.

"I'd better be getting my things together," he said.

His wife went with him but I didn't mind. At long last the operation was beginning to take shape. We had our train driver and we had a truck driver. All we needed now was an awful lot of luck.

There was another big thunderstorm brewing and even inside the hospital it was so humid the air almost had to be chewed. Beneath my doctor's smock, I could feel the sweat running down my body in rivulets.

"You'll have to come with us, you know."

"No." The doctor must have been anticipating this and he spoke like a man whose mind was made up. "I'm staying here."

"That's utter madness."

"Maybe, but it's my decision."

I kept pace with Delacroix along the corridor and wondered how best to change his mind. I didn't know him well enough to be sure whether I liked him or not but the respect was already there. He wasn't somebody I wanted to have on my conscience.

"I suppose it's the patients you're worried about."

"Precisely. I'm a doctor. I can't simply walk out on them."

"What use will you be to them if you're dead. Once we've driven off with the prisoners, it won't take very long for the officer in charge to work out the part you played. He'll stand you against a wall and have you shot."

"That's a risk I'll have to take."

Sometimes there was a very thin line separating heroism from stupidity and I knew on which side I placed Delacroix. I might have argued some more but there wasn't the time. We'd rounded the last corner and the swing doors leading to the Isolation Ward were there ahead of us. Although the guards had been changed, their weaponry was the same and I knew I'd have to take them out very quickly. I was suddenly very conscious of the Ingrams I had concealed beneath my smock.

On this occasion there was no hassle about getting past the guards and the mood inside the ward was very different too. All of the prisoners knew what was about to happen and they were so keyed up the tension was almost palpable. They were about to go over the top and, by the looks of them, several prisoners were having second thoughts. I hoped they'd be swept along by the tide.

"How's it going?"

While Delacroix ran a last check on the two prisoners we'd have to carry down, I'd gone across to Durand. Although he'd tried to keep his greeting casual, he was obviously very much on edge. So were the three men grouped around him.

"As well as can be expected," I told him. "We have a truck and there's somebody stationed at the foot of the staircase to cover us."

"How about the two guards outside?"

"I'll deal with them when we're ready to leave and until then everybody else stays out of their way. Once we're out of the ward, I'll need a man to control each of the two landings. They'll have to be men who are familiar with automatic weapons."

"That won't be a problem." I hadn't expected it would be in this particular part of Africa. Guns were a part of everyday wear. "I'll take one landing myself," Durand went on. "Felix here can take the other."

"No way. It'll have to be Felix and somebody else."

"What's wrong with me?"

Durand sounded upset.

"You're too valuable to risk. I need you to drive a train for me."

Although Durand clearly didn't like my decision, he didn't question it further. Even under stress, he was keeping his act together. It only took a few seconds to sort out another of the prisoners for sentry duty on the second landing, then I drew Durand to one side, out of earshot of the others. I nodded over at Delacroix who was still busy with his examinations.

"I'm making the doctor your responsibility."

"I don't follow you."

Durand was wearing a puzzled expression to prove his point.

"Dr. Delacroix refuses to leave with us. I admire his dedication but I think he'll be committing suicide. If he stays, he's likely to be shot."

"You want me to persuade him to change his mind?"

"I've already tried that. I don't think words will be enough."

"OK. In that case, I'll be cruel to be kind."

"Do that. He's a good man and I don't want him to suffer because of what we're doing."

"I'll handle it."

I was sure he would and now all I had left to do was step across to one of the windows. A second later a match flared in the cab of one of the trucks down below, showing that Antoine was in position. Bayliss would be ready too so it was up to me to set the ball rolling.

It was sheer, cold-blooded murder because I started using the silenced Browning the moment I stepped through the swing doors and the two guards never knew what was happening. I was so close to them that I could actually see their uniforms smouldering around the entrance wounds. Durand and his helpers were waiting to drag the bodies inside the Isolation Ward and it only took a few seconds to distribute the weapons I'd liberated. Then the men who'd be covering the landings slipped out to take up their positions.

"OK," I said. "Does everybody know what to do?"

There was a murmured chorus of assent, although several of the prisoners were making a point of avoiding my eyes. For them I'd been transformed into a monster the instant I'd shot the two guards in the back. I didn't mind too much because however much they disapproved of me as a person, I knew they'd jump to it when I gave a command.

Now that the great escape was under way, Delacroix had no further part to play and he came across to shake my hand.

"I'll be leaving now," he said. "Good luck and bon voyage."

"You're sure you won't change your mind about coming with us."

"I'm afraid I can't."

"In that case, thanks for all your help."

Delacroix was about to say something suitably modest when Durand intervened.

"Paul," he said, tapping the doctor on the shoulder.

As Delacroix started to turn, Durand swung at the side of his jaw, putting all his weight behind the punch, and I barely had time to catch the doctor before he hit the floor. The sudden violence unsettled some more

of the prisoners. Since the invasion started Delacroix had been their own
male equivalent of Florence Nightingale and there was some angry muttering before Durand quelled it, raising his hands for silence.

"Paul Delacroix is my friend." He was speaking with a certain dignity.
"If he stays behind, those FNLC animals will kill him because of the help
he gave us. I refuse to leave him behind to die."

These weren't the kind of sentiments anybody was about to argue with
and a couple of other prisoners helped to hoist the doctor's unconscious
body on to Durand's shoulders. As they were all still subdued, I seized the
opportunity to issue my final instructions.

"When I give the signal, Durand leaves first, then the stretcher parties.
After that, the rest of you leave in pairs. Once you're on the stairs, you
don't stop unless you're told to."

Everybody seemed to understand and I slipped out of the ward into the
corridor again. It was very quiet, apart from the hum of the generator,
and there was no sign of any disturbance on the staircase which was going
to be our lifeline. Not that there should have been because Delacroix had
assured me that this wing of the hospital hadn't been in use since the
invasion began, something Bayliss and I had verified through our own
observations. Our main concern had always been the parking bay, which
was why Bayliss was down there now. Although it was never a hive of
activity, vehicles were moved in and out without any apparent rhyme or
reason and outside interference was the last thing we needed.

On the landing below me I could see the top of the head of the man
Durand had introduced as Felix. He looked up sharply when I hissed at
him. Like everybody else, he was very much on edge.

"Is everything OK?" I whispered.

"It seems to be. I'm waiting for the all clear from the parking bay."

As soon as Felix put his thumb up, I signalled to Durand, who was
standing in the doorway of the Isolation Ward. He came out immediately,
still carrying the unconscious Delacroix, and the rest of the prisoners filed
obediently behind him. They couldn't have done it better if they'd been
rehearsed, remaining quiet and orderly and remembering not to bunch.
In less than a minute the last of them had left the ward and were on the
staircase.

This was where they stopped. I'd no way of knowing what had gone
wrong but suddenly the orderly column was no longer moving downwards. The leaders had already passed Felix on the landing below and
there were only half a dozen of the prisoners on the last stretch of stairs.
Although one or two of them were looking up at me inquiringly, hoping
for some words of wisdom or comfort, there was no reassurance I could

give them. The best I could do was indicate they should stay quiet and go back to watching the deserted corridor.

Down below somebody was attempting to start one of the vehicles and the engine was refusing to fire. I'd no way of knowing what effect this had on the would-be driver but by the third attempt the grinding of the engine was rubbing my nerveends raw. It wouldn't be very long before Bayliss was forced to intervene because we were faced by a very simple equation. The longer we were delayed, the greater the chances of discovery and the less the chances of escape.

After a dozen or so attempts, the man in the vehicle seemed to give up. The engine stopped labouring and I thought I heard a cab door slam but he couldn't have left the parking bay because the prisoners still weren't moving. As they had absolutely no control over their fate, the tension must have been far worse for them than it was for me and those that I could see were beginning to shift nervously.

"What's happening?" a man at the very back whispered.

"I don't know," I told him, "but stay calm. Everything is under control."

He knew I was lying almost the moment I did. Like me, he could clearly distinguish the slap of boots on tiles and the sound of two men talking together as they approached the corner of the corridor. I gestured to the prisoners on the stairs, indicating that they should crouch down, and gripped my Ingrams tighter while I prayed that I wouldn't have to use it.

Prayers weren't enough. It was the changing of the guard at Kolwezi Hospital and the two men would have gone all the way to the doors of the Isolation Ward if I hadn't been in their path. As they were caught totally by surprise, and I couldn't afford to take any prisoners, it was another act of murder. The FNLC had actually rounded the bend in the corridor before they realised anything was wrong and they were still registering their surprise when I gunned them down with one long burst, the silenced Ingrams making less noise than their bodies did clattering to the tiles. This time I didn't sense any disapproval from the prisoners. Now they were committed, they didn't give a damn what I did as long as I saw them home free.

Down below, Bayliss was evidently having his problems as well. The two shots I heard from the parking bay weren't his as his weapons were silenced like mine and the only source of encouragement was that they weren't followed by a third or fourth. Equally important, the people on the stairs had started moving downwards again. Although they were no longer quite so controlled since the shooting, none of them had given way to panic yet.

I remained where I was until the last of them had passed the landing

below before I started down the stairs myself. I wanted out but Felix
didn't show any inclination to move. He stayed on the landing, facing
down the corridor and determinedly clutching his weapon.

"Come on," I yelled as I ran past. "You're not bloody Horatius."

In any case, we were going to need his gun further down because all our
problems were in the parking bay. The sudden burst of automatic fire
sounded ominous and so was the way the prisoners were bunched at the
bottom of the stairs. They were keeping well clear of the doorway and
none of them had boarded the truck yet. By now the panic was very close
to the surface.

"What's happening?" Durand shouted.

He'd passed Delacroix on to one of the other men and he was the only
one of the crowd milling around in the lobby who seemed reasonably
calm.

"I've no idea," I shouted back, "but make sure you keep all your people
here until I say otherwise. And don't let anybody else come down those
stairs. You've got plenty of firepower to discourage them."

Now the shooting had started, the equation was even simpler and it was
all down to speed. Either we all escaped from the hospital in the next
minute or two, before the FNLC men had a chance to get themselves
organised, or Bayliss and I would have to make a break for it on our own.
Although he didn't know it, Durand would be coming with us whether he
wanted to or not.

I went out of the building at a run, crouched low and zigzagging, and I
rolled the last few yards into the cover of the nearest truck. Nobody shot
at me and once I was safely under the vehicles, I looked around, taking
stock. A few yards away one of the other trucks had its bonnet up and
there was a body in FNLC uniform on the ground beside it. Bayliss
himself wasn't anywhere in sight, nor was Antoine, and the only person I
could pinpoint was the man who'd been using the AK-47. He was behind
the wall at the far end of the parking bay where he was out of my sight but
I could hear him chattering excitedly to whoever it was he had with him.
The shouting and sounds of running feet I could hear from further away
suggested that reinforcements were on their way from other parts of the
hospital. We obviously didn't have any time left at all.

"Bayliss."

This had started as a whisper but came out much louder than I'd intended.

"I'm over here, Philis. Keep me covered."

I still couldn't see where Bayliss was, not until he rose to his feet and
sprinted from the cover of the trucks. He was angling towards the wall
and a couple of AK-47s opened up immediately but they only managed a

few shots before I dampened their enthusiasm, hosing their position with a clip from the Ingrams. Bayliss had a very good arm because he was at least thirty yards away when he threw the grenade and it was right on target. I even saw one of the bodies cartwheel into the air and suddenly there was no more shooting from behind the wall.

"Get everybody aboard," I yelled to Durand over my shoulder as I jammed a fresh clip into the sub-machine-gun. "It's the truck directly opposite the doorway."

Until I wrenched open the cab door and saw Antoine hunched down behind the wheel, I wasn't absolutely certain we still had a driver. He was keeping below the level of the dashboard and looking as frightened as any sane person should have been in our situation.

"Come on, Antoine," I shouted. "Get the engine started. By the sound of it, half the FNLC army is heading in this direction."

I didn't wait to see whether he obeyed my instructions because I was off and running. Bayliss had dived to the ground after he'd thrown the grenade and he seemed to be having difficulty getting up again, but there wasn't time for sympathetic enquiries about the state of his health. I used brute force to haul him to his feet, he slung his free arm around my shoulders and I dragged him with me as I raced back towards the truck. As far as I could tell, Bayliss had been hit somewhere in the right leg but, after a couple of faltering steps, he ran quite well. Considering the number of rebel soldiers converging on us from other parts of the hospital, he had a powerful incentive. It was the kind of situation where life-long cripples would have thrown away their crutches and become instant sprint champions.

Fortunately, Durand hadn't been idle and the last of the prisoners were clambering aboard by the time we reached the truck. I'd done my good deed for the day so I left Bayliss to find his own way to the rear of the truck while I scrambled into the cab to join Antoine. It no longer mattered whether our driver was white, black or green. We were going to have to fight our way out and Antoine didn't need any starting instructions from me. He had the truck rolling almost before I'd pulled the door closed.

"Which way do we go?" he asked.

This was a most pertinent question. The roadway followed the side of the hospital buildings and it was kerb to kerb rebel soldiers.

"Go straight ahead over the grass," I decided. "And for God's sake don't drive into any trees."

As I answered him, I was frantically winding down the window. The nearest soldiers were no more than twenty yards away as we barrelled out of the parking bay, with Antoine crashing up through the gears, and I gave them the benefit of another clip from the Ingrams. Then we were off the tarmac of the hospital roadway and bumping across the grass of the lawn. Although a lot of weapons were blazing away in our direction by now, none of the bullets hit the cab and I had to hope they were being as lucky in the back. As soon as I had a fresh magazine in place, I leaned out of the window and loosed it off in the general direction of the commotion behind us. I wasn't really bothered whether or not I actually hit anybody but I hoped it might help to keep a few heads down.

Antoine was cursing monotonously and profanely in the driving seat beside me. The rough, tussocky grass made steering difficult and the ornamental trees we had to avoid weren't doing anything to make life easier either, especially as we weren't using headlights. Nevertheless, Antoine was doing a good job. Although a lot of branches scraped along the sides of the truck, he didn't slacken speed and we hadn't hit anything solid before an extra large bump signalled our arrival on the main road. Unfortunately, he still had a lot of driving left to do because, when I stuck my head out of the window again, I could see the first of the other trucks in the parking bay starting off in pursuit. This made me very glad that Bayliss was the Boy Scout type who believed in being prepared.

"I think we've lost them," Antoine said hopefully.

I didn't bother to answer. Even before I caught my first glimpse of the headlights of our leading pursuer about a quarter of a mile behind us, I'd suspected that Antoine was the victim of his own wishful thinking.

"Oh shit," he commented, jamming his foot down harder on the accelerator.

The gesture didn't make any appreciable difference to our speed because the truck was already travelling as fast as it could without a strong, following wind. This was the way we went into the right-angled bend and, for a moment when the whole body of the truck lurched sickeningly on its chassis, I thought we were going right over. It was a good couple of hundred yards before we were back on an even keel again. We left a lot of rubber behind on the road at the next three or four corners as well but it was all in an excellent cause. The next time I checked the headlights weren't in sight.

"How far is it now?" I asked.

"It's another half a mile but you'll have to be quick. As soon as I see those headlights again, I'll be off."

"You do that."

It was less than a minute before we reached the corner I'd been looking for and I was out of the truck before it had stopped. Although there was a fire-fight going on over the far side of Kolwezi, this wasn't my concern because it wasn't heavy enough to signify the arrival of the Legion. In any case, my problems were far more immediate. The vehicles following us weren't in sight yet but I could faintly hear the sounds of them approaching at high speed and I wouldn't have much time to do my stuff. Luckily, Bayliss had prepared the Citroën for just such an emergency earlier in the day. All I had to do was release the handbrake and the slope combined with the car's own weight to do the rest. There were substantial trees growing on both pavements and when I left the Citroën in the middle of the road, it formed an effective barricade without room for another vehicle to pass on either side. Positioning the car took no more than twenty seconds but I could already see the reflected gleam of the headlights of the first of the chasing trucks.

The boot was already open and the pins of the grenades packed around the petrol tank were linked with thin cord. One sharp tug and I was running for my life, not simply to distance myself from the Citroën but because Antoine hadn't been joking when he'd said he didn't intend to hang around. He already had the truck moving at a fair speed when I jumped for the tailboard and I might not have made it if Durand and a couple of the other prisoners hadn't been there to help. A second later the grenades exploded and, for a brief instant, night became as bright as day. When I looked back I could see the whole car was burning fiercely, as were the lower branches of the trees, and it was plain that nobody would be able to follow us for several minutes at the very least.

"Old Wallinger will be pleased," one of the men commented. "That was his new Citroën you've just incinerated."

"Tough shit, Wallinger," I said sympathetically. "Is anybody in the back here hurt?"

Nobody answered, not even Bayliss. Perhaps a bullet in the leg was no more than a minor inconvenience to him. Now we were safe from pursuit we could take the direct route to the Durands' house and we were there within ten minutes. As soon as the last of our charges had clambered out of the truck under Bayliss's supervision, I went forward to speak to Antoine.

"Ditch the truck as far away from here as you can manage," I told him, "but don't take any silly risks."

"Don't worry. I won't."

Although he didn't say as much, I suspected that Antoine thought he'd already taken enough silly risks to last him a lifetime.

"And thanks for everything you've done. A lot of people owe you a large debt of gratitude. It isn't something they'll forget when this is all over."

"I know." Antoine managed his first smile of the night as he released the handbrake. "If they do, I'll make sure to remind them."

I watched him as far as the corner, then I turned and followed the others inside the house. We'd finished with good deeds for the night. Now it was time for Bayliss and me to earn the money Pawson paid us.

LONDON, ENGLAND

Ricky was wearing a patterned silk dressing-gown, loosely belted at the waist, which only came to mid-thigh and made him look slightly ridiculous. This didn't embarrass him any more than the traces of lipstick and the strong scent of opium appeared to.

"Ramona, darling." The attempt at joviality rang a little false. "I really didn't expect to see you so soon. I thought you were still playing in foreign parts. Or should I say, playing with?"

There was no response to his smile.

"Can I come in?"

"It is a trifle inconvenient at the moment, love, if you know what I mean."

"That's all right. I'm very broad-minded."

Ramona had slipped past him into the flat before Ricky had the opportunity to raise further objections and she was in the main room by the time he caught up with her. The bedroom door was open and through it she could see the young man who was sprawled across the rumpled bed. Although Ramona had never liked men with so much body hair, she doubted whether her opinion, or that of any other woman, would cause him many sleepless nights. He raised a hand in acknowledgement of her presence, making no attempt to cover himself, and lit a cigarette.

"Have you seen Philis recently?" Ramona asked abruptly.

"Mr. Philis?" Ricky was taken by surprise. "The last I heard of him he was carrying you off into the wide, blue yonder."

"So he hasn't been in touch since then?"

"I'm afraid not."

"Do you have any means of getting in touch with him?"

"With Mr. Philis? You should know better than that, love. He's the one who does all the contacting."

Ramona hesitated for a moment, biting her lower lip, before she started for the door.

"Thanks, Ricky," she said. "I'm sorry I disturbed you."

"It was nice to see you again. Now you're back, when can we start filming?"

"We can't, Ricky." Ramona had stopped with one hand resting on the doorhandle. "I shan't be doing any more."

"Surely you're not deserting poor, old Ricky for some other producer. If it's a question of money, I'm sure we can come to some arrangement."

"It's not that. I'm getting out of the business altogether. I'm retiring."

"Really?"

"Yes, really."

Ricky examined her closely for a second before he slowly nodded his head.

"He has got to you, hasn't he, love?"

Although Ramona didn't reply, she didn't need to. Ricky could read the answer in her face.

CHAPTER TWELVE

"How bad is it?" I asked.

"Bad enough," Delacroix answered, "but he was lucky. The bullet passed right through without hitting bone or the artery. Does it hurt much?"

"A bit," Bayliss grunted.

Unless he really wasn't constructed like us ordinary mortals, Bayliss had to be lying. Whenever I'd been shot it had hurt like hell.

"There's nothing I can do about the pain, I'm afraid. All I can manage is a bandage. Until you can get some proper medical attention you'll have to rest the leg and pray that infection doesn't set in."

"I can't rest. There are a lot of things left to do yet."

"Like bleeding to death, for example? The wound won't heal properly unless you take care of it."

I left Bayliss and the doctor to their argument, hoping that Delacroix was exaggerating the dangers. Not that it made much difference anyway because he wouldn't influence Bayliss. After the balls-up in Oslo, he'd be determined to prove himself. Bleeding to death when necessary was just one of the little services we were expected to provide.

Durand was still with his wife and children, huddled in a corner with them. He'd have little enough time to say hello and goodbye as it was so I didn't disturb him. Most of the other people we'd rescued from the hospital were downstairs in the main living-room and the mood there was subdued. They all knew that safety was still a long way away. It wouldn't arrive until after the Legion and the paratroopers had driven the rebels out of Kolwezi and the town was back in Zairian hands.

In the darkness it took me a minute or so to identify Felix. Once I had found him, I took him out into the kitchen with me.

"What are your plans?" I inquired. "Presumably you're not all staying here."

"Not likely. We're allowing another half an hour for everything to quieten, then we're going to disperse in small groups. Most of us live in the area so we have somewhere we can lie low."

"That's good." After all the trouble we'd been to getting them out of the hospital, I'd have hated them to be captured again. "I'm all in favour of dispersing but I'd hang on a bit longer than half an hour if I were you. Later on tonight there's going to be a hell of a lot of excitement around the station. The rebels will be far too busy there to bother about you."

"I'll tell the others. There is one thing, though. Do you have any idea when the French and Belgians will be arriving?"

Although I couldn't see Felix's face, I could tell from his voice how important the answer was to him.

"They could be here by dawn tomorrow," I told him, "but I very much doubt it. It's more likely that you'll have to hang on for another twenty-four hours."

"But they are definitely coming?"

"You can bet on it and they'll be coming in force."

"In that case we'll manage. I just wanted to be sure there was an end in sight."

"In a week you'll be thinking of this as a bad dream."

"Maybe."

And maybe he'd be having nightmares about it for the rest of his life. The thought was there but I kept it to myself as I went upstairs again. With Delacroix's bandaging finished, Bayliss was testing his leg out and it appeared to be functioning reasonably.

"Ready?" I asked.

"Any time, Philis." The smile was pure Bayliss. "Thanks for your help, Doc."

"Think nothing of it. I've learned humility through watching patients ignore my professional advice."

He sounded rather bitter and I guessed his jaw was hurting him. I also guessed that he'd be making his way back to the hospital as soon as our backs were turned but at least I could console myself with the knowledge that we'd done our best to save him from himself.

It took several minutes to disengage Durand from his family and to collect the other two men he'd said we needed to handle the points. Although one or two of the people we'd rescued did make a point of thanking us, most of them didn't bother. They had too many other things on their minds and, in any case, I didn't particularly want their gratitude. I simply wanted to be finished in Kolwezi and on my way back to civilisation.

I'd never enjoyed handling explosives and I never would. This was the reason I stood guard while Bayliss dealt with the demolition charges which had been put on the train. He was cold-blooded enough not to bother about what would happen if he made a mistake.

Although it was very dark in the marshalling yards, and darker still inside the wagons, Bayliss was working very fast. He'd made three-quarters of the wagons safe inside half an hour and, for the first time that night, we were actually ahead of schedule. At least, we were until Durand came padding back from the locomotives.

"Your friend is wasting his time," he whispered encouragingly.

"What's that you said?"

Bayliss must have had ears like a bat because he'd suddenly materialised in the doorway of the wagon beside me.

"We're not going anywhere," Durand explained patiently. "The locomotives are inoperative."

"I thought you said you could handle it."

Durand had warned us in advance that a master key was needed to unlock the controls. Although he didn't have one, he'd assured us that this was no real problem as he could manage equally well with a screwdriver.

"This is a different problem. Those FNLC bastards must have more brains than I'd given them credit for. They've removed the fuses from the compressors."

"What exactly does that mean in layman's terms?"

"I've already told you—the bloody train won't go. The compressor won't work without fuses and there's no way to build up pressure in the main reservoir without the compressor. We're stuck."

"Isn't there some way round the problem?"

"Not without fuses, there isn't."

"How about getting replacement fuses from some of the other locomotives."

The suggestion came from Bayliss. I'd started swearing under my breath but he was far more practical.

"I'd already thought of that."

"Well?"

"It's no go. All the other locomotives have been immobilised as well."

For a second or two I wasn't sure whether I wanted to laugh or cry. I just couldn't believe that what we'd been through in the last few days had been for nothing. At least, I could believe it but I didn't want to.

"Are you saying there's absolutely nothing we can do?" Bayliss asked.

"There is one possibility." Durand's pessimistic tone indicated how remote a possibility he considered it to be. "There may be some spare fuses kept in stock in the Stores."

"May be?"

"Should be, then. I can't give any guarantee."

I looked across at Bayliss but it was too dark for me to see his face. In any case, I knew what he'd be thinking. He wasn't about to give up now so there was no alternative.

"Where are these famous Stores of yours?" I inquired.

"They're inside the station."

I'd thought they would be. Although we had the marshalling yards to ourselves, there were a hell of a lot of FNLC troops in the station itself, fifty or sixty of them at least, and judging by the noise they were making most of them were either drunk or demented. Another glance at Bayliss didn't help me any more than the previous one had so I examined my watch instead. There was another three-quarters of an hour before the first of the diversions we had planned came into effect.

"I suppose I'd better go and take a look." I'd have hated anybody to think I was enthusiastic. "Are you coming with me, René?"

"I'd better." Even in the darkness, I caught the sudden flash of Durand's teeth. "Unless I'm there to hold your hand, you won't know what you're looking for."

"That's what I was thinking. Will you be all right on your own?"

Now I was addressing Bayliss.

"I don't see why not. If you hear a very loud bang, though, you'll know there's no need to hurry back."

Although I didn't wish Bayliss any harm, perhaps this would be the answer to everything. If he did make a mistake with one of the demolition charges, all our doubts and uncertainties would be at an end.

"It's over there, Philis."

We were very close to the station buildings and Durand had his mouth right against my ear. The door he was indicating was on the far side of the railway tracks and it was standing wide open. I only needed one quick glance to realise there was no way for us to get to it. Although the station didn't have any more electricity than the rest of Kolwezi, there were plenty of oil lamps burning, plus several impromptu bonfires on the platforms. One of the fires was barely twenty yards from the Stores and there were a dozen or so rebels grouped around it. It was impossible to reach the door without being seen.

"Are there any windows?"

It was my turn to whisper in the Belgian's ear.

"There's one but it's fitted with an alarm and a wire screen."

"Is it an electric alarm?"

"I think so."

"In that case, it won't be functioning. Let's go and take a look."

It took us almost five minutes to work our way around the buildings to the window. As I'd been hoping, we could forget about the alarm but there was only one way to deal with the wire mesh. It was thick wire, stretched across a solid wooden frame which was in turn securely bolted to the wall. The entire frame would have to be ripped away and this wasn't something which could be done quietly. Fortunately there was a lot of shouting and singing from inside the station and I hoped this would be sufficient to drown any noise we made.

I'd found myself a tool on the trip around the buildings, an angled length of metal which I managed to force beneath the frame. This, of course, was the easy part.

"Once I've levered the frame away from the wall and you can get a decent grip, you'd better lend me a hand. We'll take it nice and easy."

"And we'd better be ready to run like hell."

"Sure. You'll be able to follow me."

To begin with, while we were prising one end of the frame loose, we managed to be fairly quiet. Both bricks and mortar, were soft, the length of metal was a good lever and, if we'd had the time, we could have continued the same way, working slowly and methodically. Unfortunately there was only half an hour left before the first explosion was scheduled and we needed to be back on the train before then.

"OK, René," I said. "It's now or never. Are you ready?"

"Let's make it on the count of three."

Durand had a good grip with both hands, the lever was perfectly positioned and we both had plenty of adrenalin to lend strength to our arms. The frame only resisted our combined efforts for a second or two, then the whole structure came free of the wall with what seemed to be enough noise to awaken the dead.

Durand and I were off immediately, racing for the cover of the nearest wagon as if the hounds of hell were our heels. After a minute my pulse rate had subsided to the low thousands and there was nothing to suggest we'd disturbed anybody apart from ourselves. There were no flickering lights inside the Stores, nobody had come rushing out to investigate and the sounds of raucous singing continued undiminished.

"So far so good," Durand whispered. "Who's going to deal with the window?"

"Who do you think? You'd better stay under cover until I signal."

"It'll be my pleasure."

Although I didn't have any idea what song it was FNLC men were bellowing, I was pretty sure it would never make the British Top Thirty. However, there was a recognisable chorus, where all the voices were raised together, and I waited until it came around again before I used the butt of the Browning to knock a hole in the window. Where I was, the sound of breaking glass seemed very loud but, yet again, it didn't appear to disturb anybody else. After I'd allowed a few seconds to be sure, I reached through the hole in the glass and took hold of the window catch. To my surprise, it wouldn't budge and it still refused to move when I exerted more pressure. The window hadn't been used for so long that the handle was rusted solid.

This would have been a good moment to have a can of penetrating oil about my person but as I hadn't, I had to content myself with swearing viciously under my breath. A third attempt to shift the handle wasn't any more successful and I was becoming angry. None of the individual panes of the window were big enough to climb through unless you happened to be Tiny Tim and I hadn't come this far to be thwarted by a rusted window catch. By now the FNLC men were stamping as they sang and I used the Browning as a hammer, hitting the handle in time with their feet. Under this kind of treatment, the handle began to move, albeit painfully slowly, and I was halfway there when the singing suddenly stopped. I brushed the sweat from my face and waited patiently for a new song to get under way. Of course, Sod's Law decreed that there wouldn't be one. There was plenty of laughing and talking from the men grouped around the fire outside the Stores, together with the odd, good-natured bellow, but the singsong had come to an end.

My hammering was finished too so I wiped my hand carefully and took a new grip on the handle. It was a question of concentration and self-delusion. I told myself that my right arm was a rigid iron bar which wouldn't give until the handle had shifted but my right arm knew damn well I was lying. The tendons and muscles all the way up to my shoulder were doing their best to pop out of my skin and the handle still wouldn't respond.

I rubbed my sore hand and then I tried again. This time I used emotion instead of self-delusion, channelling all the anger which had accumulated from the many frustrations of the past few days. On this occasion I had the mixture right and with a last, defiant screech, the handle gave and the window was finally open.

While I waited for Durand to join me, I leaned against the the wall. The palm of my right hand was raw and bleeding and my entire arm felt drained of strength. I decided that if Durand didn't manage to find any fuses for the compressors inside the Stores, my reaction would probably be violent.

"For a moment there, I didn't think the window was going to open," Durand said.

"You weren't the only one," I told him. "Come on. You'd better go in first."

As I followed him inside, I was keeping my fingers crossed.

Durand knew roughly where the fuses ought to be. I believed him when he said that if we'd been able to risk a light, it wouldn't have taken him more than a few seconds to discover whether or not there were any fuses in stock. As it was, he was forced to rely almost entirely on touch and the search seemed to take him forever. I kept one eye on the open door and another on the window while my mental clock ticked remorselessly away. There was very, very little time left.

"For God's sake, René," I whispered. "Hurry it up."

"Stop hassling me. I'm doing my best."

I knew he was because Durand didn't want to be stuck inside the Stores any more than I did. There was some light coming in through the doorway from the flickering fire outside, casting grotesque shadows on the walls. Occasionally, when one of the soldiers walked past the door, the shadows were real and these were the moments we both held our breath.

"I've found them."

There was no mistaking the relief in Durand's voice.

"You're sure?"

"I'm absolutely positive."

"Great. In that case, let's get the hell out of here."

When I checked, it was all clear outside the window. At least, it was until I had one leg draped over the sill. Then I heard the footsteps coming around the end of the building and I temporarily abandoned any thoughts of leaving.

"What's happening?"

Durand hadn't heard the footsteps yet so he couldn't understand why I was back inside the Stores again.

"Keep quiet," I hissed. "There's somebody coming."

There were at least two people walking along the back of the station and I'd already flicked off the safety catches on the Ingrams. If it was a regular patrol, we were finished because they'd have to be blind not to notice what we'd done with the wire screen. And, when that happened, we'd be finished unless I acted very fast.

The footsteps were only a few yards away when they suddenly stopped. I thought this must mean our handiwork had been spotted and I had my finger curled around the trigger as I edged towards the window but absolutely nothing happened. Nobody shouted the alarm, there was no clicking of safety catches as weapons were made ready to fire. Instead, there was silence. I was about to risk a peep out of the window when the rhythmic slapping sound began, accompanied by the odd grunt and a lot of heavy breathing. It was Durand who grasped the significance of what was happening first, helped in his interpretation by what was an unmistakably female moan.

"I don't believe it," he breathed in my ear. "Some bastard's slipped round the back for a quick kneetrembler."

Despite the elegant way he'd phrased himself, there was no doubt that he was right, as I could see for myself when I looked cautiously out of the window. Although the couple were only dark shadows against the wall, there was no mistaking what they were doing. It could have been self-control or it could have been alcohol but they seemed to take for ever. I kept checking my watch and still they didn't stop. Worse still, towards the end they became rather noisy and the last thing we needed was for them to attract an audience from inside the station.

By the time they'd finished, I felt as limp and drained as the man outside should have done and still they didn't go. They remained where they were against the wall, arms around each other while they whispered what I assumed to be sweet nothings. According to my watch, we'd less than a quarter of an hour before the fireworks started. If they went at it again, there'd be a very different climax from the one they'd have in mind.

"I was beginning to think you'd abandoned me," Bayliss said. "What took you so long?"

"You wouldn't believe me if I told you." Fortunately, the couple hadn't stayed for a second bout. As I'd said to Durand, if they had, dying in action would have taken on a whole new meaning. "Have you finished with the demolition charges?"

"They're all safe. I've put some of the explosives and detonators in the cab like we agreed."

We'd used all the plastique we'd brought with us on the diversions and the liberated explosives were strictly a last resort. If we found ourselves in a situation where we had to use them, we'd be in deep, deep trouble.

"How about the points?" Durand inquired.

"They're all in order too. Your two friends have already gone."

"They decided not to come with us in the end?"

"They said they'd feel safer staying in Kolwezi."

I wasn't sure that I didn't agree with them because once we had the train moving, there wouldn't be any room for manoeuvre. We'd simply have to follow where the tracks took us and keep our collective fingers crossed. Although Pawson hadn't been aware of any FNLC troop concentrations along the railway and aerial surveys hadn't shown any damage to the right of way, this wasn't the kind of intelligence I had any great faith in. The information had already been out of date when Pawson had given it to us and an awful lot could have happened since then. About all we could be certain of was that there were approximately twenty-five miles of hostile territory between us and safety. In theory, Zairian forces would have pushed forward along the track, ready to greet us, but their past performances didn't give me any more faith in the FAZ than I had in Pawson.

It didn't take Durand very long to fit the new fuses in the compressors, and once he'd finished he was anxious to be off. Although he'd been bearing up remarkably well, the strain was finally beginning to get to him. After all, he'd been trained as a railway superintendent, not a commando.

"We're ready to roll," he said. "What's happened to these famous diversions of yours?"

While he wasn't actually complaining, there was definitely a querulous note in his voice.

"They should start any moment now," Bayliss reassured him, checking his watch.

He might have been giving a cue because he'd hardly finished speaking before the first explosion rocked the station area. It might have been the smallest of the charges we'd planted during the day but, as we'd anticipated, it was extremely effective. The ammunition dump we'd selected was no more than a quarter of a mile away and there wasn't simply a single detonation. With all the ammunition exploding, it sounded as though a small war was under way.

"OK," I said, tapping Durand on the shoulder. "Let's get the show on the road."

Bayliss was hanging out of the cab, monitoring developments at the station, but I stayed close to Durand because if anything should happen to him, one of us needed to know how to keep the train moving. Although he tried to talk me through what he was doing, I simply noted the sequence and allowed most of what he said to pass over my head. When it came right down to it, I wasn't really interested in battery isolation switches or reverser handles. All that bothered me were the warning lights which had come on, a bright red one labelled ENGINE STOPPED and, even more encouraging, a blue one marked ALARM. I would have commented but Durand wasn't behaving as though this was anything out of the ordinary and I didn't want to make a fool of myself. I became even more concerned when he pressed the Start button and absolutely nothing happened. On this occasion I would have spoken but just as I opened my mouth, the diesel engine fired and the warning lights dimmed.

I decided I wasn't temperamentally suited to be an engine driver and went across to join Bayliss. There was still a spectacular fireworks display coming from the ammunition dump and it looked as though one or two of the nearby buildings had caught fire. Although there seemed to be a lot of people doing a lot of running around in the station, none of this was connected with us.

"So far so good."

I was trying to maintain my record of an inanity for every occasion.

"The charge at the fuel dump will be going off in a minute or two. That should add to the general confusion."

When I turned to look at Durand, he was still fiddling with the controls. Although he was making quite a lot of noise as he started the various systems, this was more than drowned by the sound of exploding ammunition. This was all to the good but, on the debit side, we still weren't moving.

"When do we actually get started?" I asked.

"Now, hopefully, but I'd keep your fingers crossed just in case." Although Durand sounded calm enough, he was looking very tense as he seated himself in the driving seat. "I've been waiting for the pressure to build up in the main reservoir."

For a change, I knew precisely what he did next because I'd made Durand explain the sequence to me. He put the reverser handle to forward, pulled the power handle to the first notch and then released the air brake. According to what Durand had told me, we should have been off and running. Instead there was a hell of a racket from the traction motors and we stayed exactly where we were.

"She's a heavy bastard, even for two locomotives," Durand commented to nobody in particular.

He fed in more power and this must have done the trick because there was a slight jolt as we started forward. Movement might be painfully slow but we were definitely on our way.

"Hallelujah," Bayliss murmured quietly.

It was far too early for me to echo the sentiment. Although we'd definitely picked up a bit of speed, we weren't travelling much faster than walking pace and there was an awful long way to go before we were clear of the marshalling yards. It only needed one head to turn in our direction and life would become really interesting.

This was when the charge in the fuel dump detonated and what had seemed like a good idea at the time was revealed as the mistake it had really been. The explosion was followed almost immediately by a dazzling flare of light from the burning petrol which illuminated the whole of the station area. We couldn't have managed it better if we'd arranged for floodlights to be turned on.

"Jesus Christ," Durand said. "What's happening now?"

"Just keep on driving," I told him. "We'll do the worrying for you."

Both Bayliss and I were leaning anxiously out of the cab, straining to see what was happening behind us. As the long line of wagons restricted our view, it was difficult to tell. While there was a lot more shouting from the vicinity of the station, this could simply be a natural reaction to the second of our diversions. Certainly there was no immediate indication of any attempt to stop us. The locomotives reached the main line, then the first few wagons, and I began to relax slightly, actually daring to believe that we might make it unobserved. I should have known better. Nothing had gone smoothly for us so far and our luck wasn't about to change now. The instant I saw the first rounds of tracer arcing lazily towards us, I ducked back into the cab, beating Bayliss by a fraction of a second.

"You'd better step on the gas, driver," Bayliss told Durand. "We've been spotted."

Durand didn't bother to acknowledge the instruction. He simply fed more current to the traction motors and kept on praying.

Once we'd left Kolwezi behind us, the cab of the lead locomotive became a tiny world of its own, rushing forwards through the darkness outside. Except that we weren't rushing. For the past few minutes the needle on the speedometer had hovered resolutely around the 40 kilometres an hour mark and when I'd asked Durand for more speed, his answer had been equally resolute. With the number of wagons we were pulling behind us, it wasn't possible to go any faster. This was bad news because no matter how often I rechecked my calculations, 40 kilometres an hour wasn't nearly fast enough. At that speed we might be travelling through FNLC-controlled territory for as long as two hours.

"What do you think, Ray?" I inquired.

"I think I'd rather be somewhere else."

"That goes for all of us but how do you think the FNLC will react?"

"We've discussed this before, Philis. The rebels know we have the cobalt aboard. The chances are they'll try to stop us."

As he'd implied, Bayliss was merely stating the obvious but this didn't make me feel any happier. We'd always known that at some stage or other the FNLC would realise what we were trying to do and we'd also assumed that when this happened, they'd do their damnedest to stop us. This was all very well but when we'd done our planning, we'd always imagined the train would be travelling much faster. We'd banked on outrunning the opposition. It was already painfully apparent that this wasn't going to happen, not unless they came after us on tortoises.

"Isn't there any way you can find us a bit more speed?"

"Sure. I can always ditch a few of the wagons."

I looked hopefully across at Bayliss but he was shaking his head. There were definitely times when I didn't like him very much.

"Failing that, this is as fast as we can go?"

"That's what I keep on telling you. If anything, we're going to slow down a little. We hit an uphill gradient in a couple of kilometres."

"Terrific. Give us a shout when we reach it and we'll jump out and give you a push."

If I sounded a trifle sour, this was an accurate reflection of how I felt. I knew exactly what I'd have to do but I was still hoping somebody would try to talk me out of it. I certainly wouldn't have taken a lot of convincing. When I looked across at Bayliss again, I thought I could detect a certain sympathy in his expression.

"Let me guess," he said. "You're thinking about our contingency plan."

"I'm trying not to but it won't leave me alone. What do you think?"

"It's not my decision to make, Philis. Much as I'd like to, I can't manage it with a bullet in my leg."

There was no arguing with his logic. Although Bayliss was mobile, this was the most that could be said about him. As Dr. Delacroix had pointed out, his wounded leg needed rest and he certainly wasn't in any condition to jump from a moving train and then take a long stroll through FNLC dominated territory.

"Let's re-evaluate," I suggested.

"OK." Bayliss was agreeable. "The thing is, we may be all right. There's a touch of the Fred Karno about the FNLC. It'll take time for them to get a pursuit organised."

"Right."

This was exactly the kind of thing I wanted to hear Bayliss say.

"Then there's the Zairian forces," he went on. "If the FAZ patrols have pushed as far forward along the railway line as Pawson promised, we'll be covered for the last stretch."

"Right again."

There was only one minor flaw in what Bayliss had said. Our assessment presupposed disorganised rebels and efficient government troops but at Kolwezi the FNLC had completely routed the FAZ forces. This was why the Foreign Legion and the Belgian paras were having to be flown in. Bayliss was keeping quiet now, leaving me to work it out for myself. My conclusions still left me where I didn't want to be, jumping off the train.

"Do you fancy taking the risk, Ray?"

"Not really, in all honesty."

"Nor do I." I'd made my decision and I didn't feel any better for it. "René, you'd better start slowing down now. I'll be leaving you when we reach the road crossing."

"Thank God for that." Durand flashed me a smile of sorts over his shoulder. "I was wondering whether either of you had remembered the road bridge."

I didn't even attempt to muster a smile in reply as I started gathering together the explosives. My wounded knee had suddenly started to ache. Perhaps it was warning me that there was another storm on the way. Or perhaps it was reminding me that it could do without an arduous walk. Either way it didn't really make much difference. The road bridge had to go and I was the only one who could handle it.

For the first 10 miles or so the railway track cut across country and, once we'd left the town behind us, we were safe from immediate pursuit. Our problems began at the road crossing because after this there was a longish stretch where the track and the road ran side by side. Even at the modest speed we could manage, there was very little chance that our pursuers could reach the crossing ahead of us but they certainly wouldn't be very far behind. What's more, they'd be travelling much faster than the train and it wouldn't be very long before they'd overhauled us. The only way to avoid a running battle or worse was to make sure the road was impassable, although even this wouldn't necessarily guarantee the train's safety. If there was an outlying FNLC patrol which was close to the railway and in radio contact with Kolwezi, we might find the track blocked anyway but this was a possibility none of us cared to consider.

The road crossing was where I'd be leaving the train and there was no question of René and Bayliss hanging around while I dealt with the bridge. They'd be steaming full speed ahead for safety and I'd have to look out for myself. For the moment I was looking out for the crossing, leaning precariously from the cab door, and René had switched on the locomotive headlights to help. Although 40 kilometres an hour had seemed almost snail-like earlier, my attitude had undergone a profound change. Now I had to jump from a moving train in the dark, we seemed to be travelling frighteningly fast. Durand said he'd reduced speed, and he had the speedometer to back him up, but when I looked at the dark shadows flashing past we appeared to be approaching take-off speed.

"The road's coming up now," Durand told me.

"I can see it."

I tensed my leg muscles and watched the thin strip of road speeding towards us.

"Now," Durand shouted.

"Good luck, Philis."

Bayliss gave me a pat of encouragement on the shoulder as I launched myself into space, or it could have been a push to help me on my way. For a long moment I watched the dark ground rushing up to meet me, then there was the sickening jar of touchdown and I was rolling down the slope in a welter of arms and legs. As soon as I'd stopped rolling, I assumed the foetal position, my arms over my head for protection, and waited for the rest of the train to pass by. There was no explosion and once the last of the wagons was out of sight I didn't have any more excuses for lying around. Even so, I took my time about pushing myself to my feet. The Dark Continent really was bloody dark when you were out in the middle of nowhere at night and I suddenly felt very much alone.

Bayliss's aim had been spot-on and it only took a second to retrieve the pack he'd thrown after me from the side of the road. After I'd settled it on my shoulder, I started to run back towards Kolwezi, a nice, steady trot which allowed for the darkness and uneven surface of the road. Although it was no more than a quarter of a mile from the railway tracks to the bridge, I wasn't out to break any records. I'd be working with explosives when I reached the bridge and this was work which required steady hands. In any case, unless the FNLC were a hell of a lot better organised than Bayliss or I had given them credit for, I should have a little time in hand. While the railway had been constructed in a straight line, the road twisted and turned all over the place, more than doubling the distance.

Fortunately it wasn't much of a bridge I had to deal with, no more than a simple, wooden structure commensurate with the road it served. There wasn't much of a stream flowing underneath it either but over the years it had carved itself a steep-sided gulley and once the bridge was out, no vehicles would be able to travel any further. There were four main supports, two on either side of the stream, and I shared the explosives out between them, not having to bother myself about the niceties of a proper demolition job. Professional approval was the last thing I was after and I went for overkill. I fastened enough explosives to the supports to reduce the entire structure to kindling and I used fast-burning fuses as well. It was all very primitive but we'd used up the supply of C4 plastic and the chemical detonators Bayliss had brought in with him so I was having to make do with the materials the FNLC had put on the train.

Although I worked as fast as I dared, it was a very close run thing. I'd just finished attaching the charge to the last of the supports when a new sound was added to the other night noises. There were several vehicles approaching fast and I guessed that they were less than a mile away. By the time I'd lit the fuses, they were even closer and I had one especially nasty moment when I lost my footing and slipped as I was clambering out of the gulley. The slip only cost me a second but it was a second I needed to see me to the safety offered by the cover of the trees. I was still out in the open, several yards short of my objective, when I realised I wasn't going to make it and threw myself full-length. I was none too soon. The charges hadn't been properly synchronised but the separate explosions were close enough to form one continuous thunderclap of sound, tearing the night apart. Behind me, flames, smoke and debris shot high into the sky and I could feel the displaced air tugging at my clothes.

I had to wait until the smouldering pieces of wood had stopped raining down on me before I could risk a glance over my shoulder. Even with the help of the headlights of the leading truck, which had pulled up a few yards short of the other side of the stream, there was too much smoke and dust in the air for me to see clearly but I wasn't worried about the bridge anyway. With the amount of explosives I'd used, I could have dropped the Golden Gate Bridge into San Francisco Bay. I was concerned with the headlights because they left me dangerously exposed. At the moment the FNLC troops aboard should be pretty confused. They were probably thinking they'd run into an ambush but it wouldn't take them very long to work out what had really happened. After that they'd be looking for the person or persons who'd destroyed the bridge.

This was where the headlights were so dangerous. There were four trucks altogether and the two lead vehicles had come to a halt almost side by side, their lights beaming directly across the stream to where I lay. Soldiers were already jumping out of them to deploy themselves around the road and the stream. Although I sincerely hoped I was no more than a dark shadow on the ground to them, I obviously couldn't stay where I was. In a minute or two they'd be sending scouts across to my side of the stream.

The nearest trees were no more than ten yards away, five or six running strides at the most, so reaching cover was no real problem in itself. But if I ran, I'd surely be seen and if I was seen, they'd come after me. At a conservative estimate, there were 50 men with the trucks and, quite apart from the numbers, all the advantages would be with them because in a chase I'd have to keep to the trees while they could push men forward along the road to cut off my retreat. Running was definitely my very last resort.

I became a slowly moving black shadow on the ground, moving inches at a time. Behind me, on the far side of the gulley, I could hear the orders being shouted which meant that lines of command were being re-established. Fifty pairs of eyes would be straining in my general direction and although I was beyond the direct beam of the headlights, any sudden movement was bound to be noticed. I heard the scrabble of boots as the first rebel soldiers slid into the gulley while I was still a couple of yards short of cover and now I did move faster, wriggling forward on knees and elbows until the deeper shadows of the trees enveloped me. Another 10 yards and I risked rising to my feet. I was screened from the bridge and the immediate danger was past.

There were still no signs of pursuit when I reached the road crossing and once I was over the railway tracks I left the cover of the trees, knowing I'd make better time on the road itself. Adjusting the pack more comfortably on my back, I faced east and started running, a steady jog I should be able to maintain for the next two or three miles. After that, I'd only have to walk another twenty miles and I'd be home and free. It almost seemed too easy and I was still grinning to myself in the darkness when I ran into the FNLC patrol which had been attracted back towards the railway by the sound of the explosion.

LIKASI, ZAIRE

"You did well."

Bayliss didn't acknowledge the compliment. It wasn't praise he needed, it was rest. He couldn't remember when he'd last felt so tired. The thin mattress on the hospital bed and his freshly bandaged leg wouldn't stop him from sleeping the day through. Once he had the opportunity, of course.

"You shouldn't forget Durand," he said. "We owed a lot to him. He's a good man."

"So you keep saying." Pawson had perched himself on the edge of the bed. "I expect the Belgians will manage to scrape up some kind of an award for him. They're good at that sort of thing."

Not that Pawson would allow the Belgian too much credit when his report was finally drafted. He'd make it plain that it had been his operation, executed by his own men. If he didn't blow his own trumpet, nobody else would and the next appropriations review was only just around the corner.

"Is there any news of Philis?" Bayliss asked.

"Not yet but it's still early days."

"He must have managed to take out the bridge all right. There were one or two potshots at the train but no organised pursuit."

Pawson nodded in agreement.

"One of the Belgian reconnaissance groups reported an explosion in the vicinity of the bridge last night. That must have been Philis. I sometimes think he invented the big bang theory."

Bayliss shifted his position on the bed. The way he was bandaged, he couldn't bend his leg at the knee and this made movement awkward.

"I hope he makes it back."

"He will. Knowing Philis, he's probably shacked up with a dusky maiden right now. I gather that you two worked well as a team."

"We weren't too bad. For all his talk, Philis is someone you can rely on." This was a purely professional judgement. In Bayliss's book there could be no higher praise.

"He has his moments." Pawson allowed himself a thin smile. "Don't worry about him. Philis is like a bad penny. No matter how hard you try, you can't get rid of him."

Despite his outward show of confidence, Pawson had to admit to a certain private concern. He'd be relieved when Philis finally showed up. When it came right down to it, he'd be a difficult man to replace.

CHAPTER THIRTEEN

"How many fingers?"

"Four plus a thumb on each hand. At least, that's how many I used to have."

Delacroix wasn't laughing. Come to that, nor was I. Nothing about our situation was particularly amusing.

"How many fingers am I holding up?" Delacroix persisted.

"Two but I'm used to being insulted. Listen, there's nothing wrong with me. You can forget the Dr. Kildare routine."

"I'm probably a better judge than you." There was a touch of asperity in his voice. "You have a nasty head wound. You were unconscious when I was brought in."

"I was asleep," I explained. Now it was my turn to be patient. "I'd been up all night and I was tired. As for the wound, it's nothing. It hardly broke the skin."

I'd managed to duck when the sergeant in charge of the patrol had swung at my head. It was the foresight of his rifle which had done the damage, gouging a furrow above my left eye. Although I'd bled a lot, it was only superficial. The real pain came from my kidneys because my evasive tactics hadn't worked so well when he used the butt of the rifle on my back. He'd got in half a dozen good shots and I'd be looking for blood the next time I urinated. Not that it really mattered. At some time in the very near future, I'd be leaking blood all over. This was when I was stood up against a wall and shot.

With all the fuss Delacroix was making about my head, I thought it advisable to keep the bruising around my kidneys a secret. There wasn't much he could do anyway without any medical equipment. Besides, he needed the time to worry about himself. When I was standing against the wall, Delacroix would be right beside me.

"It doesn't look too bad," he admitted grudgingly.

"That's what I told you. Why are you here or don't you know?"

Delacroix pulled a face.

"I was arrested as soon as I went back to the hospital this morning. I'm not sure exactly what the charges are but I'm scheduled to appear before the People's Tribunal. How did you get caught?"

"I'll tell you later. What's this People's Tribunal you mentioned?"

I'd been wondering why I was still alive. Until now I'd assumed that I'd been brought to the command centre on the outskirts of Kolwezi for interrogation.

"The FNLC believes in justice." There was a wry note in the doctor's voice. "It's opponents aren't simply shot out of hand. Everybody is given the opportunity to present his case to the People's Tribunal. Then they're shot afterwards."

"So the Tribunal doesn't hand down too many 'Not Guilty' verdicts."

"Not that I've heard of."

"Perhaps we'll establish a precedent."

"I wouldn't bank on it."

I wasn't but it was still our best hope. I couldn't think of anything else that was likely to save us.

Delacroix was sleeping the sleep of total exhaustion and I rather envied him because being awake wasn't doing me any good. No matter how often I went over the problem in my mind, the conclusion remained the same. At some time in the very near future I'd be standing in front of a firing squad and there was absolutely nothing I could do about it. I didn't even have a straw to clutch at. There just wasn't a way out that I could see.

I'd dismissed any thoughts of escape from our temporary prison within five minutes of being booted in through the door. This was why I'd been asleep when Delacroix had joined me—there'd been nothing more useful for me to do. The room we were in had obviously been intended as a storage bunker of some kind. Walls, floor and ceiling were all solid concrete. There were no windows to allow us a glimpse of the outside world and illumination was provided by a single unshaded light bulb. The only door had a mortice lock which might not have been an insuperable problem if it hadn't been reinforced with a heavy padlock on the outside. As the door opened inwards, I couldn't even hope to kick the screws holding the padlock's hasp out of the door-frame.

In any case, unless they'd staged a wildcat strike, there were a couple of guards with AK-47s standing right outside the door. If I was going to try anything, it would have to be when I was taken out of the bunker. I'd have to be ready to exploit the slightest opportunity but I couldn't pretend to be optimistic. There were a lot of FNLC troops around the command centre, almost as many as there'd been at the hospital, and I was almost certainly classified as a dangerous prisoner. Perhaps I'd have done better to follow Delacroix's example and prepare myself to face the inevitable. I'd seldom been in a situation where I felt quite so helpless.

By my watch, it was mid-afternoon when I heard the sound of the door being unlocked. I prodded the sleeping doctor in the ribs. I had to prod him a second time before he stirred.

"We have visitors," I told him.

He rubbed at his eyes while I watched the door swing open. The first man inside was somebody I recognised, the sergeant in charge of the patrol which had captured me the previous night. He was also the bastard responsible for the pain in my kidneys. I'd have liked to think I might have the opportunity to repay the kindness.

"On your feet," he said. "You're wanted."

The harsh sunlight outside made me blink and the heat had me sweating immediately. Or it could have been fear which was responsible. I suddenly felt nostalgic for the bunker. Apart from the sergeant, we had an honour guard of four, all of them with their rifles at the ready. There weren't going to be any opportunities for me to exploit.

I'd expected to be led directly to the main building but we were marched around the side of the bunker instead. Long before we stopped, I knew why. There wasn't a wall for us to stand against, just three posts which had been hammered into the hard ground. The earth around them was discoloured by the blood spilled already and spent cartridge cases littered the ground a few yards away. The posts themselves were discoloured as well and swarming with flies which buzzed obscenely away at our approach. I'd been ready for the People's Tribunal, not this. I found it difficult to believe what was happening to me as I was stood against the middle post and my hands tied behind me. The rifles of the other guards discouraged any thoughts of resistance. Delacroix was bound to the post to my right. Although he was very pale and he was trembling, he was managing to hang on to his dignity. As the FNLC troopers formed a ragged line in front of us, I wanted to say some last words to him. Nothing I could think of seemed appropriate. Besides, my throat was too dry for me to speak properly and I didn't want anybody else to know how frightened I was.

"Take aim."

Four AK-47s were raised in response to the sergeant's command. The muzzles appeared so close that they were almost touching me. I couldn't watch and pride stopped me from closing my eyes. I looked upwards instead to where a couple of buzzards were circling lazily. Perhaps they'd had advance warning of what was about to happen. Or perhaps this had become one of their regular feeding places.

"Fire."

The dry clicks of the descending firing pins made up one of the sweetest sounds I'd ever heard. It was so completely unexpected that it was a few seconds before I registered the FNLC men's laughter. It must have been absolutely hilarious from where they were standing.

"Jesus Christ," Delacroix breathed from beside me.

He had had his eyes shut.

"Even he can't help you now." The sergeant was having difficulty fitting the words in between his guffaws. "Next time we'll remember the bullets."

If he'd been able to see into my mind, the sergeant wouldn't have been laughing at all. He'd just become a dead man. It was a promise I'd made to myself.

Five minutes later Delacroix still hadn't fully recovered. After he'd been untied from the post, his knees had given way beneath him and he'd collapsed. It had been a nervous reaction which wasn't helped by the jeers of the FNLC men. I'd had to help the doctor to his feet and half-carry him to the building housing the command centre. We'd arrived to discover that the People's Tribunal wasn't yet in session. We were left in a small office with only a couple of guards for company but I didn't mind the delay at all. I'd finally found myself a straw to hang on to.

"How do you feel?" I asked.

"The way I probably look." Delacroix was unable to keep his voice steady and he was obviously near the end of his tether. "I'm sorry I made such a fool of myself."

"Who noticed?"

"I don't think I can face it again."

He shuddered as he spoke.

"It's not something I'm looking forward to either." Although I didn't say as much to Delacroix, I'd already made my decision. Nobody was going to strap me to one of those posts again. If it came to it, I'd see how many of the firing squad I could take with me. "Can you do something for me."

"Probably." Both of us were talking quietly so the guards at the door couldn't overhear us. "Just so long as it isn't complicated and doesn't require any effort."

"It isn't and it doesn't. All I want you to do is play for time. When you appear before the Tribunal, spin the proceedings out for as long as possible."

"Why?"

"It will be dark in a couple of hours. I don't think they stage floodlit executions."

"How will that help us?"

"At the very least, we'll have a few hours longer to live."

"Is it worth prolonging the agony?"

"Don't be defeatist. I won't say while there's life, there's hope but as sure as hell there isn't any once you're dead. We may be able to find some way out during the night."

It sounded pitifully weak. This was the trouble with most straws.

"OK. I'll do my best."

He was simply humouring me, I could tell by his tone of voice. He knew that the FNLC didn't have to operate to a rulebook. Nobody could force them to stage a formal execution. A single bullet each in the backs of our heads would be equally effective.

It was easy to see why the People's Tribunal didn't have a backlog of cases. By my watch it was exactly six and a half minutes from the time Delacroix went into court until the moment he emerged. One glance at his set features was sufficient to tell me what the verdict must have been but I wasn't allowed the opportunity to check. Now it was my turn for a fraction of a day in court.

With a bit of practice, the Tribunal speeded up. All of the four men at the table were in army fatigues and fatigued was the way they looked. They knew as well as I did that the proceedings were a mockery. The faster they were through, the faster they could have me shot and get on with something more important. While one of them detailed the story of my act of sabotage at the bridge, I gazed out of the window. It was still broad daylight and there was no sign of the shadows lengthening. An eloquent plea of innocence was hardly likely to interest them, even if I was allowed the chance to present my case. I could only think of one other way to hold their attention.

Nobody, least of all me, was surprised when I was found guilty on all counts. Nor were there any gasps of astonishment when the death sentence was pronounced. The Old Bailey should have sent observers to watch the People's Tribunal in action. Kolwezi wasn't somewhere the wheels of justice ground exceeding slow. With a verdict reached, my guards thought it was time to go but I disagreed with them. As they turned away, I remained where I was.

"You missed a lot out," I said. "Don't you want to hear what other crimes I've committed?"

Previously the men at the table had had no interest in me as a person. I was simply another nuisance to be disposed of as quickly as possible. Now I'd established myself as an individual.

"Why should we?" It was the man to my far right who answered. None of them had shoulder flashes but I'd already placed him as the senior officer. "What difference would it make? We can only shoot you once."

This was pragmatism in action.

"You don't even know who I am." I was prepared to persevere. "Don't you want to know whom you're having executed?"

"Death makes all men equals."

The bastard was a philosopher as well.

"Your Russian friends wouldn't necessarily agree. Nor would the Libyans."

I was beginning to get to them. The glances that were exchanged indicated another escalation of interest.

"Why?"

"I'm the man who killed Jan-Carl Ramirez."

I wasn't being strictly accurate but Jimmy Stewart couldn't have delivered the line better. The men at the table might not like me any more but I was making an impression. This time they held a brief, murmured conference before I was brought back into the conversation. Once again, the spokesman was the same.

"What is your name?" he asked.

"Philis," I told him. "I work for SR(2)."

"That's a branch of British intelligence, isn't it?"

"It's more of a twig. There's something else for you to pass on to the Russians while you're about it. I know all about the cobalt too."

The blank expressions on three of the four faces showed that my remark had passed them by. The spokesman, however, was nodding his head thoughtfully. He knew exactly what I was talking about.

"I see," he said. "Perhaps that does justify a stay of execution. Guards, take the prisoner outside. Stay there until I send for you."

On the way out I took another look at the bright sunlight shining through the window. It was still too early to say whether I was winning or not. Delacroix obviously didn't think we were. He was slumped on a bench, showing the world what abject misery really looked like. Although I made a couple of attempts to make him talk, I was wasting my time. Delacroix had withdrawn into himself and light social banter was the last thing he needed. Nor did I, come to that. What I needed was time and I didn't think I was being allowed enough. It was less than ninety minutes before I was summoned back in front of the Tribunal.

This time there was only one man seated at the table, the spokesman from my previous visit. He wasted no time with preliminaries.

"You're not as important as you seem to think, Mr. Philis."

"So the sentence stands?"

"I'm afraid so," he agreed without noticeable regret.

Both our heads turned towards the window now. It was the beginning of the brief tropical dusk. If we'd been playing cricket, I'd have appealed against the light but I doubted if the same rules applied to executions. "You'll have a few more hours to repent your sins," he decided. "The execution will take place at first light tomorrow."

Although it didn't show on my face, I was smiling inside. The straw I was clutching at was beginning to acquire some substance.

Dawn wasn't my favourite part of the day but it was as good a time of the day to die as any. If there were any good times to die. Overnight my straw must have been blown away. We were on our way to the killing ground and I was still a prisoner. I'd been pinning my hopes on the French Foreign Legion because today was the day when they should have arrived to recapture Kolwezi from the FNLC. If I'd been in charge of the operation, the big transports would have flown in under cover of darkness, arriving over the town to disgorge their payload of paratroopers shortly before first light. The main body of troops, together with the heavy equipment, would have followed them in a couple of hours later once the strategic points had been seized. This was the strategy I'd have adopted but I'd obviously got it wrong. Kolwezi was quiet, without even the occasional shot to disturb the tranquillity. Either the rescue operation was scheduled for later or the transports had lost their way. I was glad that I hadn't mentioned the Legion to Delacroix. It would simply have raised his hopes unnecessarily. During the night he'd managed to reconcile himself to what fate held in store for him. He was walking steadily under his own steam. He was determined to die as bravely as he knew how.

Perhaps this made him a better man than me. I wasn't going to stand and look the firing squad in the eye. If I had to die, I'd be taking somebody with me and I was pleased that the same sergeant was in charge again. He'd be the very first to go.

"Only a minute or two to go now," he said.

This was simply the last sally in a barrage of merry quips, all of them designed to boost my morale. I ignored it the same way I had the rest. There weren't going to be any more jokes after I'd crushed his larynx. We'd reached the killing ground by now and one of the FNLC troopers had taken Delacroix forward to strap him to a post. I was tensed, ready for explosive action.

"Any last requests?"

I still didn't answer. Delacroix was tied to his post and it was my turn now. I watched the trooper coming towards me, the rope dangling from one hand. I was waiting for him to come close enough because he was going to die straight after the sergeant. That would make two of them at least, with more to come if I was fast enough grabbing up a weapon. Suddenly I felt as calm as Delacroix appeared to be. We'd reached the very end of the line and there was nothing more for me to lose.

It was the unexpected burst of firing which stopped me and for an instant we were frozen into a tableau around the posts. Although the gunfire was a long way away, coming from the other side of town, it was heavy and sustained, shattering the early morning calm. It could only mean one thing and I knew exactly where to look. At first the big C-141 Starlifter transports were no more than distant dots but they were becoming larger by the moment. Although it was probably imagination, I thought I could hear the faint drone of the transports' engines. It was only a second before one of the troopers had spotted the planes too and was pointing towards them, jabbering excitedly. Now everybody was staring skywards. As we watched the first stick of paratroopers exited from the lead aircraft, no more than tiny specks in the sky until their chutes blossomed above them. It was this which triggered me into action.

The sergeant was still staring upwards when I killed him, crushing bone and cartilage in his throat with the blade of my hand. In a continuation of the same movement, I grabbed his AK-47 from hands which could no longer use it and thumbed it to automatic before I hosed the three FNLC men furthest from me with a long, sustained burst which lifted them from their feet like so many rag dolls. There was only one left now, the trooper who'd pinioned the doctor, but I daren't shoot him for fear of hitting Delacroix. The trooper didn't have any such reservations and his weapon was already coming up as I turned to him. Luckily he was close enough for me to use the barrel of my rifle to knock his gun aside as I moved inside, bringing my knee up with sufficient force to squash the soft mass of his testicles against his pelvic bone. His mouth was opening on a scream of pure, undiluted agony when the butt of the assault rifle caught him full in the face. I used the butt twice more after the trooper was on the ground.

By now the drone of the transports' engines had become a roar and the sky seemed full of planes and floating Legionnaires. Some of the paratroopers would be landing very close. A couple of hundred yards away, FNLC men had started to pour out of the building which had housed the Tribunal. Many must have come straight from their beds, startled by the unexpected airborne attack, but others were armed. Safety was still a distant prospect while we were out in the open. It was a question of surviving from minute to minute.

I used the dead sergeant's bayonet to hack Delacroix free. Then I'd thrust a rifle into his hands and was shoving him in the direction I wanted. He seemed frozen into shock by the events of the past few seconds.

"Run," I yelled into his ear. "Head back to the bunker."

"But . . ."

"Run, you silly bastard," I bellowed again, interrupting him with a push that nearly had him off his feet. "Run for your life."

Delacroix ran. I'd have liked to be running with him but nobody taught doctors to zig-zag and he made too good a target for gun-happy insurgents. I dropped to one knee and gave him covering fire, shooting selectively to scatter the group outside main building. Delacroix hadn't reached the bunker by the time I'd emptied the clip. I could have continued the covering fire a bit longer but I wanted to live as well. Although the paratroopers were claiming most of the attention, I'd made enough of a nuisance of myself to be noticed as well. I'd no intention of still being out in the open after the initial panic had died down and the FNLC started getting itself organised. I grabbed as much spare ammunition as I could carry from the dead men, then I followed Delacroix, ducking and weaving in a fashion that would have made a top running back envious. There was so much shooting by now that it was impossible to tell whether I was a primary target or not but I certainly hadn't been overlooked. For all my jinking, one bullet came close enough to spatter dust on my shoes and this did wonders for my concentration.

The doctor was crouched down in the doorway of the bunker when I slid down to join him. A quick check of the ground I'd just run across showed that there was no immediate pursuit. Nearly all the FNLC men were back inside the command centre and they appeared to have lost interest in us now we were out of sight. I hoped that this was the way it stayed. With any luck, they'd have their hands full dealing with the Legion.

"It's like a miracle," Delacroix said.

He had the look of somebody who couldn't quite believe his luck. I knew exactly how he felt.

"It's not over yet," I warned him. "There's still a lot of fighting left to be done."

"What do we do?"

"We lie low and pray the Legion ends up the winner. Do you know how to use the rifle?"

"I think so."

As Delacroix sounded dubious, I gave him a brief lesson. If he did have to protect my back, I wanted him to do it properly.

"OK," I said once I was satisfied. "The gun is strictly a last resort. You only use it if you see any FNLC men coming our way. If they're simply passing by, let them be. We don't start anything unless we have to. You stay here in the doorway. I'll be up on the roof."

"Why? Wouldn't you be safer in the doorway too?"

"Not if somebody comes sneaking round the side of the bunker with a fragmentation grenade. Up there on the roof I'll have all-round vision. I'll let you know when it's safe for us to move."

Once I was on the roof, I had a grandstand view as the battle unfolded, although the Legion would probably have classified it as a skirmish. Their intelligence work must have been spot-on. At a rough estimate, no more than 500 paratroopers could have dropped in and almost a quarter of them were deployed against the command centre. They must have had somebody on the ground who had told them what the building was being used for.

The first Legionnaires had infiltrated the grounds within ten minutes of the drop and they behaved in the Legion tradition—fast, efficient and totally ruthless. They hadn't come to collect prisoners and anybody not in a Legionnaires uniform was dispatched with a minimum of fuss. When they were ready to deal with the command centre, they hit the building from all four sides at once. About 60 Legionnaires went inside and for the next quarter of an hour I could only listen to the shooting and the grenades. They cleared the building room by room and it was easy to follow their progress as smoke and flames billowed from successive windows. There must have been some kind of a last stand on the top floor but resistance didn't last very long. When men started to emerge from the burning building, none of them that I could see were in FNLC uniform. It was just over half an hour since the Legionnaires had dropped in.

If we were going to establish contact, now was the time. Although there was a lot of shooting coming from other parts of Kolwezi, our immediate vicinity was temporarily quiet. I made a last, careful check of the area, then clambered down to join Delacroix.

"The good guys are winning," I told him. "Let's go and join them. Get rid of your rifle and strip down to your underpants."

I'd already started to rip off my own shirt.

"Why do we have to take our clothes off?"

"Because the good guys belong to the Legion's 2nd Parachute Regiment. They're a mean bunch at the best of times and they're even worse once they've tasted blood. Right now I should imagine they're ready to kill just about anything that moves. I want them to know we're European and completely unarmed. That way they might give us the benefit of the doubt."

"I see."

Delacroix thought I was exaggerating the dangers but I wasn't. In a combat situation good soldiers shot first and asked questions afterwards. Whatever else they might be, the Legionnaires were bloody good soldiers.

"You start shouting as soon as you're close enough to be heard," I went on. "Your French is the genuine article. With my accent they'd probably think I was a Russian spy."

"OK." By now Delacroix was removing his trousers. "What do you want me to shout?"

"It's up to you. 'Don't shoot,' 'Vive la France,' 'I'll introduce you to my sister,' any damn thing you like as long as they know we're friends."

We went out side by side with our hands held high in the air, and we hadn't gone more than a few paces before we were spotted. A couple of Legionnaires were dispatched to cover us the rest of the way.

"We're friends. Don't shoot." Although we were still too far away for Delacroix to be heard, I didn't discourage him. It was good practice for him. "We're friends. Don't shoot."

The doctor's voice was going by the time we were within fifty metres but nobody had shot us and this was the aim of the game. A few more steps and we'd obviously approached near enough. One of the two members of the reception committee rose to his feet. His sub-machine-gun pointed uncompromisingly in our direction.

"Flat on the ground, both of you," he ordered. "Spread your arms and legs wide."

"But we're friends . . ." Delacroix began.

"Forget it," I interrupted. "Just do what the man says. He'd make the Prime Minister of France do the same."

The sun was up by now. It was very hot laying on the ground and within seconds every insect in the neighbourhood was crawling over my body but I didn't mind. We'd made it and I could begin to relax. Even the persistent ache in my kidneys seemed a small price to pay.

It didn't take the Legionnaires long to satisfy themselves that we really were unarmed. When we were asked to identify ourselves, Delacroix told the truth and I said I was an English businessman. It saved a lot of awkward explanations. Satisfied that we were harmless, the Legionnaires escorted us to their captain, a hard-looking man with half of one ear missing. If the injury had come from a bar-room brawl, I hated to think what must have happened to the other fellow.

The captain was far more interested in Delacroix than he was in me. There were a lot of questions about conditions at the hospital and the other European residents of Kolwezi while I stood quietly in the background, sipping brackish water from a canteen one of the paratroopers had handed me. This suited me fine. I found it very comforting to have a hundred armed, battle-hardened men around me who'd help me keep myself alive. There had been no signs of an FNLC counter-attack, although there were plenty of firefights going on in Kolwezi itself, and the main body of French and Belgian troops should be hitting town soon. Unless I did something very stupid, I was home and dry.

It was almost five minutes before the captain had finished with Delacroix and turned his attention to me.

"You're English, aren't you?"

"That's right."

"But you don't live in Kolwezi."

"No."

"So what the hell are you doing here then?"

"I'm like you," I told him. "I'm trying to forget."

Although Delacroix laughed, the captain didn't even crack a smile. He must have heard all the Foreign Legion jokes before.

RITCHIE PERRY is the author of eleven previous novels, including *Macallister, Foul Up, Fool's Mate,* and *Grand Slam.* He lives with his wife and two children in Bedfordshire, England.